DRAKO'S FIRE

MAYA UNADKAT

SILVERDUST PRESS

The
AURA
REALM

DRAKO'S FIRE

MAYA UNADKAT

First paperback edition January 2023

ISBN 978-1739703417 (Paperback)

First Edition

Map Illustration by Aryan Durgale

Published by Maya Unadkat

**ALSO BY
MAYA UNADKAT**

<u>The Aura Realm:</u>
Asyra's Call

for the readers who took a chance on me

CONTENTS

CHAPTER ONE

An Unexpected Visitor

Ellora Artemer woke up to the sun shining brightly into her room on this unusually hot morning in late June. After a full hour of tossing and turning, she finally gave up and hopped into the shower, planning to go for a morning stroll in the shade. Being the first one awake in the house, Ellora decided to go to her favourite cafe and get some freshly baked breakfast for herself and her parents. She put on a loose dress and set out, sighing at the pleasant feel of the cool breeze across her legs.

In no rush, Ellora turned into the park, determined to take the long route to the coffee shop. The bright, low-hanging sun cast a golden glow over the vibrant blades of grass swaying in the breeze. The air was fresh and cool, and the luscious green leaves provided a glorious shade from the blazing sun above. She strolled along the winding path, sneezing as pollen fell from the trees above. Birds chirped happily from the branches, and flowers bloomed perfectly in hedges. The sweet scent of flowers filled the air, and Ellora could hear the distant sound of a small river flowing nearby.

On any other day, she would have asked her friend and colleague Dan to join her for a chat over coffee and pastries at the cafe, but he had gone back to the Madori Kingdom to visit Belle, his girlfriend and Ellora's best friend, for a few days. Although Ellora wished she could have gone with them, she was already returning to Madori in just two weeks for additional training. The thought of returning filled her with excitement, and she had a letter from Oriel confirming her return pinned to her wall with a stack of post-its counting down the days.

Although she was looking forward to returning to the Madori School of Aura, there was no doubt it would be completely different to her usual time there. Belle was busy with her Madori Mistress training with Oriel and loving it. Meanwhile, her roommate Melody was suffering the awful Princess Liviana's presence back in the Glassi kingdom, and her childhood friend Clara was staying with Hazel in Hawaii, in The Human Realm.

By the time Ellora arrived at the school, Dan would be back home in London, and the only other one of her friends who would be around was Hunter Nash.

Ellora wasn't sure how she felt about seeing Hunter again. After all, their relationship had been so strange the year before. First, she had wrongly accused him of trying to Kill their Madori Mistress and steal the Kingdom's Aura source. Then, even though she had been a horrible friend to him, he had fought her ex-boyfriend for cheating on her. And to top it all off, she had discovered his secret identity. He was the Prince of England who had been hiding his identity from the public for years to live as normal a life as possible.

The thought of seeing him again caused a strange fluttering sensation in her heart, like a butterfly trapped in her chest. She couldn't decide whether it was a good or a bad feeling. They had left on good terms but with zero correspondence since, and she had no idea now he would act.

Finally arriving at the familiar, air-conditioned cafe from her childhood, Ellora greeted the owners, Ryan and Romina, with a wide smile.

In no rush and with nothing in particular to do that day, she decided to make the most of the chilled building and settled down with her coffee at one of the small, wooden tables looking out the window. There was nothing Ellora found more peaceful than people watching. With each passing minute, the crowds grew bigger, and the streets became busier. Ellora watched them, losing herself in the hustle and bustle of city life.

Ellora wondered what it would be like to return to the grand castle and spend time with Belle, even though they would both be busy. Oriel had told Ellora that Master Rainclarke would oversee her training and schedules while she was training Belle, so Ellora was sure they would also work on her dreams.

She had only had three since coming home.

The first had been on her second night back, and it was a dream she had already had multiple times before.

As usual, she was running from an unknown presence. While she couldn't see the presence, she could feel it. It was a chill that ran down her spine, making her hair stand on end. She could feel it in the bones under her skin, in the blood running through her veins, in every breath she took. And she could hear the footsteps, slow and deliberate, echoing in her mind like a drumbeat.

So she ran. She ran up the stairs, into the dark room and under the bed. The silence was so thick, so sickening, that it was all she could do not to scream. Each heavy thud of a footstep was louder and heavier than the last. Whoever it was was getting closer. With each step, Ellora's chest tightened.

She held her breath, knowing that even an exhale would be heard in the deafening quiet. Just when she thought she couldn't take it anymore, when Ellora was sure she was about to burst, she woke up, drenched in sweat and panting for breath.

A week after the first dream, Ellora had another nightmare in which she was being chased by fire in the corridor outside her baby sister Ophelia's room.

However, it was the third dream that had awoken her early that morning, a vision unlike any she had ever had before.

It started in her family's garden, which was usually a bright and cheerful place where Ellora and Ophelia used to play when they were younger—running around, riding their bikes, and splashing about in the inflatable pool their parents would put up during the Summer. But in the dream, the garden was dark; a thick inkiness blanketed it as if even the moon and stars had abandoned it. All the lights were off, and Ellora was alone. She couldn't remember how she got there, but the door was locked, and no matter how hard she tried, it wouldn't budge.

An echoing giggle from behind her made Ellora jump. She spun around, but the sound had come from the back of the garden, hidden in the shadows of the trees where even the moonlight couldn't reach. The giggle came again, louder this time, and Ellora slowly backed up, pressing herself against the hard brick wall on the other side of her kitchen.

She heard rustling on her left and inhaled sharply, turning towards the sound. A shadow darted to the right, and Ellora tried to follow it with her head. The crunching of leaves at the back of the garden made her look back, but there was nothing there. Nothing that she could see, anyway.

"What are you doing?" asked a little voice behind Ellora.

"Argh!!" Ellora shouted, twisting around sharply and clutching at her chest. Ophelia stuck her head out of the kitchen window and leaned towards her. "Ophelia, what are you doing? You scared the Aura out of me!" She panted heavily, trying to recover her breathing.

"You're the one who was lurking out here in the dark, Ellie. I just wanted a glass of water," Ophelia replied, her young voice twisted into a higher pitch than usual. She tilted her head to the side and cocked up one eyebrow as she narrowed her eyes at her big sister.

Ellora frowned as she shivered from the cold, rubbing her hands together to warm them up. "Right, well, it's freezing out here, and I think I've locked myself out. Could you open the door, please?"

Ophelia hopped down from the counter she was perched on and scurried around to open the garden door.

"Thanks," Ellora said as she walked inside, instantly feeling a cloud of warmth settle over her icy skin.

"Were you sleepwalking again?" Ophelia asked as Ellora poured a glass of water for each of them.

"I don't sleepwalk," Ellora uttered, furrowed her eyebrows.

Ophelia sighed as if her big sister was being ridiculous. "Yes, you do, Ellie," she insisted. "You must do – where else would those muddy footprints upstairs come from?"

"What footprints?" Ellora asked, her confusion deepening. She had never seen any muddy footprints around the house; their father would never allow that.

"The footprints that come up the stairs to my room," Ophelia explained in between gulps of water. "Last night, you even woke me up because you came into my room, and I could hear you saying weird words near my bed, but I knew you must have been sleepwalking, and dad says it's dangerous to wake a sleepwalker, so I just ignored you. I was too tired to get up, anyway."

Ellora's skin crawled at Ophelia's words, an uncomfortable pit settling in her stomach. She was sure she hadn't been in Ophelia's room the night before.

"You were only there for a minute, anyway," Ophelia continued. "Then you left again, and I could hear you walk back down the corridor." She looked at Ellora with a frown. "You're being weird. Maybe you're tired."

"Maybe," Ellora nodded, but she wasn't convinced. An unfamiliar ball of nausea was growing in her stomach. She swallowed thickly and took a heavy step towards her sister. There was something wrong here.

"Well, I'm going to sleep. Goodnight."

"No!" Ellora cried desperately, her hand shooting out to grab Ophelia's wrist as she got up from the table.

"Ellie, let go of me!" Ophelia shrieked, trying to wriggle her wrist free from her sister's grasp.

"I'm sorry," Ellora whispered, her voice shaking as she stumbled back, releasing her hold on Ophelia. "But please don't go to sleep yet. I just... I have a bad feeling, Ophelia."

Ophelia's eyes widened, her deep brown irises shining curiously. "What's wrong with you?"

"What do you mean?" Ellora murmured.

"Your hand...," Ophelia poked it lightly with the tip of her finger, "it's boiling."

"Is it?" Ellora asked, resting a palm on the counter to steady her wobbling legs. "Maybe I've got a temperature. Maybe that's why I don't feel good."

But Ophelia took a slow step backwards, her eyes filled with fear and her mouth curled downwards. "Mummy!" she screamed. "Mummy, come quick!"

"Ophelia, what is it?" Ellora asked, reaching out for her baby sister. But as she saw her hand, a scream of terror escaped her lips.

She was on fire.

As a bell jingled, announcing the arrival of a customer, Ellora snapped out of her reverie. She frowned as she looked back at her coffee, the dark liquid now cold and uninviting. Glancing around to ensure nobody was watching, she hovered her hand above the mug, wiggling her fingers as she focused on her Aura. Slowly, the coffee began to steam and warm under her touch, the rich aroma filling her senses. Satisfied with her handiwork, Ellora took a few more sips of the now-hot coffee before choosing breakfast.

Scanning the display, she selected two fresh croissants for her parents, two more coffees and an apple danish as a treat for herself, the warm scent of cinnamon and apples making her mouth water.

It was still early when she arrived home again, carrying the warm drinks and pastries, and pleasantly surprised by her brief outing. The crisp morning air and the hustle of the city were exactly what she needed. Since Ophelia died, the house had been like a weighted blanket, suffocating her and her parents without them even realising it, a constant reminder of their loss. This quick trip was like a breath of fresh air, a welcome escape.

She unlocked the door quietly in case her parents were still sleeping but was surprised to find her mother waiting for her on the other side, her features carved into a frown as she paced the doorway.

"Ellora, where have you been?" her mother hissed. "Mr Rainclarke has been waiting for you for over half an hour, and you wouldn't even pick up your phone!"

Ellora, taken aback by the presence of emotion in her mother's voice, was too surprised even to consider what her mother said, too shocked even to care that it was anger.

"Mum, it's *Master* Rainclarke. He's an Incendi *Master*," Ellora mumbled as she walked into the kitchen and set the pastries and drinks down on the dining table. "Wait." She wrinkled her eyebrows and looked up at her mother. "What did you say?"

"Ellora, how nice of you to make an appearance," came a familiar, amused voice behind her. Ellora spun around, her eyes widening when she spotted her Incendi teacher standing in her living room. She cursed inwardly, realising she must have missed him as she walked past and into the kitchen.

At the same time, she sent a silent 'thank you' to the Spirits, grateful she had woken up early enough not to have to face her strictest teacher, even though he was also her favourite, in her Winnie The Pooh pyjamas.

"Master Rainclarke," Ellora stammered out in surprise.

"Ellora. I thought we already covered pleasantries," Master Rainclarke tried to joke, and Ellora narrowed her eyes at him. He never did that. "And please, Mrs Artemer, call me Noah. No need for formalities." He smiled politely at her mother, who offered a faint twist of her lips before leaving the room.

"Sir, what are you doing here?" Ellora asked in a trembling voice, her first thought that something might have happened to Belle.

"Ellora, I don't want you to worry," Master Rainclarke replied, locking eyes with her.

"You know that's only going to make me worry more," Ellora told him, trying to keep her voice calm and even.

"Yes, I'd better explain," Master Rainclarke sighed apologetically. "I'm afraid Oriel has sent me to collect you. We didn't want you coming back by taxi; you need an escort."

"An escort?" Ellora took a step back to lean against the table. "Why? What's going on?" Her heart began to race, and her hands quivered by her sides.

"We need you back at the school. Within the next two hours, actually," he told her. "I'm sorry we're pulling you away from your family two weeks earlier than we planned, but I'm afraid we don't have a choice. I'll give you more information when we're in the car."

Ellora's worries only intensified as she hurried up the stairs to pack a small suitcase and place Lucifer, the tiny penny pet Clara had gifted her the previous year, in her pocket. Luci let out a little grumble of protest, unhappy at being woken up. As she made her way out of her childhood bedroom, she couldn't help but glance back at Ophelia's bedroom. Since the day her baby sister died, she had been too afraid to enter the room to revisit those memories. But something about today made her want to return, to run her hands over the polka-dotted bedding and trace the dents and carvings on the wooden toy box at the foot of the bed.

But she didn't have the luxury of time at the moment.

She hastened down the stairs as Master Rainclarke finished explaining the situation to her parents.

"Be careful," her father told her, pulling her into a tight hug.

"I will, dad," Ellora replied, hugging him back.

"Take care, now," her mother added vacantly with a stiff smile.

Ellora gathered her two suitcases and, giving in to his insistence, allowed Rainclarke to carry one of them to the car.

As soon as they were both in the car and Ellora had placed Lucifer safely in her lap, she turned to Rainclarke. "What's going on? Why did you come to get me?"

Master Rainclarke hesitated. "Oriel was planning to tell you herself." His lips curved into a frown and his eyebrows lowered. Around them, the cars slowed to a complete standstill. With a sigh of resignation, Rainclarke turned to look at her. "There's been another attack."

For a moment, Ellora said nothing as she stared out the window, her mind racing with all the potential implications of Rainclarke's words. It couldn't be Oriel because she was the one who requested for her to come.

"Is it Belle?" Ellora demanded, taking a deep breath and turning to him with quivering lips. "Is she okay?"

"Belle is fine," Rainclarke assured her, although he hesitated before continuing. "The attack took place in the Incendi Kingdom."

"Clara?" Ellora cried, her eyes wide with fear. "No, it can't be. Please tell me she's okay. She was in The Human Realm the last time we spoke."

"Ellora, it's not Clara. But Clara is on her way back to the castle as we speak."

"Thank the Spirits," Ellora sighed, her shoulders relaxing.

"Ellora, listen. It was Melody. Melody Sotto."

CHAPTER TWO

Return to Madori

B y the time they arrived back on the shores across from the Madori School of Aura, Ellora had just about finished filling in Master Rainclarke on her latest and most peculiar dream.

"That certainly does sound very different from any of your other nightmares," Rainclarke remarked as he drove the car off the sand and onto the surface of the water. "Do you think any part of that dream might have been a real memory?"

Ellora's heart warmed at the sight of the majestic castle ahead of them, its glistening white walls reflecting on the sparkling water below.

"Do you mean to ask me if I can turn into a ball of fire, sir?" Ellora asked, only partly joking. After attending the Madori School for several months, she learned that almost nothing was impossible in this realm.

"I'm more concerned about the sleepwalking and the muddy footprints your sister saw," Rainclarke clarified. "And the strange chanting she heard in the middle of the night."

"I'm not sure, sir." Ellora's brows furrowed in thought. "I suppose it's possible, but if—"

Before she could finish her thought, Master Rainclarke pressed his foot harder on the accelerator, speeding up and driving past the entrance to the castle, swerving left instead of stopping.

"Where are we going?" she exclaimed, her knuckles turning white as she gripped the armrest.

"The car park, of course," Rainclarke answered before plunging the car into the water at an angle.

Ellora braced herself and looked around frantically, expecting water to come rushing in at any moment. It was only when she noticed Rainclarke continue to drive calmly that she realised he intended to go into the water. They weren't sinking or under attack. Instead, it felt as though they were moving along any other road.

"We have a car park?" Ellora asked in surprise as she settled back into her seat, her pinks tinged a faint pink in embarrassment at her reaction.

"Some of the teachers do own vehicles. And it's not publicised, but we have official Madori School vehicles for... well, for times like this, I suppose," he explained calmly, guiding the car effortlessly along the unseen road.

They continued driving, or rather, sinking, through an invisible tunnel in the water until they hit the bottom, where Ellora could make out a large, blurry rectangular shape towards their right. Rainclarke drove through the body, and they emerged into a small garage-like room.

"Are we under the school right now?" Ellora asked in awe as they climbed out of the vehicle. She had no idea there was anything under the school, apart from the strange caverns beneath the fountain that a former prefect, Julia, tried to escape through with the Madori Orb just a few months before. Ellora remembered the incident well, as Julia's theft of the source of Madori Aura nearly killed their Madori Mistress, Oriel.

"This way, Ellora," Rainclarke gestured towards a lift Ellora hadn't noticed. "So, do you?" he asked as they stepped into the lift, and it began to ascend.

"Do I what?"

"Do you think the dream was a real memory?" he repeated as they stepped out of the lift and into the unnaturally quiet library.

"I'm not sure," Ellora replied, scanning the vacant expanse of the library. Usually bustling with students and faculty, the room was eerily deserted. Not even Wendy, the librarian, was there. Ellora had expected it to be somewhat quiet since most of the occupants were away for the summer, but she at least expected to find Hunter, who often holed up in the library and buried himself in his books. In the absence of her friends, the dimly lit space with its dark carpets, towering ceilings, and endless shelves of books felt more daunting than inviting.

"Dreams can be bizarre, Ellora," Rainclarke commented, breaking her reverie. "It's very possible your brain did make it up, but I suppose we can't assume anything for the moment. Nothing can be ruled out at this stage."

"Elle!" cried a familiar voice behind them. Ellora turned to see her best friend, Belle, running towards her from the door to Oriel's office. Belle wrapped Ellora in a hug, nearly toppling her over. "I can't believe you're here!"

"I've missed you," Ellora said, hugging her friend back. "How's Melody?" she asked as soon as Belle let go.

"She's been better, but she's no longer in danger," Oriel answered, walking over to them with a warm smile. "How was your journey?" she asked, standing next to Master Rainclarke.

"It was fine, but Master Rainclarke wouldn't tell me much," Ellora responded hurriedly, more concerned about Melody than small talk.

"Yes, well, I'm afraid that's my own fault," Oriel said, giving her a sad smile and placing a comforting hand on her shoulder. "I thought it would be best for you to get the full story from me and see Melody for yourself." Oriel gave her a sad smile and placed a comforting hand on her shoulder.

Ellora felt a vague sense of reassurance wash over her, her anxiety beginning to fade as she stood in the place she considered her home, surrounded by her best friend Belle, Oriel, and Master Rainclarke. If nothing else, they were all safe there.

"Why don't you freshen up, and then we'll talk properly in my office?" Oriel suggested. "I'll have tea ready, of course."

As much as she wanted to argue and demand answers right then and there, she had been stuck in the car for a while and was desperate to use the bathroom.

After Rainclarke assured Ellora that he would see her later, Belle insisted on helping Ellora carry her bags up to her room, and they jogged up the familiar stairs together.

"It was scary, Elle, I'll be honest with you," Belle told her as they walked. "When they first brought Melody in, Oriel and I were not even sure she would make it."

Ellora swallowed at the thought of her friend in such a critical state. Tears began to blur her vision, but she blinked them away. She didn't have time to cry right now. "I can't even imagine how it must have felt to see her like that, Bee," she whispered, feeling a pang of guilt for not being there for her friend.

Belle shook her head. "It's Mr and Mrs Sotto who I'm really worrying about now," she added. "They've barely slept in days and are refusing to leave Melody's side, even now that she's stable."

"Oh, they're here?" Ellora questioned, feeling thoughtless for not even considering Melody's parents.

Belle nodded. "After the attack, they contacted Oriel directly and asked if she would bring them and Melody here to be healed. It made sense to Oriel because she's a student here, and of course, we are known for having the best Healers in the Realm. I don't know if you remember, but they work for Liviana's parents, the King and Queen of France."

Ellora nodded. How could she forget? Liviana would always take the opportunity to remind everybody that she was a princess and that Melody's parents worked for her own.

"Well," Belle continued, "Oriel also managed to convince Liviana's parents to give Mr and Mrs Sotto time off work to be with Melody until she recovers. Paid time off," Belle added, raising an eyebrow.

"Now that's impressive," Ellora huffed out a breath of laughter. Considering what an awful person Liviana was, Ellora figured her parents couldn't be much better.

"I actually think she has something over them. Even Master Rainclarke was surprised she managed to get them to agree."

"Yeah, or they're worried Oriel will kick Liviana out of the school," Ellora suggested. "Let's be honest, she doesn't deserve to be here in the first place, and Oriel could easily transfer her to another school if she wanted to."

When they finally made it to their corridor, Ellora felt her stomach warm. The familiar blue-grey walls welcomed her, even as Ellora purposely avoided looking at the door to the Prefect's room. It used to be occupied by Julia before she was sent to Mistfall, in the Realm of the Dead, for her betrayal, and it was still a sore subject for most of them.

"Is she okay, though?" Ellora asked Belle, hoping for an honest answer.

Belle hesitated before sighing and looking Ellora straight in the eye. "I don't know."

Ellora let out a deep breath and leaned against the door to the room she shared with Melody.

She needed her to be okay.

"Elle, you should put your stuff away and then go and speak to Oriel," Belle said, giving Ellora a quick squeeze on the shoulder. "She'll tell you everything, and then you can go and see Melody for yourself." She looked down at her shoes and chewed on the inside of her cheek before looking back up at Ellora with a deep breath. "They don't know who did it," she whispered, shaking her head. "That's all I know."

With a half-smile, Belle turned and headed back down the stairs, leaving Ellora to turn the doorknob to her room.

"Feeling better?" Oriel asked with a tight-lipped smile as Ellora sat on the leather seat opposite her, on the other side of the dark mahogany desk.

Ellora nodded. Being back in the large room was a comfort, a familiar corner in a land of uncertainty. She looked over at the bare, navy-blue wall on the other side of Oriel's office with a nostalgic grin. Once upon a time, that wall had been home to a rather ghastly painting of the Madori School's founder, Arellia. Until Melody took it upon herself to tear the painting up, convinced the mythical Madori Jewel was inside. As it turned out, the Madori Jewel was *not* inside the painting, but fortunately, Oriel hated it enough to find the incident amusing.

The grin faded from Ellora's lips at the thought of Melody, once so bubbly and chatty, who was now lying unconscious in an infirmary bed. "It feels like I never left in some regards, but I will feel a lot better when I find out Melody is alright," she answered with raised eyebrows.

"Of course. Let's not waste any more time. So, what we know so far is that Melody was attacked in the Glassi Kingdom. We don't know by whom because the other person she was with... well, he didn't make it." Oriel's lips twisted at that. She swallowed heavily.

Ellora inhaled sharply. Somebody else had been with Melody. "Who? Who was it?" The realisation that it could have been Melody who didn't make it made her stomach twist painfully.

"We don't know. Ellora, I know this is difficult, but you must know that we are all, every single one of us, doing as much as we can to figure out what happened and stop this from happening again. We all love Melody to pieces and want nothing more than to keep her safe." Oriel's eyebrows creased with concern.

"How is it that we don't know the identity of the other person Melody was with?" Ellora asked, swallowing down the shock. "Surely there must be some way to find out who they are?"

Oriel let out a heavy sigh, sinking back into her chair and rubbing her forehead. "It's suspected that the victim was a friend of Melody's from before she attended the Madori School of Aura. But it's taking a while to identify the body because they were..." she trailed off and swallowed before continuing, "they were burnt. Completely. Whoever it was, they are now unrecognisable."

Ellora's stomach churned, the bile rising in her throat. She swallowed hard, choking down a gulp of the hot lavender tea sitting in front of her in an attempt to calm her stomach. She always had been prone to nervous vomiting, but now was definitely not the time.

Someone died. Someone actually died. Not only had they died, but their body had been burned away, their bones charred beyond recognition. And that someone had very nearly been Melody.

"Burned?" Ellora's voice trembled and the words caught in her throat. "In the Glassi Kingdom, the Kingdom of ice of all places? I've heard that even candles don't burn in the Glassi Kingdom."

"They don't," replied Oriel, her eyes hard and shadowed by dark circles. She took a deep breath and a sip of her own tea before leaning forward and speaking in a hushed voice. "Do you remember when I told you about the strange things happening in the Realm? The day the four of you caught Julia? I think this is linked. It has to be."

"Oriel, what in the name of the Spirits is going on?" Ellora questioned in a shaky voice.

"That's what I'm trying to figure out," Oriel answered in a tone that could only be described as a mixture of determined and utter terror. Her eyebrows knitted together in a frown as she absentmindedly chewed on her bottom lip.

"How is Melody doing now?" Ellora asked after a few silent minutes, clasping her hands together in an attempt to stop them from shaking.

"She's in a coma," Oriel replied, her tone matter of fact. At least she wasn't sugarcoating the truth. "Neither I nor Healer Amare think it's anything to worry about. She was severely injured in the attack, and although we've managed to heal her burns, concussion and all other physical injuries, her mind needs time to recover. I think Melody's Aura put her into this coma to protect itself and to allow itself to heal and repair faster."

"So, she'll wake up?" Ellora implored eagerly, hope creeping into her voice as she sat on the edge of her seat, her foot tapping rapidly against the floor.

"I believe so. It's just a matter of when."

There was a quick light rap at the door, and Rainclarke rushed in without waiting for a response. His shoulders were stiff and rigid, his eyebrows furrowed, and his teeth clenched. "I'm sorry to interrupt you both," he glanced apologetically at Ellora. "But this really can't wait," he said, holding out a sheet of paper.

"Would you mind giving us a minute, Ellora? And then we'll head straight up to see Melody," Oriel suggested, her tone gentle and a small smile on her lips.

Ellora nodded, leaving the small office and closing the door behind her, walking through the dark shelves of the library, lost in thought.

Somebody died. Ellora turned a corner, weaving in and out of the shelves in the history of Aura section. Melody almost died. She ran her fingers absently along the spines in the section of Human legends. Melody was in a coma. She grasped the edge of a shelf in the history of the Spirits section, pressing her head against the cool wood.

"Ellora," a deep voice muttered her name from beside her, and she looked up to find Hunter frowning down at her in concern. "I didn't know you were back." His dark hair hung over his eyes as he tilted his head.

"Melody—" Ellora started to say.

Hunter said gently, his eyes softening. He placed the book he was holding on the closest shelf and walked closer to Ellora, then did something that surprised her more than it should have; he hugged her.

Ellora froze, stiffening up at the unexpected contact.

She didn't know what to do, and knowing Hunter wasn't a very touchy person, he was the last person she would have expected to hug her. But she quickly leaned into him and wrapped her own arms around him.

Even though he didn't talk about it, Ellora knew Hunter had a soft spot for Melody. Everyone had a soft spot for her, really, but Melody had been the only one to really try to talk to him when they all first met at the First Form welcome dinner last year. Ellora knew he appreciated and remembered her effort.

And she knew he must have been struggling too. "She'll get through this," he whispered comfortingly into her hair. "She'll be okay."

The door to Oriel's office opened, and Ellora heard Oriel and Rainclarke talking, their footsteps approaching. She and Hunter broke apart, and she shot him a brief but grateful smile.

"Ah, Hunter, you're here too," Oriel chimed as she came around the corner. "Perfect timing."

"Yes, I could use your help, Hunter, if you've got a few minutes," Master Rainclarke requested.

"Of course. I'll see you later, Ellora. Oriel," Hunter nodded to both of them before leaving with the Incendi teacher.

"Ellora?" came a whisper from behind her.

Ellora had been sitting next to Melody's bed for a couple of hours already in the silent and unmoving infirmary. At first, she sat quietly, uncomfortably. Then she cried. And then more silence. Eventually, Ellora decided it would be a good idea to try and talk to Melody. It was possible her friend could hear her, so Ellora spoke. She told her about seeing Hunter earlier, she spoke about her Summer and what she had been doing, she read to her, and finally, she went back to sitting in silence.

She turned around to see Clara standing stiffly in the open doorway. "Clara, when did you get here?" she asked, giving her oldest friend a tight hug.

"About twenty minutes," Clara replied, clasping her arms across her chest. "Oriel just filled me in. I came as soon as I heard." She peered in at Melody, lying in the pale blue sheets, but stayed where she was, leaning against the door frame. "How's she doing?"

"Okay, I think," Ellora answered as she moved back to the chair, but even she could hear the uncertainty in her voice. "She hasn't moved since I've been here, but that's not unusual. Oriel managed to convince Mr and Mrs Sotto to have something to eat and maybe try to squeeze in a nap. They argued but looked so exhausted that I think they'll conk out the second their heads hit the pillow."

"It must be difficult for them to see her like this," Clara whispered, furrowing her eyebrows. "Have they been here the entire time?"

"Yeah, they asked Oriel if they could stay, and she managed to arrange it for them."

"I mean, can you blame them for wanting to stay?"

"Not really," Ellora replied.

There was a moment of heavy silence before the sound of Clara shifting broke it as she finally entered the room. "It's weird around here, isn't it? With the school so empty? Kind of creepy, actually," she said, sitting on the chair next to Ellora.

"Much better, zhank you, Oriel," the strained voice that belonged to Melody's mother came from outside the room. It seemed they had woken up from their nap already. "Zhank you for staying wizh 'er, Ellora," Mrs Sotto spoke, attempting a smile that didn't quite reach her shadowed eyes. "Oh, and you must be Clara. Melody mentioned you as well." She walked into the room with Mr Sotto following behind.

"Ellora, Clara, why don't we grab a bite to eat?" Oriel suggested, smiling tiredly from the doorway of the infirmary. The strange light in the room masked the fatigue that Ellora noticed earlier, making Oriel look almost like her usual self.

As they made their way out of the infirmary and through the winding corridors of the castle, Ellora felt a sense of dread burrowing into her stomach. But as they entered the almost empty dining hall, Ellora was greeted by the friendly faces of Belle and Dan, who were already seated at the table. Despite her exhaustion, comfort warmed her as she joined her friends at the table. She was starving.

CHAPTER THREE

The Madori Spirit

"I can't remember," Ellora insisted with a heavy sigh, pinching her lips together and fixing her gaze on the dark burgundy walls in front of her as she paced.

"Okay, Ellora, that's quite alright," Master Rainclarke responded soothingly, his voice easing the dull throbbing in her skull. She thanked the Spirits for the dim lighting in his office—anything brighter would have made the pain unbearable.

She swallowed and pressed the palms of her hands into her eyes, taking deep, slow breaths. "Why can't I remember anything?" The words came out as a shaky whisper.

"It might take some time, Ellora," Master Rainclarke reassured calmly, placing a warm cup of tea on the glass coffee table for her. "It's got sugar in it."

Ellora nodded gratefully, taking the tea and sitting down once again. With each sip, she could feel the sugar restoring her energy, the steady pounding in her head slowly beginning to alleviate. "I just don't understand why I can't remember," she repeated after another sip of the tea. Rainclarke's words were filled with reassurance, but the slight furrow of his eyebrows and the downward curve of his lips did nothing to help her nerves. She was concerned that he was concerned.

"There's no need to push anything, Ellora."

Ellora ran a hand through her smooth hair, massaging her aching skull with the tips of her fingers as she did. "It's just frustrating. I'm so close. I can feel it. I know this one was important. I don't know how I know, but I do."

Master Rainclarke pursed his lips. "Ellora, it's easy to be angry with yourself and feel like you'll never get there, but look at how far you have already come. Not even a year ago, you were not sleeping because of these nightmares, and your Aura was entirely blocked. And now, you have unlocked your affinity for your Madori Aura and know so much more about these dreams, these memories."

He had a point. A year ago, Ellora was convinced she had been accepted into the Madori School of Aura by mistake.

"You need to take it easy," Master Rainclarke told her kindly, taking the empty cup from her when she drained the rest of the silky liquid. "You're clearly in pain, and we don't want to drain you. Why don't we take it step by step, hmm?"

"What's the first step?" Ellora asked.

"Well, the beginning. Do you remember where the dream began?" Rainclarke leaned forward, his elbows on his knees and his eyebrows raised into his forehead as he questioned her.

Ellora took a steadying breath as she closed her eyes. Whereas only this morning she was able to remember the dream as clearly as if she had just lived it, all she could see now were grey swirls of smoke in her mind. It was as though she had been reading a story when the words were suddenly stolen, torn, right from the page, leaving behind blank, stained paper that made no sense whatsoever.

But between the smoky trails in her memory were glimpses of red. Ellora gasped but forced her mind to remain focused. There was something there, something covered by the fog. She ripped through the dark wisps, forcing them aside to reveal the deep, dark red that was hiding behind them. "Red," she whispered. "Flames. They're flames." And just as suddenly as the smoke appeared, it was consumed by a raging inferno, the heat so intense that it singed Ellora's skin.

She yelped and stumbled backwards, snapping her eyes open to examine her poor, charred hands. Only to find they were unscathed and unharmed.

She exhaled through her nose, wrinkling her forehead at the sight of her olive-toned skin, free from any marks or blemishes.

Master Rainclarke leaned in to place his hand on Ellora's shoulder. "Are you alright?"

"Fine," she breathed. "I'm fine."

He walked over to his desk and retrieved a chocolate bar from the drawers. "Why don't you eat this, and we'll call it a day? It's almost dinner time anyway."

She looked up at him and blinked.

"Ellora?" he droned, the sound of his voice snapping her out of a trance.

"Yes. Thank you." She took the chocolate from his hand and walked to the door. "See you tomorrow."

Master Rainclarke frowned at her. "You mean at dinner?"

"What?"

"You'll see me at dinner? In just under an hour."

"Oh. Right. Yes."

"Ellora, are you sure you're alright?"

As she twisted the door handle, a wave of dizziness hit her and her knees buckled beneath her. The chocolate fell out of her hand, and nausea rose into her throat. "Ellora?" a familiar deep voice called to her as she leaned against the wall, forcing her legs to stay standing. "I've got you," Hunter told her. She felt herself falling and readied herself for the impact against the floor, but a strong pair of hands grabbed her just before the collision.

And then there was black.

Everything was a blur when Ellora woke up. She couldn't recognise the pale ceiling above her, the bright walls surrounding her, or the pale blue material covering her. To the right was a dark blur that looked as if it was moving slowly, up and down.

"Is it true?" an unfamiliar, muffled voice rang from somewhere nearby.

"Zella, you know I can't say anything about it." Ellora knew that voice—it belonged to Oriel. She let out a grateful breath; at least she was still in the castle.

"But surely we have the right to know," complained another voice, this one more high-pitched and frantic. "We've already seen a minor impact in our own Kingdom. Mistfall, even in our own school, of all places! But if it's starting to hit the other kingdoms this badly, it will only get worse for us, too."

"We don't even know what *it* is," responded a calmer and steady voice. Those low tones could only belong to Master Rainclarke. "How can we expect Oriel to provide answers if she doesn't have them herself?"

Ellora gritted her teeth and tried to lift her head, ignoring the sharp pain coursing through her skull in an attempt to hear them better. She had a feeling that whatever they were talking about was related to Melody in a way. And, possibly, to whatever happened to the water supply last year.

The water supply had suddenly vanished, which was completely unheard of in the Madori Kingdom, the kingdom of water. They all assumed it was something to do with the Madori Orb being stolen, but when they found and apprehended the suspect, Julia, a Prefect at the school, the water supply did not return.

And there was also the matter of Daphne's attack, which remained unsolved. Ellora's stomach still churned at the thought of how Daphne looked when she found her, with a long and deep gash diagonal across her body and begging Ellora to end the torture she endured, begging Ellora to kill her.

Ellora pushed herself too hard, her head spinning as she forced herself into a seated position. Another sharp pain pulsed through her skull, and Ellora groaned.

"Ellora, stop," Hunter sighed, his voice coming from the right.

She looked over and saw him heaving himself up from a chair. If his messy hair and the handprint on his cheek where he had been leaning were anything to go by, he had fallen asleep next to her bed, which she now recognised was in the infirmary.

He got up and carefully supported her back with one hand, gently lowering her back onto the bed. "You need to take it easy," he ordered. "You all but collapsed when I saw you in the corridor earlier."

"Did you—Do I remember you carrying me around the school?" Ellora demanded, her voice low and tired as the memory of being lifted flashed across her mind.

"I did not carry you *around the school*. I carried you here. A 'thanks' wouldn't be amiss, you know. It's not like you could walk yourself," Hunter joked, his eyebrow lifted playfully, but his jaw relaxed.

"Ellora, you're awake!" Oriel cried, hurrying in through the door with Master Rainclarke no more than two steps behind her. "How are you feeling?"

"I'm alright, I think. My head feels awful, though. What happened?"

"You collapsed after your session with Noah earlier," Oriel explained as she chewed on her lips, "Healer Amare and I did some diagnostic scans on you, but the only thing that we could see was that your Aura drained away very quickly, in the space of a minute or so."

"Ellora," began Master Rainclarke in a strained voice, his arms crossing over his chest and his face wrinkling in a way that created a knot of anxiety in Ellora's stomach, "it seems that something about that dream we were discussing is still being partially blocked. I believe that's why you are unwell."

"But that would mean... my own memories are blocking my memories? How can that be?" she asked, pinching the bridge of her nose tightly. "It doesn't make any sense."

"Well, Ellora, you know your case isn't quite like any we have seen before," Rainclarke replied. "I have no clue how these things work, and I know you're frustrated, but if you're really desperate, there might be somebody you could ask for guidance." he raised his eyebrows knowingly at her.

"Asyra," she whispered.

"I'm not sure this is the best idea, Artemer," said Hunter, his voice tense and his shoulders stiff. Despite Oriel and Rainclarke's warnings to stay in bed and rest, Ellora hopped out of the infirmary bed the moment they left, determined to seek help from the Madori Spirit, Asyra. Her headache had become excruciatingly painful, and she needed her to make it stop.

As she tried to stand, a searing pain shot through her head, and she stumbled, grabbing onto the edge of the bed for support. She took a deep breath and tried again, gritting her teeth and forcing herself to breathe deeply.

"Okay, well, if you're going to be stubborn, at least let me help you," Hunter muttered with a sigh. He helped her off the bed and through the door of the infirmary. "I'll come with you; there's no way I'm letting you go alone."

"You'll come with me to Asyra? Can you do that?" Ellora panted, stopping to catch her breath and lean against the wall.

"Have you forgotten? I've known her all my life," Hunter murmured, his voice tinged with bitterness as he put his arm around her waist. "If you lean on me, we might make it down there a little easier."

"Oh, right. Wasn't your grandfather the last Madori Master?" asked Ellora, gratefully shifting to share her weight with him.

"He was. I happened to spend a lot of time with him, and he used to bring me with him on his visits to Asyra when he could."

After what must have been the longest and most painful walk Ellora had ever endured, the two finally made it to the East Courtyard. Through the shadows, and with the moon barely visible above them, the East Courtyard had an entirely different atmosphere to it. A shiver prickled against her skin, making each hair stand on edge.

"We're almost there," Hunter reassured her as they hobbled to the door that hid the secret lake. A faint glimmer of light emanated from below the door, casting an unusual glow across the courtyard and illuminating the shadows cast by the majestic branches of the trees. The corners of the square were plunged into darkness.

"It looks different," Ellora whispered to Hunter as they shut the door behind them. "It looks creepy."

The moon shone down from above, creating a layer of ghostly mist that hovered over the magnificent, inky lake before them. The pebbles that bordered the lake, which would normally sparkle in the moonlight, were now dark and shadowy. The surrounding grass was dull, lacking its usual brightness and lustre.

Ellora looked up at Hunter when he didn't reply. He was silent, but his face was etched into a deep frown, and his eyes narrowed ever so slightly as he stared out into the water.

"Asyra!" Ellora called out, stepping closer to the lake, trying not to put too much weight on Hunter and wincing as she did so. "Are you there?" she called out again but grabbed her head with a pained yelp as it throbbed sharply.

"Asyra!" yelled Hunter.

"Well, well, it appears I have visitors," a cool voice echoed in their minds before they heard the swishing sound of water as Asyra rose from the lake in front of them, her eyes narrowing as she spotted Hunter. She fixed her lustrous, blue orbs on Hunter, her pale irises hardening.

"Asyra, please, I need your help," groaned Ellora as she unsuccessfully tried to separate herself from Hunter. "I don't know what's going on. Please."

Finally, Asyra acknowledged Ellora's presence, her gaze softening with a hint of warmth. Rising out of the water, she towered over Ellora by an entire foot and beckoned her forward with a graceful gesture. Ellora stepped closer, leaving Hunter's side, but he remained close, never straying more than a metre away from her.

Asyra rested her forefinger on Ellora's forehead and closed her eyes. Ellora felt a warmth first in her skull, spreading out from the point of Asyra's touch to the far corners of her head. Just as Ellora allowed herself to close her eyes and bask in the freedom of a clear and painless mind came a strike of pain. She doubled over, clenching her head in agony, barely aware of the choking sound coming out of her mouth.

"Ellora!" Hunter called out her name and two firm hands wrap around her arms, but she couldn't bear to open her eyes or speak.

A soothing, melodic voice echoed in Ellora's mind, singing a familiar tune that seemed to absorb her pain and ease her suffering. She inhaled sharply as the last remnants of agony dissipated, her eyes fluttering open to find Hunter's worried gaze fixed upon her. "I'm okay," she murmured, nodding reassuringly. Wobbling, she rose to her feet, her legs still unsteady from the intensity of Asyra's cure. But just as abruptly as the pain subsided, it surged back and Ellora cried out in agony, clutching her head once more.

"What caused the pain to start?" asked Asyra, her voice chilled as it sounded in their heads. She lowered herself into the water so that she was at Ellora's height once more. Lines formed between the eyebrows on her pale and shimmering face as she tilted her head to the side.

"I had a dream last night that I was trying to remember," Ellora answered in a strained whisper. "The moment I tried to remember what happened, the headaches started, and they have only gotten worse."

Asyra nodded, a thoughtful expression on her face. "Let me try something," she suggested after a moment. Ellora took a deep breath and looked back at Hunter, whose brows were knitted together but said nothing to stop her. She took a step closer to Asyra again, the floating mist engulfing the bottom half of her legs, and leaned forward so the Madori Spirit could reach her. She placed a light finger on Ellora's forehead, and Ellora gasped as a burst of coolness spread from it and through Ellora's skull, instantly easing the pain.

"Yes," Asyra's voice was gentle and soft in Ellora's mind. "I can feel something there." There was a pulse of pain before the coolness overcame it again. "There's some sort of blockage."

"Can you remove it?" that voice belonged to Hunter.

"I can," answered Asyra, "but the pain alone would most likely kill you." Ellora swallowed. There was no way she could keep going like this. Surely, there must have been some sort of solution that would allow her to live. Asyra pressed her lips together. "I believe I may be able to make a secondary blockage. It would stop this one from causing you pain. Similar to a barrier, if you will."

"What does that mean? Will that affect my memories?"

"It won't alter them," Asyra replied through their thoughts, "but it will prevent your memories from returning to you. As of right now, there is the slightest chance you could remember your dream. But if I put up this barrier, that opportunity is gone."

Ellora swallowed. All the hard work she and Rainclarke had put in to try and unravel these memories would be for nothing; she would likely never find out the truth of her sister's death. She would never even be able to remember who did this to her. But in such agony, she wouldn't know anyway.

With a shaky exhale, Ellora nodded. "Please, put up the barrier."

For a moment, nothing happened. But suddenly, a hot intensity overcame the coolness that was keeping Ellora's headache at bay. It was fire, burning through her skull and scorching her mind. Flames engulfed her every thought. The pain was unbearable, akin to acid burning through her bones. A scream, filled with terror and agony, tore from her throat.

But then, just as suddenly as it began, it ended. The fiery torture came to a halt, replaced instead by a blanket of warmth and comfort. Her throat was raw and sore from the scream she let out. A soft blue light filled Ellora's vision, just as it had when Asyra had first touched her almost a year ago to unlock her Aura.

As the glow slowly ebbed away, Asyra released Ellora, allowing her to stumble clumsily back into Hunter's arms for support. She swayed on her feet, thankful when Hunter supported her once again, overwhelmed by the power that travelled through her.

"Feeling better?" the Spirit asked.

"Much," replied Ellora gratefully, with a sigh. "Thank you."

"Thank you, Asyra," said Hunter with a nod.

As if Hunter's voice sparked something in Asyra, she suddenly snapped her eyes onto him. "While you are here, there is something I need to discuss with you."

Ellora looked between the powerful being before her and Hunter. Why was Asyra staring at him like that? "Yes?" she asked, a feeling of uneasiness settling deep in her stomach. She swallowed.

"Where is Julia being kept?"

Ellora certainly had no idea what Asyra was going to ask, but she most definitely was not expecting her to ask about Julia, of all people.

"Why?" demanded Hunter, rather bluntly in Ellora's opinion, to the Madori Spirit who had potentially just saved her life.

"After everything I did to help you to find that traitor and catch her, one would think you would be grateful enough to give me an update on the person who tried to *destroy my kingdom,*" Asyra's voice became dangerously quiet. Ellora could feel the power and the anger seeping off her as she raised herself out of the lake. She had no idea how tall the Spirit was, as she usually kept herself at eye level, but she was already twice her size and staring down at them.

Ellora gulped and stumbled backwards, away from the water, and felt Hunter grab her hand from behind. "You're right, Asyra.

It was thanks to your help and guidance that we were able to stop Julia before she escaped," she said, hoping that flattery would be enough to calm the Madori Spirit. "We're sorry; we didn't mean anything by it."

Although Asyra's eyes softened slightly, she didn't lower herself back into the water.

"The truth is," Ellora continued, "we don't know, ourselves. We haven't been told what has happened. Only we have been assured that we are safe, and she has been locked away somewhere. The Kingdom is no longer in any danger," Ellora lied. Oriel had, in fact, told them that Julia had been taken to Mistfall, the one place Ellora hoped she would *never* have to visit, dead or alive. She prayed to the Spirits, or the other Spirits, at least, that Hunter would follow her lead and lie.

"We don't have any more information than that," Hunter said, making Ellora silently thank the Spirits. "But we're no longer in danger."

"That's where you're wrong," Asyra communicated into their heads. "You may not realise it, but the threat has not finished with Julia. If Oriel believes Julia was acting on her own accord, she cannot even begin to comprehend the potential dangers that await."

Ellora and Hunter exchanged an alarmed glance but made no move to go anywhere. Even with the two of them using their Aura, they would not be able to leave if the Madori Spirit did not allow them. Asyra was no mere Aurum—she was the Madori Spirit, and in this state of anger, there was no telling what she would do.

Asyra's eyes remained hard and narrow as she analysed them, her shoulders stiff and her nostrils flaring with each slow inhale and exhale. "If you knew what was good for you, you would tell me where Julia is being kept," she told them in a low voice, the corners of her lips upturning with each slow and venomous word.

"But Asyra, like Ellora said, we truly don't know where she is," Hunter replied.

"Yes, you *did* say. But the problem is, Hunter," she spat the words into their minds, pronouncing his name with venom in her tone, "I think you're lying to me," she conveyed coldly, rising from the water even higher above them. "Do you think an Aura Spirit is a good enemy to have? I have helped you, and I have supported you. So far. Together, we have stopped the Madori Kingdom from crumbling to dust. But be aware that that was *my* choice."

"You're right, Asyra," Ellora quickly cut in when she felt Hunter tense, knowing he would have said something foolish or something that would prevent them from leaving that night. Besides, for whatever reason, it seemed that Asyra liked Ellora more than Hunter, and Ellora wanted to use that to their advantage. "But you should know, we—*I* would never lie to you."

That seemed to pique Asyra's interest, and she started to sink back into the water. "But you understand how imperative it is that I receive this information about Julia's whereabouts?" she asked, raising an eyebrow.

"Of course!" answered Ellora sweetly. It seemed to work, as Asyra had sunk back to their height again.

"Good," Asyra replied curtly. "In that case, I will look forward to seeing you back here soon to tell me the answer."

Before Ellora or Hunter could protest or make an excuse, The Madori Spirit sank straight back into the lake and vanished.

"Let's get out of here," grunted Hunter, pulling a stunned and nervous Ellora with him by the hand before she had the chance to blink, let alone question what just happened.

CHAPTER FOUR

A Hidden Danger

E llora woke with a start, her heart pounding like a drum in her chest. She was sure she had heard someone calling or speaking to her, drawing her out of her restless sleep. But as she scanned the dimly lit room, taking in the stark white walls and the row of pale blue, empty beds, she saw no one.

Swinging her legs over the side of the surprisingly comfortable infirmary bed, she walked to the small bathroom, splashing cold water on her face to wake herself up. After the strange and somewhat terrifying ordeal with Asyra, Hunter insisted on taking Ellora back to the infirmary for the night to rest, despite her feeling better.

"Just in case," he had said. Although, she at least convinced him to let her collect Lucifer from her room. Belle had been looking after him and feeding him, but Ellora missed him and knew she would feel a lot better with him by her side.

Ellora sat up at the little table next to her bed and found some paper and a pen, deciding to write out the dream so she could show Master Rainclarke before she had the chance to forget.

4ᵗʰ July.

I was a young child again, and the dream began with me running up the stairs.

Nobody was shouting at me this time, telling me to run. There was nobody chasing me, no heavy footsteps marching up the stairs behind me. But I still felt the urge to move forward.

I didn't go to my bedroom. I went straight to Ophelia's. There was a strong feeling, an instinct, telling me to go there. The house seemed empty because it was so quiet, but I could feel it wasn't. There was somebody else in there with me. I couldn't see anyone, but I could just sense them.

When I got to Ophelia's room, I saw her. I saw her. My baby sister. She looked straight at me, and she looked terrified.

She didn't say anything, though. She just stared at me, begging me with her eyes to help her. She looked so helpless, so young, in her pyjamas and tucked up into her polka dot bed sheets.

Suddenly, her eyes widened, and her mouth opened. She looked terrified. Slowly, so, so slowly, she turned away from me and looked towards the opposite corner of her dark room. I tried calling to her, but I couldn't seem to speak. No sound was coming out of my mouth. I also tried to go inside, to go to her, but it was like there was some sort of barrier at her door stopping me from going in.

I looked over to the corner of her room, where she was staring. I saw something green, like some sort of green light or something. I don't know what it was, but it was floating in the air, it was glowing, and it was green. It looked strange.

Suddenly, a flame appeared from nowhere. Like the floor has just combusted or something, burst into fire. But a very controlled flame. Now that I think about it, it kind of looked like when Master Rainclarke creates fire in his hand. Almost.

It wasn't moving about like a candle flame would, but it was also a lot bigger than a candle flame. It was huge.

It stood still at first, but then it started moving. It moved in my direction. It didn't grow. It just kind of shifted or floated along, I suppose, is the best way to describe it.

It started getting closer to me, and I knew I needed to get out, so I started calling for Ophelia again. I shouted her name again and again and again, but still, no sound would come out, and she was completely focused on the green thing in the air. She wouldn't look at me.

The fire got so close that I should have been able to feel the heat. But I couldn't, weirdly enough. Maybe because of that barrier.

I wanted to stay. I wanted Ophelia to come with me, but it was too late. The flame blocked the entryway and was getting closer.

I had to run. I ran through the corridor, and that was when I heard something behind me. Footsteps.

I turned and saw the fire pursuing me. I screamed, my throat finally able to make some noise somehow.

And then I heard someone scream my name back at me, and that was when I woke up.

It was now far too late in the morning for Ellora to go back to sleep, not that she would have been able to, anyway, after that dream. On the bright side, though, Ellora could spend some time with Melody since her parents were sleeping in a guest room and wouldn't return to the infirmary until after breakfast.

"You'll be okay, Melody", Ellora said, watching Lucifer curl up in Melody's hair, his grey tail dusting the tip of her nose. It was no secret he loved her, probably because she fed him and stroked him every time she saw him. "Healer Amare said you could wake up at any moment. She's the best around; we both know that."

Melody's eyes remained still, her skin pale and her breathing even. She had lost a lot of weight in the small amount of time she had been here.

"As soon as you're able to," Ellora whispered, "you and I are going to eat all the chocolate cake and chocolate mousse in the world. And Lucifer misses you, too. I think he especially misses the fact that you always treat him with strawberries. It's not the same without you, Melody," Ellora sighed, knowing she was pretty much talking to herself by now but also not caring much.

"Your mum told me that your brother Jason is coming to visit tomorrow. I'm sure he'll be happy to see you. Your mum said he's finally been able to get some time away from Asclepius' Academy for Healers to come and see you. Apparently, they have a rigorous programme, and they were worried about him leaving, but he promised to catch up on his work, so they made an exception. I'm sure your mum has told you all this already."

She sighed, leaning back in her chair and looking at Melody, who seemed so peaceful that if she wasn't so pale, Ellora could easily have convinced herself she was only sleeping.

"I can only imagine how difficult the healer training must be. I mean, I've seen Healer Amare work a few times now, and the most simple procedures look so complicated. I think you would have made a fantastic healer if you didn't have such a strong Ferri affinity, don't you think, Melody? Well, either way, I'm looking forward to meeting Jason; you've spoken about him so much, I feel like I already know him!"

"Genevieve, Thomas, I hope you both enjoyed your breakfast," Oriel's voice drifted in from the hallway.

"We did, zhank you again, Oriel," replied Mr Sotto as the three of them entered the room.

"Zhank you, Ellora, for keeping 'er company," said Mrs Sotto, placing a hand on her shoulder.

"Not at all, Mrs Sotto," replied Ellora with a small smile. "I had a lot to catch Melody up on, anyway." Melody's parents were such lovely people; the thought of them stuck working for Liviana and her parents made her nauseous with anger.

"Ellora, would you like to join me for breakfast?" Oriel asked, walking over to her with a strange expression that was both worried and amused. "I'm afraid the others have all eaten, but I was otherwise occupied, so I'm hungry. And you look surprisingly better, certainly well enough to venture out and into the dining hall." She raised an eyebrow at Ellora, indicating that she knew about her and Hunter's trip to the courtyard the night before.

"Hunter filled me in," Oriel confirmed her suspicions as they walked down the stairs, their footsteps clattering loudly in the silent corridors. "You shouldn't have gone last night when you were in such a state, but I'm glad it helped you, at least."

Ellora hesitated, wondering if she should tell Oriel about Asyra's weird reaction the night before.

"Hunter told us about what... *happened* while you were there, too," Oriel added upon seeing the hesitation on her face. "He came to Master Rainclarke and me as soon as you were asleep."

"Why do you think *that* happened?" asked Ellora, surprisingly unbothered that Hunter had gone behind her back.

"To be perfectly honest, Elle, I have no idea. But I also don't think it would be a good idea for you to go and see her again."

"But Oriel, I told her I would come back and tell her about Julia. Hunter and I lied last night and pretended we knew nothing, but she expects me to come back and fill her in. Besides,

I didn't get a chance to find out anything about my dream before she went a bit crazy. I need to know."

"I know, and you will. But we'll find another way. Just trust me, okay?"

Of course Ellora trusted Oriel as the Madori Mistress and their headteacher. Without her, Ellora would have left the school a year before, and her best friend would have died. But she also needed to know what was going on and wasn't sure how much longer she could go without reporting back to Asyra before she started appearing in her dreams again like she did when Ellora first joined the school.

She piled a stack of waffles onto her plate and smothered them with chocolate sauce, strawberries and a generous helping of whipped cream before picking up a cappuccino and sitting at the table.

Oriel looked at her and her plate of food in amusement. "I'm hungry, okay?" Ellora mumbled defensively. "Besides, I missed dinner last night and the chocolate cake that went along with it, so I've got to make up for it."

"You deserve all the chocolate in the world. Who am I to deprive you of it?" Oriel chuckled. "How was your time at home, by the way? We haven't had a chance to have a proper conversation since you arrived."

"It was alright." Ellora shrugged. Nobody other than Clara, Belle and Dan knew about her parents, and that was only because they each witnessed it themselves.

Clara never mentioned the emptiness that filled her mother's eyes since Ophelia died. Dan never commented on her inability to focus on a conversation anymore. Belle never asked why she slept or sat all day, every day, why she never received more than a 'hello'.

And, of course, nobody would bring up her father's obsession with work. It was his way of coping; not only had he lost his youngest daughter, but he had somehow lost his wife in the very same moment.

"Master Rainclarke may have told you already, but my dreams didn't stop while I was away like I hoped they would. How has everything been here? What's going on with the whole missing water and other weird and unexplainable things happening situation?"

Oriel frowned. "Not great, actually. I think we—"

"Oriel, would you mind coming out for a second? I've just found something I need to show you," interrupted a frantic-eyed Master Rainclarke, poking his head into the room.

"I'll just be a moment," Oriel told Ellora with a smile.

Ellora ate her waffles in silence, taking Lucifer out of the little makeshift nook she made for him in her bag and putting him on the table in front of her. She cut up a couple of strawberries and put the pieces on a small plate in front of him for him to nibble on.

As if watching Lucifer munching on the juicy strawberry crossed wires in her head, Ellora suddenly remembered a part of the dream she had a few nights ago, and she jumped up, itching to tell Master Rainclarke as soon as possible. She wasn't sure how important it would be, but he had, after all, insisted that she tell him every detail she possibly could.

She ran to the door, so she could tell him before she had the chance to forget the details once again. When she opened the door, Oriel's and Master Rainclarke's voices reached her instantly. They couldn't have been too far from her, as what they were saying was fairly clear, but she couldn't see them when she looked around.

Too late, she realised they were actually having an argument, and Ellora turned to go back into the dining room before she could intrude any further, only she heard something that she couldn't ignore.

"She's in danger, Oriel," Master Rainclarke's voice hissed in frustration.

"You don't think I know that, Noah?" countered Oriel, sounding just as frustrated.

"You need to get her out of here."

Ellora froze. *Who* was in danger? Could it be Melody? Had something happened while she and Oriel were eating breakfast?

Could that be why Master Rainclarke needed to speak to her so urgently? But surely he would have told Ellora too? If he came all the way to London to tell her about Melody and bring her back, why would they keep this from her?

What if it was Belle? Ellora panicked. If there was something wrong with Belle, she didn't even know what she would do. Maybe something went wrong with her Aura. Master Rainclarke was currently playing a huge part in her training since everything happened with Melody, so it was possible that he came to tell Oriel something happened.

"I know that," Oriel said again with a sigh. There was a soft thud, and Ellora guessed one of them had slumped against the wall. "I just don't know *how* to get her out of here."

"The King and Queen," Master Rainclarke replied quickly. "You can take her there."

"I did need to go anyway, to see *you know who* about *you know what*," Oriel considered. Ellora had no idea what "you know who" or "you know what" were, but she was incredibly intrigued. "We would have to leave immediately," Oriel spoke again, apparently closer to a decision. "Will you be okay without me?"

"Yes," Master Rainclarke replied. "And I will take care of Belle's training until you get back; you don't need to worry about that. She can't complete all of her training without you, of course, but you know there are parts I can deal with."

So, Belle wasn't the one in danger.

"What about Hunter?" asked Oriel, her voice still sounding unconvinced.

"I'll sort something out. Maybe he can join the two of you later on today."

A short silence followed, along with another sigh of exasperation from Oriel, but then Ellora heard the soft padding of what must have been their footsteps along the carpet, returning to the dining room, and Ellora darted back inside to sit on her chair, stuff her mouth with waffles, and pretend she hadn't been eavesdropping on them.

"Master Rainclarke," Ellora mumbled after gulping down the waffles, "I remembered something from my dream the other day."

This caught Master Rainclarke by as much surprise as it had Ellora. They had both made peace with discovering nothing more from that dream. "That's great, Ellora," he said, taking a seat at the table next to Oriel, "what did you remember?"

"There was a woman," replied Ellora. "She had long, red hair, a vibrant, fiery red. I'm not sure if it's important, but I remembered a flash of her. I think the strawberry reminded me."

"Everything is important in the right context," he replied with a smile. "I'm glad you were able to remember."

"Ellora, there's been a slight change of plans," Oriel said quickly. Ellora looked at her with feigned nonchalance. Ellora raised her eyebrows in question. "I need to visit a contact in London," Oriel continued, "and I would like you to join me."

Oh.

"To speak to your contact?" asked Ellora, surprised.

"No," Oriel answered hastily. "Just to London."

"Okay," said Ellora, watching the relief flash across Oriel's face that she agreed so readily. So it was *her* that was in danger. "But why?" It would have been so much easier if Oriel would simply tell her what was going on rather than have to admit she essentially spied on them.

"Will you just trust me, please?" asked Oriel. The worry and fear on her face were so genuine that Ellora felt terrible for questioning her. Although, she was becoming slightly sick of the 'trust me' line. "I'll fill you in on the way. We're going by car."

"Car?" Ellora repeated, furrowing her brows. "Why don't we just take the Gate?" As much as she hated travelling through Gate between Realms because of her Gate sickness, it was by far the most efficient way of doing so.

"Because I'll need the car when we get there," Oriel replied, although Ellora figured there was something else that was not being said. But she decided she would ask on the way there since Oriel and Rainclarke both looked anxious enough already.

Ellora nodded. "When do we leave?"

"Does two hours from now work for you?"

"What do you think they were talking about?" Belle asked after Ellora told her about the conversation she overheard. Ellora was packing a small bag while Belle sat on Melody's bed. She was allowed a break from her training while Oriel prepared for the trip, and Rainclarke helped her and ran up to Ellora's room as soon as she heard Ellora would be going too.

"I don't know, Bee. I really don't. I mean, the first thought that came to mind was Julia, but she's... you know... in *Mistfall*," she whispered.

"But what if this has nothing to do with Julia?" Belle asked.

"But then who? Who else would be a threat to *me,* of all people?"

"What if this is all to do with the weird, secretive stuff that's been going on through the Realm? That stuff you heard while you were in the infirmary?"

"It could be. I suppose it wouldn't be linked to Julia, then."

"Yeah, but do you remember how this all kind of kicked off when Julia had already taken the Orb? I mean, nothing like that has ever happened before. Ever. And now this? Surely it can't just be a coincidence?"

"I suppose so. I'm hoping Oriel will fill me in properly on the journey."

There was a moment of silence.

"Do you think what's going on is related to what happened to Melody?" Ellora asked in a low voice, interrupting the silence.

"To be honest, I think it could be. But there's no way to know if we don't even know what's going on in the kingdoms."

"You're right; we need to find a way to figure out what's going on."

"Can't you ask Asyra?" Belle suggested.

"No," said Ellora quickly. "Hunter and I went to see her yesterday, and she was... different. She seemed angry."

Belle frowned at that but didn't push for any more information. "I can ask my sister," Belle suggested. "I'm sure she would have some sort of idea, being the Incendi Mistress and all."

"That could work, Bee!"

"I'm seeing her in a few days—Oriel said all of the Upper Council members are coming here for a meeting, and she asked Kris to come a bit earlier so that I could see her too."

"That'll be so nice, Bee! With both of you being, or training to be, Upper Council Members, you don't get to see enough of each other."

"True. I miss my parents too; I'm hoping to get them here for a visit soon since I can't leave. Oh, but before I forget, there's something weird about this Upper Council meeting," Belle lowered her voice.

"What do you mean?" Ellora followed her cue and spoke in a hushed voice, too.

"As the Madori Mistress in training," Belle began, "I'm supposed to be attending all of the Upper Council meetings with Oriel. But she said I don't need to go to this one."

"Maybe it's a boring one or something," Ellora suggested, but even she wasn't convinced. Considering everything that was currently happening in the Realm, she doubted any of their meetings were too dull at the moment.

"It's possible," replied Belle. "But we both know that's not the likely reason."

"Whatever it is, if it's to do with Melody, we need to figure it out. I have a feeling there's something important we're not being told."

≈≈ ≈≈ ≈≈ ≈≈

"Ellora!" a voice called to her above the chirping of the birds as she sat against her favourite tree in the West Courtyard. Ellora turned around to see Hunter trying to catch up to her, waving a stack of papers.

"Hunter, what's wrong?" she asked, standing up and brushing the dust from her shorts.

"Ellora, my father sends me a copy of the Aura Times each week, and I just received yesterday's publication. You need to take a look at this." He opened up the folded paper and handed it over to her.

"*Death comes to Caeli*," She read the title aloud. "What?" she asked, looking at Hunter for clarification.

"Keep reading," he nodded towards the article.

"*A young boy, age six, was found in the North-Western territory of the Caeli Kingdom. He was, at first, thought to be unconscious by the merchant who found him. According to many people who live near the area, it is common, if unsafe, for children to play around the abandoned, rocky ground.*

"*After calling for help and turning the body to search for a pulse, it was clear that he was, in fact, dead.*"

Ellora looked up at Hunter in horror.

"Keep going," he said in a hushed tone, his voice thick.

"*The young boy was almost torn apart, bleeding from many jagged scratches and slices across his body, wounds, unlike anything many people living in our peaceful realm have ever seen before.*

"*His family have been notified*," Ellora finished, her hands shaking as she dropped the newspaper to the ground.

She looked back up at Hunter, feeling dizzy at the memory of the time she had ever seen wounds like that before. If this were true, it would mean they had all been wrong. About everything.

Hunter nodded grimly at her, having come to the same conclusion as her.

"It's happened again," she whispered.

CHAPTER FIVE

The Aura Attacks

To say she was angry was an understatement. Ellora could feel her hands trembling as she paced in front of Oriel and Master Rainclarke.

Slowly, she took a steadying breath and turned to face them, leaning her back against the chair behind her and gripping the sides with tight fingers to keep herself stable. "How could you keep this from us?" she finally asked, surprising herself at her own calm, if trembling, voice.

Oriel and Master Rainclarke looked up at her from their seats in Oriel's office. Rainclarke's eyes were filled with fear and concern, while Oriel's face was plastered with resignation, her eyes tired and guilty.

But Ellora couldn't care less. She had never felt such betrayal in her life, not when she thought Hunter was a deranged murderer and thief, or when her boyfriend, the idiotic Prince of Japan, cheated on her. She hadn't even felt this way when she found out

Julia was the one trying to destroy the Kingdom and kill Belle and Oriel.

This was different. Oriel *knew* what Ellora witnessed that day in the library. She knew Ellora was still haunted by the memory of Daphne lying limp and lifeless. The image of Daphne's tear-streaked face still twinged Ellora's heart. They were tears of agony pouring down her face, tears for her life, tears for the life she thought she would never have, tears of fear. She could still picture the deep, gruesome gashes covering Daphne's abdomen, crimson blood oozing out of them. The metallic scent of blood still lingered in her nostrils, and if it was too quiet, she could still hear the sound of Daphne's laboured breaths.

She had been alone when she found her. Alone with Daphne's head in her lap as she slowly bled out, her trickling blood pooling beneath them. Alone as she desperately tried to reassure her everything would be alright.

Completely and utterly alone.

And yet, neither Oriel nor Rainclarke had thought to share with her the fact that whoever had done that was still out there. Whoever almost killed her friend could be walking the streets, looking for another to slaughter.

And to make matters worse, Oriel all but confirmed that Melody's attacker was likely Daphne's attacker. *Melody* almost died. It was certainly not something that should have been kept from any of them, no matter the reason why.

Oriel sighed. She stood and placed a comforting hand on her shoulder. "Ellora, I understand how you feel, but—"

"No, Oriel," Ellora interrupted, throwing off her hand with a violent shrug, "you *don't* know how I feel. That's exactly my point. None of you have any idea what that was like, so who are you to keep this information from me? Especially after what has happened to Melody."

"I wanted to tell you," said Oriel in a soft voice, with frowning eyebrows and honest eyes. "I knew you needed to know, *all of you*, and I was going to tell you as soon as I could."

"What do you mean?" Ellora asked.

"This is not just Madori School business, Ellora; it's not even just *Madori* business. This concerns the entirety of the Aura Realm, and since Oriel is the Head of the Council, she's the last person who would have been allowed to tell you," Master Rainclarke said in an even tone. Oriel sat down and pinched the bridge of her nose between her fingers.

"Ellora, we don't even know how the journalist who wrote that newspaper article knew about it," Oriel told her, looking up again. Ellora felt the fear inside of her intensify at the urgency in Oriel's face." The only people who were supposed to know were myself and the other Upper Council members, as well as the merchant who discovered the boy, his family and the authorities who figured out what happened. I didn't even tell Noah," Oriel gestured to her husband, "until the article came out."

Ellora took a seat. "How do you know it wasn't the merchant, or the family, or someone who told the newspaper?" The fact that the information had been leaked did not change the fact that Oriel should have told them the truth, at least *after* the article came out, but that seemed less important now, knowing the entire Realm was at risk.

"It could be," Oriel began, "but I don't see that happening. The family had no reason to share gruesome information like that about their son to the public; the merchant is still being interrogated, and the authorities would also have no reason to do that."

Ellora nodded, her gaze dropping as she lost herself in thought and her hand absently running through her hair. After a brief moment of contemplation, she lifted her eyes to meet her Madori Mistress once again. "What else has been going on in the kingdoms?" she asked. Oriel raised an eyebrow, her calculating eyes staring at her curiously. Finally, Ellora sighed. "I heard all of you talking outside the infirmary." She bit her bottom lip in hesitation. "Please don't lie to me. I'm just scared. And I think we have a right to know."

"Very well, I suppose you're right," Oriel said with a small, tight-lipped smile as she stood up from her seat. "But I think it's only fair to have this discussion with the others too."

When Ellora, Belle, Hunter, Dan, Master Rainclarke and Oriel were settled into the common room, all gathered around a table on sofas and chairs, Oriel began. "You all remember the issue with the water supply, I assume? It caused quite the commotion, as I recall," she looked at the group for confirmation that they did remember the incident to which she was referring. After receiving scattered nods, she continued, "well, the water supply wasn't the only issue. Daphne, for example."

"You mean whoever attacked Daphne was responsible for the water supply?" hissed Belle. "Why? Why would someone go from cutting off the water supply to attempted murder?" She looked just as confused as Ellora felt.

"And why would they attack again? In the Glassi Kingdom and now the Caeli Kingdom, too," Hunter added. "At least, those are the attacks we know of." He glanced at Oriel, but in calculation, not accusation.

"I didn't actually see a connection until what happened in the Caeli Kingdom to that little boy. I truly felt they were isolated incidents," Oriel explained, ignoring Hunter's comment. "But that's not all. I'm not sure if any of you remember, but there was an incident in our Terrari gardens here last year."

"The strawberries," Ellora recalled, looking at Hunter, who nodded in agreement.

"I remember that," he said. "Henry Fischer and I spent an entire evening looking for Mistress Patel because all of the strawberries had mysteriously died. Nobody could figure out why."

Oriel nodded. "Exactly," she said. "And then there was the issue with the Leitocks."

"I think it was Violet who mentioned the Leitocks at the Winter Ball last year. Didn't they go crazy or something?" Belle asked.

"They went crazy," Oriel confirmed, biting her lip once again. "And then they were all found dead."

"What in the Realms," Hunter whispered, his eyes wide.

"And you're saying all of these events are linked?" asked Dan.

"That's what we think," answered Oriel. "And there's been more incidents like these in other Kingdoms. Like in the Ferri Kingdom, the cows started mysteriously dying one by one."

"The *Ferri* Kingdom of all places?" Clara asked.

Suddenly, something clicked in Ellora's head. "Is that why the Upper Council members were here so often last year?"

"Yes, that's why I was so worried every time any of them made an appearance. I knew it meant something else had gone wrong," replied Oriel. "And to think, at first, we thought this was all to do with the Madori Orb. How foolish we were," the last sentence was spoken in a hushed whisper that Ellora wasn't sure Oriel meant to say aloud.

Oriel pinched the bridge of her nose with her fingers, resting her head in her hands. "You can't blame yourself, Oriel," Master Rainclarke said gently. "You aren't a Magi Aurum; there's no way for you to have known."

Turning to face him, Oriel sighed. "I know, Noah, but that doesn't change the fact that, on paper, this is all my responsibility. And most of the Upper Council members are expecting me to have this sorted out." She was quiet for a few moments, and nobody else knew what to say until she spoke again. "There's one more thing I should tell you all – I'm inviting all students to come back here early."

Hunter widened his eyes. Ellora was not as familiar with the Aura Realm or the Aura schools as he was, but the look on his face meant this was not a regular occurrence. "Why?" asked Ellora.

"I think it's safer here than out there. Even if we have had incidents, now that we are aware of the danger, we are much better equipped to handle things and keep everyone safe. I've already prepared the letters asking for students to come back, so when you and I are back, Ellora, they'll be sent out ready for everybody to return."

CHAPTER SIX

A New Castle

The day was breathtaking, and Ellora gazed out the window, basking in the warmth of the sun's rays as they journeyed through the Madori Kingdom. Vast bodies of water surrounded them, the sun illuminating the surface and creating a mesmerising play of light and shadow. She squinted, her eyes drawn to the sparkling water of the sea they had come from, reflecting the sun's glare back at her. It danced and shimmered with the movement of the fish and other aquatic creatures that swam just beneath the surface. The sky was a brilliant shade of blue, with fluffy white clouds dotting the expanse. The wind blew through the open window, bringing with it the sweet scent of sea salt and seaweed.

The drive would be a long one, and after the way she had spoken to Oriel and Master Rainclarke, she wanted to clear the air. After all, Oriel had a point – if this was a matter of danger to the entire Realm, she could have hardly told a group of students, especially when she hadn't even mentioned it to her own husband, a trusted teacher.

She sighed and, in an attempt to make the drive comfortable, decided to strike up a conversation. "So, how do you know the King and Queen of England?" she asked.

"I've known Louisa for a very long time," Oriel answered, her tone casual and with no hint of upset or anger. "We were very good friends back when we attended the Madori School of Aura ourselves. Best friends, in fact, even though she was a few years older than me. Louisa happened to be the Prefect on my corridor."

Ellora thought about what it would be like to have such a relationship with her Prefect; her own had turned out to be a traitor and a thief.

"I didn't have many friends in my own form when I first started at the Madori School of Aura."

Ellora looked up at her with raised eyebrows. Oriel was one of the kindest, friendliest people she knew, and she found it difficult to believe anybody didn't want to be her friend.

Oriel looked at her and huffed out a small laugh. "Thank you, Ellora. That look says a lot. But it's true; they were all rather jealous. Almost as soon as I stepped into the Madori School of Aura, my own Madori Master, Hunter's grandfather, identified me as the next Mistress of the school. He took me under his wing immediately and began to train me. So not only did I not have a chance to really meet others in my form and make friendships, but everybody disliked my power before they could get a chance to know me."

Ellora didn't know how she would have even made it through the first year without friends. "How did he know you were to be the next Madori Mistress?"

"The moment I walked through the doors, I felt something. Like a cool sea breeze brushing against my skin. Everyone was staring at me, and I had no idea why until I looked down and saw a trail of water, kind of floating around me like a belt and trailing out the door. It turned out that the water surrounding the school had been following me. I was put into training the same day. I felt so alone, and it was even more difficult with such a busy and overwhelming schedule.

"That's why I tried to wait before I announced Belle would be the next Madori Mistress. I knew from the moment you brought her to my office after she spent too much of her Aura, and Master Graynor knew when she was fully able to control the water so soon after joining the School. But I didn't want her to suffer the way I did. Looking back, I didn't need to worry; Belle has much better friends than I could have ever dreamed of at that age," she smiled at Ellora.

Ellora smiled back, but the smile was empty. She couldn't help feeling a little sad, as well as impressed at Oriel's clearly incredible Aura, that Oriel had been made to feel like that rather than proud of herself as she should have been. She should have had friends encouraging her and sharing her happiness.

"Luckily, I met Louisa on one of my first days, and we immediately became very close friends. She told me she thought I was inspiring and that she was proud of me. Of course, I was a little confused; how could someone who didn't even know me be proud of me? But Louisa told me she didn't need to know me to see what a kind person I was and what an inspiring leader I would make.

"I didn't know at the time that my best friend Louisa was actually Princess Louisa Winnashire of England, the daughter of my mentor, but I suppose it didn't matter much when I found out. Louisa had such a huge impact on my life, and I will be forever grateful."

"What about the King? Do you know him very well?" asked Ellora.

"Actually, I didn't meet him until he and Louisa started officially dating. He graduated the year before I joined the Madori School. But he's a kind man. I was over the moon when Louisa told me he proposed; I knew how happy he made her."

"And what about your contact?" Ellora continued, fully aware that she was bombarding Oriel with questions but too eager for answers to resist. "You said earlier that you would fill me in on the journey."

Oriel looked at her hesitantly. "Look, Elle. There are some things I can't tell you, no matter how much I would like to. For your safety, for mine, but especially for the safety of my contact."

"You think I would leak that information?" Ellora asked Oriel, feeling a slight pang of upset, but she could hardly blame Oriel for being wary—she had also trusted Julia. Spirits, all of them had, and she had essentially tried to kill her.

"No, no, it's not that," Oriel said quickly. She sighed, the dark circles under her eyes once again prominent and visible. "We shouldn't really be discussing these things while we are still in the Realm. Ellora, you know as well as I do that there are certain *people* out there who can access that information whether or not you share it willingly."

"*People?* You mean like Asyra?"

"We really shouldn't be discussing this here," Oriel said quickly, shooting Ellora a look that quite clearly said, 'we can discuss this later'. "Even if I can't share the details of my contact, I can at least explain why I am going to see them. I'm hoping to get some more information on what's going on in the Realm. And, for reasons I cannot share, they refuse to come to the Aura Realm, and therefore, I have to go and see them myself."

"Oh, right," said Ellora, feeling as though she had somehow been left with more questions than answers. She wanted to ask a few more questions, but the soft shimmering of the Gate to the Human Realm was now visible up ahead.

"Oh, Spirits," she grumbled, her lips curving downwards in disgust, "I hate this part." She took a deep breath and willed herself, *begged* herself not to throw up this time.

"You get nauseous too?" Oriel asked with a sympathetic glance.

"Nauseous is an understatement."

"Here, take one of these." Oriel pressed a button on the steering wheel, and a small compartment emerged from below the radio. She pulled out a little tub of what looked like chewing gum from the Human Realm and held it out to Ellora. "Put one in your mouth, and you should be fine."

"What are these?" Ellora asked, looking into the tub filled with different coloured squares. She pulled out a bright green one and popped it into her mouth while Oriel chose a pink one. "Mmm, watermelon," said Ellora.

"Yes, the watermelon ones are good, but I can't risk taking a green one because, most of the time, they're apple flavoured," said Oriel, making a face.

"I take it you don't like apples, then?" Ellora laughed.

"And you would be right. They're Gate Pastils, one of the hybrid products from Ferrari. Not many people know about these, but I also get nauseous from Gate jumping in the car, so I wouldn't be able to live without them."

"Hybrid products?" Ellora had never heard of anything like that before.

"Some clever Aurum technicians have managed to combine the use of modern Human technology with Aura to create products like these. The Pastils are one of many. Back when a Magi Aurum had invented them, they used to be a lot more common, but they were only really used for walking through the Gates rather than driving. And, when the Magi Kingdom and Aurums were wiped out, some Terrari Aurums managed to combine their Aura with Human anti-nausea medicine, tweak them a little, and create these!"

"What in the Realms is Magi Aura?" Ellora asked, this time feeling bombarded with information herself. "As far as I was aware, there are currently six Auras: Madori, Incendi, Terrari, Caeli, Glassi and Ferri. I've also heard of the Lynchi-Obscuri war, so I assume before the war, there was Lynchi Aura and Obscuri Aura, but even those are hardly ever mentioned."

"Yes, now that I think of it, I suppose it's surprising you've even heard of Lynchi and Obscuri, let alone Magi." She was silent for a few minutes as she navigated through a particularly busy roundabout before continuing. "How can I explain it? Magi Aura... it was unlike any Aura you know of today. It was spectacular, almost a unique combination of different Auras. Magi Aurums could do all sorts of things, different to what we can do. Stronger things – *powerful* things."

"Like what?" Ellora had never heard any talk of Magi Aura, not even from Belle, whose family had been living in the Aura

Realm for generations and knew almost everything about Aura history.

"Well, the Magi Kingdom was primarily known for two things – enchantments and potions. Their potions saved so many lives and helped so many people. It was outstanding."

"That sounds amazing."

"It was. But even more than their potions, their enchantments were also Realm-renowned. In fact, the Gate Room keys that each Upper Council Member has for their school," Oriel said, gesturing to her own key, which hung as a small, sapphire-like stone on an elegant chain around her neck, "were enchanted by Magi Arurums."

"Wow," said Ellora, fascinated by the idea. "The possibilities of their Aurum sound endless."

"Oh, they were! The Magi Kingdom were constantly churning out new items and tools for the Rest of the Realm to use."

"If they were so Realm-renowned and helpful, what happened to them?" asked Ellora.

"You know how it is, Ellora," Oriel said with a sigh, her shoulders tensed. "While all the Kingdoms lived in harmony, some Aurums just couldn't accept that the Magi Aurums, with all their skill, simply wanted to help others. They couldn't accept that the Magi Aurums wouldn't use their Aura for power. There were only a handful of Magi Auras that could do more than you or I could, but their Auras were different and unexpected, and some people didn't like that.

"When some Magi Aurums began to master their enchantments, there was fear in the Realm. Rumours began to spread—toxic rumours, lies about what they were doing. Rumours that they were harnessing their Auras in unnatural ways—harnessing it from other Aurums, from Humans, from children who had Essence that had not converted to Aura. I cannot tell you who was so against them, who started the war, but one thing was for sure – whoever it was was a *very* powerful Aurum."

"But if one thing is certain, it's that whoever it was that started all of this had someone working for them from the inside. Someone betrayed the Magi."

"Magic, like what the Humans refer to as magic?"

"Similar, I suppose," answered Oriel. "When Humans think of magic or enchantments, they think of witches and wizards. I suppose all of us Aurums could be considered witches and wizards to the Humans, but it wasn't quite the same. I mean, most Magi Aurums, as I said, couldn't do much more than us; it was just the rare few that had this particular ability.

"I'm sure you've heard of a few famous Magi Aurums, Elle."

"I don't think so...."

"You've never heard of Merlin?" questioned Oriel.

"From Arthurian legends?" Ellora asked, jaw dropped. Human mythology and legends were somewhat of a forte of hers, and she had never stopped to think that any of the stories could be related to the Aura Realm.

"The very one. In fact, he trained at the Madori School of Aura. The Magi Kingdom never had an Aura School since they were the smallest, so he came to train at ours. Rumours *also* have it that Asyra had quite the soft spot for him," she chuckled.

"Asyra?" asked Ellora excitedly.

"Yes?"

"Asyra, as in our Madori Spirit, the *mermaid* Asyra?"

"Yes, Elle, what are you getting at?"

"Well... I was just thinking about the stories of Nimueh, the Lady Of The Lake. Could those stories be about Asyra?" Ellora asked.

Oriel laughed. "I'd never considered it before, but I suppose you may be right. The Humans don't realise it, but more often than not, there is some element of truth to all of their tales."

"You don't have to tell me twice," scoffed Ellora. "I had a face-to-face meeting with a Hydra under our school last year, remember?"

"How could I forget? Oh, pop another pastil in your mouth, Ellora; we have another Gate here that will take us all the way South to the outskirts of the country. Might I recommend the red ones? They're usually cherry flavoured."

"Why are we going so far away?" asked Ellora, popping a red pastil into her mouth. "I thought we were going to see the King and Queen."

"Yes, well, while their public lodgings are in the palace in London, they don't usually stay there. They have a hidden home that you can only access via this Gate, here," she said. The familiar soft shimmer of the Gate hummed around them before Oriel drove straight through. On the other side, they emerged onto a long, gravel drive.

Ellora still felt a little lurch in her stomach, but thanks to the Pastils, she didn't feel the urge to vomit. She needed to find a way to get some for herself.

The castle was a stunning sight to behold, even if it was much smaller than the Madori School of Aura. Built from bricks of grey stone, it stood tall and proud, its lofty spires reaching high towards the sky. The walls were adorned with intricate carvings, and the castle had a fairytale-like quality. With its turrets and crenellated battlements, it looked like something from one of the children's storybooks Ellora loved growing up.

Ellora couldn't help but feel surprised, as she assumed that Hunter's family, the royal family, lived in an extravagant estate similar to the Madori School and the other famous castles dotted around England. But this one was much more quaint and, Ellora figured, much easier to navigate.

Still, as they approached, Ellora couldn't help but feel awestruck by the grandeur of the castle. The sparkling pond, big enough to be considered a lake, was located right in front of the doorway. It was a picturesque sight, with swans and ducks gracefully paddling across its surface. The sun was shining high in the sky, casting a golden glow over the castle, making the grey stone walls sparkle and shine. The castle had a serene and peaceful atmosphere, the perfect place for a fairytale ending.

Tall, ancient trees added to the castle's charm, their branches stretching out to frame the walls. The castle's entrance was grand, with a large wooden door that was intricately carved with the royal crest and was flanked by two stone statues of fierce-looking lions.

As Oriel drove around the pond and parked directly in front of the door, Ellora couldn't help but wonder at the lack of soldiers on the estate.

The very moment they got out of the car, the heavy wooden door flung open, and a dark-haired woman ran out, speeding directly towards Oriel to give her a hug. Ellora felt a wave of panic wash over her. From the way Oriel laughed and hugged the woman in return, it was clear that this woman was Louisa, the Queen of England. But what made her even more nervous—although she couldn't quite put her finger on why—was that this woman was also Hunter's mother.

She smoothed out the light t-shirt she was wearing, inwardly cursing herself for not changing into something more intelligent than a t-shirt and denim shorts to meet the Queen and King of England.

She considered curtseying. After all, that was what you were supposed to do upon meeting royalty. At least, she thought it was. But Hunter didn't like being on the receiving end of such attention. Even Mason and Livianna never expected it. But this was different—this was a Queen she was meeting, not a spoiled princess. Yes, she decided it would be best to curtsey, and she did so the moment Queen Louisa turned around to face her.

The Queen was a striking figure with raven black hair that cascaded down her back in loose curls. Hunter certainly inherited his locks from her. But her face was round, and her cheeks bright and pink. She definitely hadn't passed those features onto her son, whose face was pale and angular. Her dress was the deep, rich colour of emerald green and was adorned with intricate beading and embroidery that sparkled in the sunlight.

Ellora immediately felt the anxiety fade as Louisa approached her, a warm and welcoming smile dancing on her lips.

She bobbed into a low curtsey, surprised when Queen Louisa laughed as she did and told her not to be silly, that curtseys were entirely unnecessary. Ellora looked up slowly, only to find Queen

Louisa holding her arms stretched towards her, offering a hug. Ellora glanced hesitantly over at Oriel, who simply raised her eyebrows and shrugged before deciding *not* hugging her would be more offensive than anything else.

"It's so lovely to finally meet you, Ellora," Louisa said honestly after letting go of Ellora. "Hunter has told us ever so much about you.

"He has?" Ellora asked. "Oh, well, I—yes, we—we're friends," she blurted out awkwardly.

Louisa chuckled, the warm sound pleasant and angelic. "So I've heard."

Fortunately, Oriel stepped in before Ellora could say anything else to embarrass herself. "I think Ellora may be slightly nervous about meeting you," she laughed gently. "Although I have assured her that you and Archer are lovely people, it's not every day that you meet the leaders of a country. And I'm sure it has absolutely nothing to do with a certain someone who happens to be your son." Oriel and Louisa both shot Ellora knowing looks, and she could feel her cheeks burning, even though she knew the red colour wouldn't touch her olive-toned skin.

"Not at all," she said, finally finding her voice and silently thanking the Spirits it sounded steady and casual. "Why would your being Hunter's parents matter?"

"Well, Ellora, there is nothing to worry about. I promise, Oriel is right, and Archer and I are, in fact, lovely," Louisa joked, a small and elegant chuckle escaping her lips as she did. If it were not for the hair, Ellora wasn't sure she would believe that Louisa was Hunter's mother. "Please, don't feel any formalities with us; while you are staying here, you are as welcome as Oriel, so don't hesitate to ask for anything," she said warmly, with a kind smile. Ellora was beginning to think at least one Disney princess was based on this woman; she was so lovely.

"Anyway, these human formalities mean nothing in the Aura Realm. As you know, it's only here in the Human Realm that our titles even mean anything," she chuckled. "If anything, *we* should probably be curtseying to *you*, Oriel!"

"Don't be ridiculous, Louisa."

"Well, anyway, the two of you look rather tired, and with all that Gate jumping, you must be feeling a little unsettled, Oriel. Why don't we go straight through to the parlour, and I'll get a pot of tea started."

She led them through the doors and down a corridor on the right, all the way to the end and into a quaint parlour lined with pale grey walls. "Archer!" She called through another door to what, through the little glimpse Ellora could catch, looked like a library. "Archer, Oriel and Ellora are here."

She left them to settle in and stated she would be back soon with some tea. Ellora was surprised, still, that there were no servants about or anybody working there to bring the tea for

Louisa, although she certainly respected it and liked the fact that Louisa had gone to make it herself.

"See, Elle, I told you she was friendly," Oriel laughed.

"She seems so lovely," answered Ellora. "I suppose after meeting Mason and Liviana, and since I still don't really think of Hunter as a prince, my natural instinct was to be nervous."

"Well, you know I'm not exactly supposed to say anything negative towards any of my students, so I'll just say that's a fair enough stance to take."

"Oriel, it's lovely to see you again. I trust your journey went well?" King Archer greeted, walking through the door at the back of the room from what looked like the library.

"As well as can be with that much Gate jumping, Archer, thank you," Oriel smiled at the King, but Ellora noticed she didn't attempt to approach him for a hug or even to chat with him any further. "This is Ellora Artemer, one of my students."

"Ah, yes, Hunter's friend, aren't you?" He offered a hand to shake to Ellora, who took it.

"I am. It's a pleasure to meet you," she replied, hoping that was respectful enough, even if there was no need for formalities. Ellora felt less at ease around Archer than she had with Louisa, but for some strange reason, she also didn't have the same nervous urge to make him like her.

"Look who just woke up from her nap," said Louisa, walking back into the room carrying a child who was rubbing her eyes.

"There's my favourite Winnashire!" Oriel cooed, getting up from the sofa she had been sitting on to take the giggling and excited toddler into her arms. "Hello!" She played with Sapphire. "And how is my Goddaughter doing?"

"She's well," answered Archer.

"Oh, Alana," Louisa said, catching the attention of a girl who was walking past the room, "I made tea, but I left it in the kitchen. Would you mind bringing it all in?"

"Yes, of course, your Majesty," the girl, who couldn't have been much older than Ellora, answered, dropping into a low curtsey.

"Please, Alana, how many times do I need to tell you? You can just call me Louisa."

"So, I assume you're here for a reason, Oriel?" asked Archer. "Is everything alright?"

"There are some issues in the Aura Realm, as I am sure you both know of already," answered Oriel, sitting back down but keeping Sapphire, who was playing with Oriel's hair, in her lap. Ellora shifted uncomfortably; of course they knew—Hunter's father was the one who sent them the newspaper about the attacks in the first place. "Until recently, Noah and I, as well as the other Upper Council members, were convinced we had it all under control. As it turns out, we were wrong. I'm worried about the situation and about how quickly it's escalating, so I am here to meet with one of my contacts. They have some information for me that I think will be pertinent to all of this."

The Queen nodded, her eyebrows etched into a frown. "Which contact?" she asked.

"I can't share that information this time around." Apparently, that reply hit like a brick. Archer's eyes widened and his back straightened. Louisa's frown grew deeper. "It's that serious?" she whispered. Oriel's lack of an answer seemed to be enough.

Ellora looked between the three of them. Should she have been more concerned about this situation? She knew she had been in danger when she was in the Madori School of Aura, although from whom she still didn't know. But surely that was just her? Yes, there had been devastating attacks, but she didn't realise it was escalating even further. How could it get worse?

"Well, you're always welcome here, whether the Realm is in danger or not." Louisa smiled tightly in an attempt to break the tension. "In fact, Ellora, we heard from Noah today, who told us Hunter will be coming home for a while too, and he should be here later this afternoon. We'll celebrate his coming home with a dinner party for us all since it's the first time we'll be seeing him in Spirits knows how long," she looked at Oriel with a joking glare.

"I gave him a choice," Oriel replied with a defensive chuckle. "You know very well that boy has far too much Essence in him for it to convert to only one Aura."

"Yes, yes, you're right," replied Louisa. "I am joking, of course, although I do miss him greatly. Almost as much as his sister misses him." She gestured to Sapphire, who was thoroughly entertained fiddling with a ring Oriel was wearing.

"Unfortunately, I won't be able to attend your dinner party, which is a huge shame because they're always spectacular. But I need to meet my contact this afternoon, and I'm not sure how long I will be gone. And then, possibly, the two of us will be out of here by tomorrow morning."

Ellora snapped her attention to Oriel with one brow raised. Oriel didn't mention them staying for less than 24 hours, and if she was in danger, how was she supposed to go back to the Madori School of Aura? She hadn't yet had the chance to tell Oriel about having heard her and Rainclarke outside the dining room because they arrived a lot sooner than Ellora thought they would, thanks to all the Gate jumping, but they definitely needed to discuss it.

"Oh, so soon, Oriel?" Louisa asked sadly. "As long as you promise to visit again soon, I'll have to forgive you. Let me take the two of you up to your rooms. Ellora, then you'll be able to settle in, and Oriel, you can get ready to leave."

She led them up only two flights of stairs to the top floor and down a corridor. She opened one door for Ellora and the opposite door for Oriel. "Do let us know if you need anything," she said with a smile before turning back and leaving the same way they came.

"Oriel," Ellora said, knowing they needed to talk before the following day when they would leave.

"Ellora, I'm sorry, but I'm going to have to postpone any further conversation until I get back. If I don't leave in the next ten minutes, I'll be late and miss any opportunity to talk to them."

"Okay, we can talk later; when will you be coming back?"

"I shouldn't be too long. It's not too far from here, so I shouldn't return too long after dinner. But there's also a chance I won't be back until late tonight or maybe even early tomorrow morning, depending on how it all goes." She offered a quick reassuring smile, then closed her door behind her as soon as she finished speaking.

Ellora didn't know what that meant, but she sighed and made her way into her own room. She would at least be able to ask *who* she was in danger from before they returned to the Madori Kingdom.

CHAPTER SEVEN

Alana

Ellora heard the door across the corridor from herself open and then close, the sound of Oriel leaving, and knew she had to figure out a way to kill time before Hunter arrived. She definitely didn't want to get stuck with either of his parents, even if they weren't as bad as she thought they would be; it still felt wrong to have met them without Hunter being here, too.

She poked her head out the door and looked in both directions to ensure she wouldn't accidentally run into Louisa or Archer. She walked out of her room and turned in the direction of the library that she saw Archer emerge from earlier. She saw a couple of maids and servants on the way, who all lowered their heads as she walked past, but otherwise, the halls were quiet.

Ellora assumed Louisa was preparing for the dinner party or maybe even Hunter's arrival, but she had no idea what Archer could have been doing. She just had to keep her fingers crossed that he hadn't gone back into the library.

She made it into the library, which happened to be empty, without any more encounters and sighed in relief. Being the guest of a Queen was not something she was familiar with, and she had no idea how to act. Until Hunter arrived, the best thing she could do was keep her head down and stay out of anybody's way.

The library was much smaller than she was used to at the Madori School of Aura. While the Madori library was enormous, almost the size of a ballroom, and filled with rows upon rows of shells that extended from floor to ceiling, the books all filed and stored meticulously, this library was a single room. It was still substantial, there was no doubt—certainly larger than her bedroom—but fortunately, much easier to navigate.

White wooden bookshelves lined the walls, leaving gaps only for the windows to let in natural light. On the far left of the room was a group of four armchairs arranged in front of a grand fireplace made of dark, polished stone. The warm glow of the fire under the intricately carved mantelpiece gave the room a cosy feeling that filled Ellora with warmth and comfort.

A desk and a comfortable chair stood in front of one of the windows, providing a perfect spot to read and study. The room was the perfect blend of style and function, and, surrounded by the musty smell of old books, Ellora couldn't help but feel in awe.

She walked around the room, browsing the books in the Winnashire family's collection. She wasn't sure what she wanted to read but knew some fiction would keep her occupied for a few hours until Hunter arrived. Perhaps she would even take two, just in case he took longer than expected. Picking one romance title and one mystery, Ellora opened the door to return back to her room, only to spot Archer on the other side.

"This is not acceptable," he demanded, and she froze in the doorway.

Was he on the phone?

Ellora decided she did not want to deal with that and shut the door again, closing herself into the library. She settled into one of the armchairs, knowing that soon enough, Archer would either come in or leave. While the latter was preferable, both options were better than exiting the room while he was arguing with somebody over the phone. But before she could even open the first book, something caught Ellora's eye.

Tucked away in a corner which could only be seen from this side of the room, was a little brown bookshelf. The dark, worn-out wood didn't match the rest of the room, which was pristinely white, and it was short, holding only a small handful of old-looking books that looked as though they would fall apart at the touch.

She crouched down in front of the bookshelf, leaving the two she previously chose on the chair, and scanned the titles; they were all about Aura. She picked one about the history of Aura and opened it, having to cough away the dust that blew into her face. It seemed nobody read these titles.

She picked up another, one whose title was too worn to be read and flicked through the pages, this time keeping it away from her face. Her jaw dropped open. This tiny, discarded tome was all about harnessing and practising Aura. Not only did it explain how to control Aura, but it also had a significant section on unlocking Aura and converting Essence. Ellora removed the cardigan she was wearing and carefully wrapped the book in the cloth, making sure not to damage it, before placing the covered book in the sage green rucksack she had brought down with her.

She had one more browse at the little bookshelf before leaving and, at the last minute, also decided to bring along a little book about Magi Aura that she discovered, wrapping that one as well. Apparently, even if it wasn't widely spoken about, it was documented. The book was short, only 100 or so pages, but nonetheless, Ellora thought she would give it a go.

These were books she certainly did not want to be caught reading by anybody who walked into the library; Ellora prayed to the Spirits that Archer would be gone as she cracked the door open and peered through the small crack. There was nobody there. She thanked the Spirits and hurried back to her room, once again afraid of bumping into anybody but also very eager to examine the information she had discovered. So much for some light reading.

When she returned to her room, she carefully peeled the cardigan away from the first book, determined to start there and move on to the other once she became tired and her Aura was beginning to drain.

On second thought, it would probably be best to have some tea ready. She certainly didn't want to drain her Aura and be unable to reach the kitchens in time to get some tea. She would end up waiting for ages—until Hunter arrived. And even then, she doubted he would even know she was in there if she was passed out. He might even assume she had left or gone for a walk or something else.

Before going on a hunt for some tea, Ellora decided to have a quick glance at the instructions in the book. The first step was to gather materials, so Ellora figured she should get a vase of water, too. She wouldn't try the other Auras just yet, but she would figure those materials out when she was ready.

Hearing soft padding outside her bedroom, Ellora rushed to open the door and stick her head out. "Excuse me!" she called, actually excited to see someone for once, so she wouldn't have to struggle to find the kitchen and, knowing herself, probably get lost in the process. "I don't suppose you could tell me where the kitchen is?" she asked the girl.

"Of course. But what is it that my lady needs from the kitchen? I would be happy to fetch it for you."

Ellora realised it was the girl Louisa had spoken to in the parlour earlier. "It's Alana, right?" The girl nodded her head timidly. "Please, call me Ellora. I'm certainly no member of the nobility," she smiled kindly.

"If that would please you," Alana said, nodding and dropping into a mini curtsey.

Ellora had to force herself not to laugh. She wasn't used to hearing *anybody* being spoken to like this, let alone herself. "I just wanted to make myself a cup of tea, Alana."

"I can make it for you!" Alana announced, practically jumping to offer.

"No, really, it's no trouble," said Ellora, "I don't mind at all getting it, myself. Besides, I would love to see more of the castle and could do with a little walk."

After some back and forth, Alana agreed to let Ellora make her own tea, but only if she allowed Alana to come with her to make sure she didn't get lost and get her safely back to her room after.

"Could you show me where you keep the honey?" Ellora asked, having put the kettle on to boil. She had no idea if those who worked here came from the Aura Realm or the Human Realm, so she didn't want to risk heating the water with her Aura. She filled a mug with earl grey tea before adding a generous dollop of honey. It was nothing like Oriel's lavender blend, but she had to make do with what she had.

"Thank you for helping me, Alana," she said kindly to the girl, who also filled a vase with water for her. "I think I can make my way back, though, if you've got other things to do."

Ellora hesitated upon seeing the bright pink shade that flushed Alana's cheeks. Did she say something wrong?

"Sorry," Alana said in a voice barely louder than a whisper. "I didn't mean to intrude by offering my assistance."

"No, no, no!" Ellora said quickly, shaking her head. "That's not it at all! I just didn't want to bother you, is all, Alana, spending so much time looking after me that you don't have the chance to get your own stuff done!"

"Oh," Alana said, the pink beginning to ebb away. "Well, you're not bothering me, my lad—I mean...Ellora. I've enjoyed your company."

"I'm glad to hear it," laughed Ellora.

They walked back through the corridors and up the stairs together, Alana having insisted on carrying the tea and barely allowing Ellora to take the water. "So, how did you end up working here?" asked Ellora.

"Oh, I was very fortunate to be able to get a job working here, Ellora. It was so very sought after. I originally applied to be Sapphire's "nanny" when she was a baby. But, now that she is a little bit older and I do not spend so many hours with her, I asked Her Majesty if she could give me some more responsibility. I like to be useful. And, besides, The Queen gets to spend so much more time with Sapphire these days, and I am not needed so often."

"Well, that sounds great, Alana. I take it you like babies and children, then?"

"Oh, I do! I always have. I just think they're adorable, and it's such a privilege to be able to help them grow up and to learn, don't you think? Well, I'd like to think I'm rather good with babies, too, but I'm certainly not as good with Sapphire as her brother is." At that, Alana's cheeks flushed lightly with that same colour that Ellora had seen earlier, and her stomach twinged.

"Oh, you know Hunter?" she blurted out, her attention captured by that last sentence. "What a silly question; of course you know Hunter!"

"I haven't seen him for a while, though, because he hasn't visited in a while. I suppose you already know that. I'm blabbering on now," she laughed nervously. "But The Queen said he is coming back today for a short time, so I'm sure Sapphire will be happy to see him and as will we all, here at the castle."

At that point, the two of them reached the door to Ellora's room. She cleared her throat awkwardly before opening the door and taking the tea from Alana's hands. "Well, thank you, Alana, for helping me today. I almost certainly would have gotten lost if it weren't for you," she attempted a lighthearted laugh.

"I'm sure you would have found your way, Ellora," Alana laughed, obviously now feeling much more at ease in Ellora's company.

"Hopefully, I'll see you at the dinner party later?"

Alana nodded and smiled before turning and padding back down the corridor. Ellora closed the door behind her as she entered her room and set the things down on the table with a sigh. It was time to get to work.

CHAPTER EIGHT

The Dinner Party

Before trying anything else, Ellora decided it would be best to practice what she could already do. With one more look over her shoulders to ensure she closed the door properly, she focused all of her attention on the vase of water in front of her.

Like Belle taught her so many months ago, Ellora took a deep breath and imagined the water floating up in bubbles from the vase. It took a few minutes of intense focus and breathing, but eventually, the water started to rise out of the vase. At first, there was only one bubble, barely big enough to be the size of a pea, but as Ellora communicated more with the Aura inside her, as she got into the rhythm of controlling it, the bubbles were emerging larger and larger each time, growing to the size of a peach pit, then a plum, a tennis ball, and eventually, the size of an actual football. She lifted all of the bubbles into the air together, prepared to merge them all into one, and lowered them back into the vase.

The bubbles danced in the air, shimmering and sparkling as they caught the light, creating a mesmerising display of light and movement. Ellora's concentration was unwavering as she guided the bubbles with a graceful gesture of her hands, her eyes fixed on the water as it obeyed her every command. She felt the power of her Aura flowing through her, and it was a heady feeling of control and mastery. She was in complete control, and it was a feeling of pure exhilaration.

A loud knocking at the door startled Ellora, and she jumped backwards, falling from her chair and breaking her concentration. All the water in the air, which was the entire quantity of the vase by this point, came splashing down directly on top of her.

A loud, persistent knocking at the door startled Ellora, causing her to jump backwards in surprise. She lost her balance and fell from her chair, breaking her concentration. All of the water that she had levitated and was holding in the air, which was the entire quantity of the vase by this point, came crashing down on top of her in a drenching deluge. The water soaked her clothes, drenched her hair, and made her shiver as the cold water made contact with her skin. She struggled to get up, her clothes sticking to her body as she tried to shake off the excess water. The sudden interruption and the unexpected soaking left her flustered and disoriented, unable to stop herself from cursing under her breath as she made her way to the door.

She swung the door open forcefully, only to find Hunter on the other side of it. Whatever it was that she was going to say was immediately forgotten. All that came out of her mouth was an awkward little squeak as Hunter stood there, hand raised to knock again before the door opened. His mouth curved into an amused, yet confused, arch as he looked her up and down and folded his arms, leaning against the door frame.

"Did I interrupt a fully-clothed bath?"

Ellora looked down at herself in embarrassment, at the denim sticking to her legs and the light grey t-shirt, now a completely different shade of dark grey. She glared at him before grabbing him by the wrist and yanking him into the room, closing the door behind them. "I was trying to practice my Aura," she grumbled, pointing to the vase and the water splashed around the floor. "You startled me, and I lost focus. As you can plainly see, the water went all over the place. Thanks for that."

Hunter covered his mouth with his hand, his ears turning a shade of red and his shoulders shaking up and down, and Ellora glared even harder. "I'm sorry," he said in between laughs. "I don't mean to laugh at you. Really, Artemer, I don't. But If you could see yourself... you look like an angry Leitock, with your hair sticking up all over the place, and...." He couldn't stop laughing by now, and it appeared Ellora's stare was not helping.

"Do—you—know—how—long—it—will—take—for—me—to—do—my—hair—Hunter!" She smacked him on the arms to punctuate each word.

"Relax, your hair will be fine!" Hunter said, finally having calmed down. "Your hair always looks great," he said teasingly.

"Yes, because I spend two hours washing it and taming the frizz twice a week, Hunter. I don't have two hours right now because I need to get ready for the dinner party!" She wasn't really *that* annoyed, but being angry at Hunter felt a lot more natural than being happy to see him.

"Here, let me help," Hunter said, reaching out a hand towards her and advancing.

"What are you going to do?" Ellora stepped back before he could come any closer, raising her arms in a defensive position that she was sure looked more amusing than threatening.

"After all this time, you still don't trust me, Artemer?" he laughed, one eyebrow raised.

Ellora frowned but acquiesced and allowed him to come closer. "Sit," he instructed, pointing to the chair in front of him. Ellora sat but watched him warily through the mirror on the wall in front of them.

Hunter put his hands above her head. At first, nothing seemed to happen, but suddenly Ellora felt a rush of warm air envelop her. It lasted only five seconds or so, but the warmth remained even when he removed his hands. "What was that?"

"Shh," Hunter cut her off. This time, he put his hands into her strands, and again that warm air enveloped her, but it was different this time. It was like a warm wind was caressing her skull while Hunter ran his hands through her hair. The warmth felt so lovely, and Ellora closed her eyes with a sigh, savouring the sensation. But before she could fully appreciate it, it was over.

"Hey," she complained, snapping her eyes open to glare at Hunter again. But as soon as she saw herself in the mirror, her jaw dropped open. Her clothes and hair were dry again, and her hair was flowing gently down her shoulders in soft, voluminous and, most importantly, frizz-free waves.

"Where in the Realms did you learn to do that?!" she exclaimed, looking at Hunter, who had a pleased and somewhat smug look on his face. She knew he was pretty good with his Caeli Aura, but she didn't even know something like this was possible.

"Please," he scoffed jokingly, "did you think *this* happens naturally?" he asked, pointing towards his hair.

Ellora rolled her eyes. "Shut up, Hunter." She looked at him for a minute before busying herself with tidying up the desk. "I'm happy to see you."

"It's nice to see you too, Artemer," Hunter replied, folding his arms again and leaning against the wall. "According to my mother, you've been a delight, so I'm assuming you've been enjoying your afternoon here?"

"I have, actually," replied Ellora. "Your parents are lovely, by the way, and so is your sister. I've heard she's quite fond of you." Hunter shrugged at that, but his lips were twisted into a small, secret smile. "I found these in the library earlier. That's why I was practising my Madori Aura." She brought out the two books to show him, starting first with the one about harnessing Aura and then showing the one about the Magi Aurums.

"I don't think I've ever seen these before, actually," Hunter said, leafing through the first book. "Could be helpful, though." He placed both books on the little stand next to Ellora's bed rather than on the desk by the wall. "I have some exciting news to share."

"Already? I've not even been gone a whole day!" Ellora laughed.

"Watch this." Hunter lifted his hand, holding it between them and closed his eyes. Out of nowhere, a tiny flicker of fire, like a candle, appeared in his palm. It lasted a few seconds before flickering away, after which Hunter closed his hand and looked at her, excited yet looking significantly more tired than before.

"Hunter, some of your Essence converted to Incendi Aura? That's amazing!" Ellora said excitedly.

"It's going to take some time and practice before I can do much more than that, but Rainclarke confirmed I've got Incendi Aura now," he said, his lip twitching into a reluctant grin.

"Your parents must be very excited."

"My mother was. Almost as excited as she was about me being home."

"And have you managed to see Sapphire yet?"

"No, she was eating when I arrived, and she never eats if she sees me—she gets too excited. My mother thought it would be best if I waited. I'm sure she's finished now," he said, glancing at the clock above the windows. "Would you like to come with me?"

"Oh. That's okay, Hunter. You hardly ever get to see your family."

Hunter scoffed. "Sapphire will be happier seeing you than me as long as you play with her. And having you around might just about make speaking with my father tolerable."

"You don't get along then?" Ellora asked hesitantly.

Hunter made a face. "It's not that we don't get along... I suppose we just have different ideas about what my life should entail."

Ellora could see Hunter's jaw tense and decided it would be better to drop the subject. "Well," she stood up from where she was perched on the edge of the bed and raised her eyebrows, gesturing to the door, "Sapphire awaits."

"Ah, I'm glad I caught you two," Louisa called to Hunter and Ellora, who were taking a stroll in the gardens after playing with Sapphire before they needed to get ready. "Guests will begin to arrive for dinner in about an hour."

"We'll be there in 45 minutes then, mother." Hunter nodded at her with a smile. He was acting like he was dreading the dinner, but Ellora had a feeling he appreciated the effort his mother put in. Louisa was apparently pleased with his response as she left with a content smile.

"When you said you wanted to show me the gardens, I thought you meant *flower* gardens if I'm honest," Ellora joked, waving out towards the rows and rows of different vegetables in front of them.

Hunter didn't laugh, but the corners of his mouth twitched upwards. "My mother is a Terrari Aurum. She grows vegetables all year round, and they all get taken and donated to those who require food."

"That's kind of her," Ellora said, feeling impressed by this act of kindness.

Hunter shrugged. "She sees it as her duty to help her country, as the Queen, so she doesn't mind. Besides, if she can help, what sort of Aurum would she be if she didn't?" He began walking in another direction, this time along a path that Ellora didn't notice before, that led to some of the trees, and Ellora followed behind. "My grandfather taught her to be a kind and fair leader."

"As you will be when you are King," Ellora added confidently. But she noticed his shoulders stiffen slightly.

"By the way," Hunter said. "Tonight at dinner... there are going to be some, well, some prominent members of The Aura Realm present."

"What does that mean?"

"It means that there will be a lot of people in that room tonight with information neither of us could find in any books or even from any other people. Not to say that they will all be willing to share, of course. I'm just saying it would be a good idea for us to keep an eye and an ear on what goes on this evening, especially because Oriel isn't here to do so herself. And I know Rainclarke has been helping you with your nightmares and your Essence and Aura; you might be able to get some information about that, too."

"I have no idea what I'm going to wear," Ellora whispered frantically. She called Alana to her room to ask for her help with doing her hair, incredibly nervous after seeing how Queen Louisa had gotten ready but had overlooked the most crucial part.

"We'll find something, Ellora," Alana said to reassure her, although Ellora could tell she was just as nervous.

Just then, a knock sounded at the door. "Who is it?" Ellora called, praying to the Spirits it wasn't Queen Louisa; she didn't want her to see her panic.

"It's me." The smooth, deep voice could only belong to Hunter. Ellora felt a wave of relief that only lasted for a moment before she realised that now, Hunter would realise how unprepared she was. She ran over to the door and yanked it open, gesturing for Hunter to enter.

He looked worriedly over her before snapping his eyes to her face. "You know we're supposed to be down there in a few minutes, right?"

"Yes, I know that, Hunter!" Ellora snapped in a whisper, flinging herself back onto her bed and running her hands through her hair.

"Ellora has nothing to wear," Alana stated when it was clear neither Hunter nor Ellora were planning to say much else.

"Why didn't you say so?" Hunter asked with a frown. "Come on." He opened the door again and walked out. Ellora hopped up in confusion, wondering where in the Realms Hunter thought he was taking her in her denim shorts. "Do you want something to wear or not?" Hunter asked, poking his head back into the room.

Ellora looked at Alana, who shrugged, before following Hunter out of the room. "Alana, please do come with us."

Hunter led them through two corridors and down a flight of stairs to another room whose interior was very similar to Ellora's guest room. "Mother always keeps spare gowns, suits, and general clothing for guests here. I'm sure we'll be able to find something."

He opened a set of double doors on the left side of the room, revealing a walk-in wardrobe filled to the brim with fabrics of all colours and sizes.

"What in the Realms would I do without you?" Ellora asked Hunter, grateful that he had saved her from looking like a lunatic in front of his parents and some of the most influential people in the Aura Realm. Impulsively, she grabbed him by one shoulder, pulled his face down towards hers and planted a kiss on the cheek. As soon as it happened, her eyes widened, and she dropped his face, staring at him in horror at what she had done as his face became bright red. She stared at where her fist was wrinkling his pristine suit and let go immediately, swallowing hard. She knew that she should have said something, addressed the fact that she acted on impulse and she should not have kissed him, but it was as though she had a frog in her throat; she just couldn't get any words out.

She blinked twice while Hunter's eyes went from wide to narrow and uncomfortable. "Well, stop staring, Artemer; get in there, get dressed, and let's go," he grumbled.

"Yes, right," Ellora mumbled, pulling Alana into the room with her. She couldn't believe she had just done that, and she could feel her own face heating up.

Alana cleared her throat awkwardly behind Ellora, who turned quickly, having forgotten she was not alone. "Well, it's a good thing Queen Louisa keeps these around, huh?" Ellora asked with an awkward laugh.

Alana gave her a tight-lipped smile and began to filter through the fabrics. "Would you prefer a dress?" she questioned.

"Yes, I think so," Ellora replied and began to sort through the dresses with Alana. There was an entire section for ball gowns, another section for cocktail dresses, another section for summer dresses... the wardrobe just seemed endless.

"What about this?" Alana asked, pulling out a long, flowy, white dress with thin straps.

"I think it might look a little *too* bridal for dinner," Ellora replied after considering. "What about this one?" she proposed, pulling out a gold, ballgown-style dress.

"Maybe a little too formal?" Alana suggested. She was right; she didn't want to turn up looking more overdressed than the Queen.

They both continued searching until, at the same time, their eyes landed on a sleeveless, lilac, a-line dress that was cinched in at the waist and flowed subtly outwards, with a tulle layer on top. They looked at each other with big smiles. This one was perfect.

"Finally!" Hunter exclaimed as Alana emerged from the wardrobe ahead of Ellora. "You were taking so long I was considering sending in a search party to look for you. Come on, we need to leave, or we'll be la—" His words cut off when Ellora walked out, the dress sitting perfectly on her frame.

"You like it then?" she teased, doing a little twirl.

Hunter cleared his throat quickly. "You look lovely."

"Oh, look, you have managed to coordinate your clothes," Alana commented awkwardly, pointing to Hunter's tie, a pale purple colour that happened to match the lilac shade of Ellora's dress. Ellora and Hunter exchanged amused looks. This was not the first time they accidentally coordinated their outfits.

"Well, as I believe you were about to say, we had best get going, or we'll be late," Ellora said, hooking her arm around Hunter's. "Thank you so much again for your help getting ready, Alana." She smiled at Alana, who was staring vacantly at the point Ellora's arm linked with Hunter's, eyebrows etched in a furrow.

She quickly snapped her eyes away and up to look at Ellora. "You're welcome."

"Oh, good, you're both ready," Louisa said with a smile, ushering Hunter and Ellora down the remainder of the stairs. "You look lovely, both of you. Like the perfect couple."

"Oh, we're not—"

"No, that isn't—" Ellora and Hunter spoke over each other, but Louisa simply smiled knowingly at their pink faces before walking away to talk to one of the waiters.

"I didn't tell her—" Hunter began.

"I didn't think you did," Ellora interrupted. "The room looks lovely," she said abruptly, looking around at the elegant changes that had been made. A large, rectangular table had been brought in and was covered in a pristine, white tablecloth. There were floral centrepieces which must have been picked just minutes before because they looked so fresh.

"Yes," Hunter chuckled. "If there's one thing that cannot go disputed, it's that my mother knows how to throw a good dinner party.

"Are those guests arriving?" Ellora asked, nodding towards the front door, which was being held open by one of the servers.

"Yes. We'd better move to the parlour. That'll be the reception room, where we'll have drinks before dinner." They walked over together to find King Archer on one of the leather armchairs, glass in hand. Ellora guessed from the colour of the liquid that it must have been some sort of scotch or whisky, definitely something from the Human Realm rather than the Aura Realm.

"Hunter. You're back safely, I see," Archer said. Ellora looked at Hunter with one brow raised. He had been here for an entire afternoon and hadn't seen his dad yet?

"Yes, father. Thank you for keeping me updated on current events while I am away. It's certainly been useful to receive The Aura Times weekly."

He didn't receive much of a response. Archer nodded his head, and that was that. Ellora looked at Hunter, trying to see if he had any sort of reaction to the lack of affection, but Hunter didn't even seem to notice.

"Aadan!" exclaimed Archer, getting up from his chair to greet the man who had just entered the room.

"It's been a while, Archer, my old friend," Aadan replied, patting Archer on the back. "And Hunter. It's a pleasure to see you again, my boy."

"Aadan. It has been far too long. May I introduce you to Ellora Artemer, a very good friend of mine? Ellora, this is Aadan Abara, the Minister of affairs in the Ferri Kingdom."

"Ellora," the Minister said with a polite smile, taking the hand she offered out to him. "Any friend of Hunter's is a friend of mine."

"What can we get you to drink, Aadan?" Archer asked, motioning for one of the servers to come and take his order.

"Be careful around him," Hunter murmured so quietly that Ellora was partly convinced she imagined it. "He's not who he seems to be, and I wouldn't wish his presence upon my worst enemy."

Ellora swallowed.

Louisa came through very soon after, closely followed by more guests. Judging by the size of the table Ellora saw in the dining room, they would only be waiting on one or two more people.

As Hunter and Ellora made their rounds, Hunter introduced her as his friend and colleague at the Madori School of Aura, and Ellora shook everyone's hands politely with a smile.

While Ellora was having a particularly fascinating conversation with one of the guests, a political leader from some part of the world, about the structure of the Incendi School of Aura, she noticed Hunter slip away from the corner of her eye. "Yes, actually, the Incendi Mistress, Kristen, is my best friend's sister."

"She is?" the politician asked her. "Well, you'll be happy to see her this evening, in that case."

"Kristen is coming tonight?" Ellora asked. "I didn't realise she and Lousia knew each other."

"I believe Kristen is a new acquaintance of my mother's," Hunter said, returning to them with two glasses of purple wine in hand. He handed one to Ellora, who accepted it gratefully. "Unless I'm mistaken, they met recently when my mother was in the Incendi Kingdom to acquire a fire ruby for my sister. It's been rumoured to grant luck."

"Well, Belle will be happy to know that her sister is doing well," Ellora said with a smile. It was at that moment that Kristen walked in, heading straight over to greet Louisa with a warm hug. Over her shoulder, she spotted Ellora and her forehead creased. "Ellora?"

"Kristen! It's lovely to see you." Ellora smiled as Kristen walked over to them, overjoyed to see another familiar face.

"Likewise! What are you doing here?" she asked.

"I came with Oriel—"

"Is Oriel here, too? Thank the Spirits; I've been trying to get a hold of her—"

"No," Ellora interrupted. "Oriel isn't here. We came together, but she needed to go and see someone; she left earlier today, and I stayed here. She's expected to return later this evening or early next morning. Why have you been trying to get a hold of her?"

"You don't know?" Kristen asked, her voice now a hushed whisper.

"Know what?" Hunter asked softly.

Kristen looked over at him, noticing him for the first time. "This is Hunter," Ellora explained. "Louisa's son and a friend of Belle and I."

Kristen nodded, looking between them and then around the room as if worried they were being listened to. "Oriel trusts the two of you. And that's saying a lot; there are many she wouldn't even trust with making her tea, let alone anything serious. But we need to talk. In private. Urgently."

"Follow me," Hunter said, nodding towards the door. They looked around themselves to make sure they weren't being observed, and it seemed as though everybody was absorbed in their own conversations. They slipped out quietly, and Hunter led them up the stairs and to another room, which Hunter opened up for them.

After they entered and closed the door behind them, Ellora noticed the furniture; there was a dark bed in the middle of the room, and a table in the corner, with four chairs placed around it. There were a few doors on the far side of the room, probably leading to a changing room and a bathroom, and there was a large sofa with a couple of armchairs and a coffee table in front of a large fireplace on the other side.

"Is this your bedroom?" Ellora asked.

Hunter shrugged, gesturing for them to make themselves comfortable. "It was the one place I knew for sure we would have privacy."

"Okay, first of all, where is Oriel?" Kristen asked, sitting down and leaning forward, her arms resting on her knees.

"We don't know," Ellora said quickly. "What's going on that's so serious?"

"Before I say anything else, there's something the two of you need to know. About the Upper Council members."

Ellora looked up sharply at that. She and Hunter exchanged a look of worry, and they sat on the sofa, placing their wine glasses on the coffee table in front of them.

"What I am about to tell you should be repeated to absolutely nobody apart from Oriel; I shouldn't even be telling the two of you, but there is no other way I will be able to get the message to Oriel quickly enough. But, especially, you *cannot* tell any of the Upper Council members about this at *any cost*. Neither Oriel nor

I trust the rest of them," Kristen said, speaking in a hushed tone even though they were alone.

"None of them?" Ellora asked, shocked. These were supposed to be the Aurums leading the Realm, the Aurums running the Aura Schools and responsible for the future Aurum generations. How could it be that Oriel didn't trust them?

"Elliott Vaughn. He can be trusted to an extent. But, still, I wouldn't seek him out unless absolutely necessary."

"Who's Elliott Vaughn?" Ellora asked.

"The Terrari Master and Upper Council Member," Hunter replied.

"Exactly. Now, I spoke to Belle earlier today, and she told me Oriel filled you in on everything going on in the other Kingdoms. But what we are trying to figure out—Oriel and I—is who is causing it all."

"That's where Oriel is right now. She said she has a contact who might have some information," Ellora said.

"I thought as much when you told me she was visiting someone," Kristen frowned. "The thing is, Oriel and I are certain that whoever is doing this has got to be someone powerful, someone who has easy access to all Kingdoms."

"Someone with easy access to the Gates," Hunter added.

"An Upper Council Member," whispered Ellora.

"Precisely," answered Kristen. "So when I found out earlier today that somebody tried to access my Gate Room, it worried me. I came tonight after being unable to contact Oriel in the hopes that she might be here."

"But if that was another member of the Upper Council, wouldn't they have access to their own Gate Rooms? Why would they try to go through yours?" asked Hunter.

"Because they tried to come into my Gate Room from The Under."

Ellora heard Hunter inhale sharply. "So that would mean—"

"Yes. A dead Aurum has somehow figured out a way to come back from the dead to the Aura Realm. And if they get through to another Upper Council member, we'll all be in danger."

CHAPTER NINE

The Madori Mistress Returns

The rest of the evening passed relatively uneventfully. After Ellora, Hunter and Kristen rejoined the party, the final guest, a friend of Archer's and the Monarch of Hawaii, arrived, and dinner began. The food was delicious, the conversation pleasant, and Ellora felt relief course through her body at the realisation that she would be spending the evening in the company of Hunter and Kristen.

Despite the relaxed atmosphere and interesting conversation, Ellora couldn't help but constantly chew her bottom lip and drum her fingers on the table as she waited for Oriel's return. Each time a door opened, Ellora turned, hoping it was her. Every time she heard a voice come from outside the room, she prayed to the Spirits that it was Oriel, only to be disappointed. Whenever Louisa left the room, Ellora was filled with the hope that when she returned, Oriel would be with her.

But she never arrived.

Ellora stood with Hunter and his parents by the door as the guests left, joining them in wishing each guest a good evening, when Kristen leaned down and whispered in her ear, "Remember, it's imperative Oriel is informed the very moment she gets back." Ellora nodded with a straight face, taking in Kristen's urgent eyes and slightly furrowed brows. As if she could have forgotten.

"Surely she should be back by now?" Ellora asked as she paced from window to door and back again. She and Hunter decided to wait in her room for Oriel, figuring it would be the best place to hear her when she returned.

Hunter's gaze was fixed on the ceiling, his body flat and motionless on the bed, still in his suit from the evening but with his tie removed and his top button undone. "I'm sure she'll be here soon," he replied, not bothering to sit up as he did. "She did tell you she could be back late, didn't she?"

Ellora ran her hand through her hair. "Yes, but something doesn't feel right."

With a sigh, Hunter sat up, running his hand through his mussed and messy hair, his eyebrows etched into a thoughtful curve. "Did you hear what some of the guests were saying this evening? About receiving letters?" Ellora shook her head but stopped walking and leaned against the desk as he spoke. "They've all already received letters to return to the Madori School of Aura."

"How soon?" Ellora frowned.

"I suspect some of them have already returned."

"Master Rainclarke must have sent them out after we left yesterday," Ellora said, her frown deepening. "Why would he do that?"

"He didn't mention anything before I came here."

"So he must have sent them late afternoon or early evening yesterday. But why?"

His eyes snapped to hers suddenly. "Something must have happened."

"We've not even been away for one day," Ellora whispered. "What in the Realms could have possibly happened?"

"Whatever it is, we need Oriel."

Ellora took a deep, steadying breath.

"I know you're worried, but everything will be fine," Hunter said, standing and walking over to place his hand on Ellora's shoulder. "It's Oriel. She would never let anything happen to the Kingdom."

"You're right," Ellora said. She was still nervous, but she could do nothing before Oriel returned. She considered telling Hunter about the conversation she had heard between Oriel and Rainclarke. She still hadn't had the chance to speak to Oriel about it and was struggling to keep it in.

Rolling his eyes, Hunter sighed at her, crossing his arms over his chest and tapping his foot against the floor. "Out with it, then,

Artemer. I can practically see the thoughts flashing across your face." Ellora felt her cheeks warm but knew it would be right to talk to him about what she heard.

"I don't know what's going on," she said after recounting the conversation she overheard.

Hunter frowned. "There's no doubt they were talking about you; Oriel practically dragged you out of there at the earliest opportunity. But who could be putting you in danger?"

"That's what I've been trying to figure out," said Ellora, slumping into one of the chairs. "I didn't get a chance to ask her on our way here."

"Do you think..." Hunter began but stopped. "Do you think it could be Asyra?" He asked in a hushed voice and with his eyebrows lowered in concern.

"Asyra?" Ellora asked in shock. "Why... why would she...?"

"I know she helped you last year, with your nightmares, with your Aura, with catching Julia, but she's not always so friendly, Ellora. She seems to have taken a special liking to you for whatever reason."

"What do you mean?"

"We both saw how she calmed down when speaking with you rather than with me. At first, I just thought she liked you more than me; fair enough. But maybe it's more than that..." Hunter got up and came to sit in the chair next to Ellora, leaning forwards, his arms on his knees. "What if it's not that she didn't *like* you more, but she wanted to protect you? As in, she didn't want to harm you."

"But then, how could I be in danger? As you said, she seems to have taken a strange liking to me and if she does want to protect me, won't I be the safest in the Madori School of Aura?."

"I don't know, Ellora, none of it makes sense. But maybe... maybe she wants to *use* you."

Ellora gulped. Why in the Realms would Asyra want to use her? There was nothing that she could do that most others couldn't. If she wanted to use anyone, surely it would be Belle.

A loud knocking at the door jolted Ellora awake. She lifted her head drowsily from where she had apparently fallen asleep sitting at the coffee table and looked around, rubbing her eyes. Hunter seemed to have fallen asleep sitting on the floor, with his back against the bed, and was now rubbing his neck tenderly as he blinked away the sleep.

"We fell asleep," she yawned.

Hunter grumbled something Ellora didn't understand as he stretched, rolling his head from side to side, before hopping gracefully up onto his feet.

"Good morning, Ell—Oh!" It was Alana walking in with a mug of tea in hand. "Sorry, I didn't—I wasn't—Your Highness,

I didn't know you were here. I didn't mean to interrupt." She turned bright red and shifted awkwardly between her feet.

"Don't be silly, Alana. You're not interrupting anything. Please, come in," Hunter said, holding the door wider to allow her inside before stepping out and crossing the corridor to Oriel's room.

"I made tea the same way you did yesterday. I thought you would like to have some when you wake up," she told Ellora stiffly, her eyes fixed on her feet and her cheeks still tinged a faint pink.

"That's really nice of you, Alana. Thank you." Ellora smiled gratefully at her but frowned when she saw Alana swallow, nod awkwardly and silently place the mug on Ellora's table.

"If she's in there, she's not answering," Hunter declared with a frown as he returned to Ellora's room.

"Maybe she's already downstairs?" Ellora asked, grabbing a jacket and heading out the door.

"What about your tea?" Alana called after the two of them. Ellora hurried back quickly, grabbed the mug, smiled at Alana, and took it with her.

"Mother," Hunter greeted Louisa as they walked into the dining room, where she sat at a large, square table filled with plates of food, feeding Sapphire.

"Good morning," Ellora said politely, forcing herself not to ask about Oriel straight away. Louisa didn't even know about their conversation with Kristen the previous evening, so she wouldn't understand how vital and urgent her return was.

"Has Oriel returned yet?" Hunter asked. Ellora shot him a grateful look; she was itching to ask herself.

"Good morning. You are both up early. Not as far as I'm aware," Louisa replied. "But I'm sure she'll be back any moment now." Ellora fought the urge to sigh in disappointment and looked at Hunter worriedly. His wrinkled forehead and clenched jaw didn't make her feel better. "Why don't you both sit down for breakfast? Archer is still sleeping, but I had to get up and feed Sapphire, so I asked for breakfast to be made."

Ellora wasn't sure she would be able to eat. Her stomach was churning with a panicked ball of nausea and nerves, but she couldn't explain that to Louisa. Instead, she sat next to Hunter at the table to have the cup of tea Alana made her, if nothing else. She watched as he put an egg, some mushrooms and tomatoes, and a couple of slices of toast onto his plate before pouring himself a black coffee. He raised a brow at Ellora, who sat with only her cup of tea, flicking his eyes between her empty plate and the table full of food. But when she only raised her eyebrows stubbornly in response, he sighed. Rolling his eyes, he picked up her plate himself, adding a couple of small pancakes, a spoonful of blueberries and a generous helping of maple syrup before putting the plate in front of her once again.

She felt her stomach flutter at the fact that he knew her well enough to know what she would want for breakfast but tried to argue nonetheless. "I'm too nervous to eat," she whispered, making sure Louisa couldn't hear her.

"You barely ate last night," he murmured back at her. "You've got to eat something to keep your energy up."

"Did you two enjoy the dinner party last night?" Louisa asked, picking at a bowl of fruit in front of her in between attempting to feed Sapphire, who, sure enough, stopped eating the moment Hunter entered the room and was now trying to crawl her way across the table over to him.

"Very much," Ellora answered. "I still can't quite believe you managed to plan everything so quickly." She forced herself to take a bite of her pancake and glared at the smug smile on Hunter's face.

Louisa smiled at her. "Well, I've had a lot of practice, and I just thought it would be a nice way to spend Hunter's first evening back in a while. I—" she turned quickly to look at the door which led from the dining room to the hall. "Oh, you know, I would be willing to bet that's Oriel!" she chirped, hopping up and handing Sapphire over to Hunter as she walked out of the room.

"Uhh... what just happened?" Ellora asked Hunter as she wiped a trail of jam from Sapphire's chin with a tissue.

"Wards. We've got them set up around the perimeter, so when one is activated, we can sense it."

"That explains how your mum came out to meet Oriel and me before we—"

A blood-curdling scream pierced the air, cutting off Ellora's train of thought. She and Hunter locked eyes, Ellora's wide with fear and Hunter's in shock, before they both bolted out of the room, Hunter gripping Sapphire tightly with one hand. At the same time, the other was extended and ready to unleash his Aura if necessary.

"What's going on?" he demanded as they approached the hallway at the entrance to the castle.

Louisa burst through the main door, her breath coming in ragged gasps. Her hands were smudged with a thick, dark red, and her eyes were wide with fear. Tears poured down her face, leaving wet trails of mascara on her cheeks, yet she seemed not to notice. "Get Sapphire out of here," she whispered, her voice trembling with a mix of fear and emotion.

Hunter immediately took charge of the situation. "Alana!" he called out. He handed Sapphire over to her as soon as she arrived, giving her strict instructions to take Sapphire to her room, hide and make sure to lock the door behind them until he, and only he, gave the all-clear for them to come out. His voice was firm, but his eyes betrayed a hint of fear and uncertainty.

Louisa looked at the two of them nervously for a moment, and just when Ellora was ready to shove past her and see what was going on, she nodded and motioned for them to follow her out the door.

Ellora felt her heart sink straight into the pits of her stomach when she saw her.

Oriel.

CHAPTER TEN

A Secret Trip

O riel was slumped against the brick wall, her eyes closed, her skin ashen, and her ankle twisted at an unnatural angle. The sleeve of her blouse was torn off her shoulder, revealing a gash, and a pool of blood was slowly growing underneath her. It was an unsettling sight, that was for sure, but what made Ellora promptly vomit into a bush on her left was the shiny, blood-stained metal dagger still embedded in Oriel's abdomen.

Hunter scanned the area with panicked eyes but ultimately steadied himself and bent down to take Oriel's pulse and feel her forehead.

"Is she..." Ellora could not finish the question, her voice trembling as tears threatened to spill over.

"She's alive," Hunter murmured. "Barely. Her pulse is weak, and she has a high fever."

Louisa looked just as stricken as Ellora felt. Still, if Ellora were in her right mind at that moment, she certainly would have admired the way she suddenly collected herself and took control of the situation, moving past her feelings to work in the best interest of her best friend. She supposed that was why she was the Queen of England, after all.

"You need to get her back. To Healer Amare," she ordered, looking at Hunter.

"How?" Ellora whispered, trying her best not to look at her Madori Mistress lying helplessly in a heap.

"We have a Gate here, and Oriel has the key to get through to the Madori School of Aura," Louisa answered.

"Around her neck," Ellora said. She couldn't bring herself to remove the necklace, so Hunter reached down and removed the thin chain carrying the little gem that was the Key to the Madori Gate.

"We need to move quickly," Louisa muttered, mostly to herself, as she opened the door again to call for more help.

It took multiple servants to carry Oriel while Hunter supported Ellora on her shaky knees. Carefully but hurriedly, they managed to climb the steps to the Gate room, which happened to be located in one of the towers. Ellora couldn't say how long it took them to get to the top; time moved like a blur in the panic.

She couldn't believe this was happening.

"Listen to me," Louisa put one hand on Hunter's shoulder and one hand on Ellora's as she looked at the two of them with wet eyes. "There's a reason why I left that Realm; there's a reason why your grandfather left, why all of the remaining Lynchi and Obscuri Aurums went into hiding in the Human Realm. Don't trust anybody. I mean it.

"I wish I could come with you both; I wish I could tell you not to go, but I can't. You need to save her. And you need to stop them, those Upper Council members. Just... they're not to be trusted."

Ellora took the key from Hunter, as he took over from the servants in supporting Oriel. Her hands were shaking, but she managed to open the Gate, unable to appreciate the majestic sight of the shimmering blue Gate appearing before them.

"Go, find someone!" Hunter demanded the second they stepped through the Gate, as the Gate closed again behind them.

Ellora wasted no time in replying. She ran from the room, her heart pounding so hard she was sure it would implode at any moment. She ran to the first place she could think of – Master Rainclarke's office. It was late enough in the morning that she was almost certain he would be there. She repeatedly slammed her fists against the wooden door, all but throwing herself against it. The handle would not budge, no matter how much she twisted it.

"Master Rainclarke!" she cried through the wood, pounding on the door with open palms. Her heart was beating like a drum in her chest, her palms clammy and her stomach churning.

Even in the short period between finding Oriel and getting her through the Gate, she had become so much paler and even more blood had seeped out of the wound. "Master Rainclarke!"

"Elle?" it was Belle who appeared behind her. "What's going on? Why are you back already?"

"Belle! Belle, Master Rainclarke! Where is he?!"

"He's having breakfast, but—" Ellora didn't give Belle a chance to finish speaking. She grabbed Belle by the wrist and dragged her along as she ran through the corridors, down the stairs, and flew into the dining room, the shakiness in her limbs replaced by a rush of urgency that kept her moving.

"Master Rainclarke, quick, it's Oriel!" she cried, ignoring all the stunned faces staring back at her and not giving him a chance to ask questions or even think before following her, as she ran once again, not dragging Belle this time, but allowing her to follow. She led both of them to the Gate room, where Hunter had managed to lay Oriel down on the ground and elevate her head in his lap. He had made an effort to place her ankle in a way that it wouldn't injure her any further.

Rainclarke stared at her for a few silent seconds, eyes wide, before jumping straight into action. "Run ahead and let Healer Amare know we're on our way." Ellora wasn't sure exactly who it was that he was directing, but she and Belle left to explain the situation while Hunter remained behind to help Rainclarke.

It wasn't long before Rainclarke walked into the infirmary, carefully cradling Oriel in his arms. Healer Amare quickly directed him to an empty bed that she had prepared. With a calm yet firm tone, she asked Belle to stay and assist her. As a future Madori Mistress, Belle's training included learning healing enchantments, and with Oriel's condition, Healer Amare knew she would need all the help she could get. She allowed Rainclarke to stay while she checked Oriel's vitals but made it clear that Ellora and Hunter would have to wait outside.

They both did as instructed and sat on two of the chairs outside of the infirmary, knowing arguing with her would only cause delays.

"Ellora, 'Unter! What are you doing, sitting out 'ere?" They both turned around to see Mr and Mrs Sotto walking towards them, coffee cups in hand. Their expressions changed when they saw the blood covering Hunter's previously white shirt and skin, as well as a small trail on Ellora's hands and the tear streaks on her face. "What 'as 'appened?" Mrs Sotto demanded, rushing over to them.

"It was Oriel," Ellora whispered, her voice still shaky.

"We don't know what's happened," Hunter added in a low voice.

Mrs Sotto turned from them to look at the infirmary door and back again. Without a word, she sat in a chair next to Ellora while Mr Sotto sat in the next chair along.

Ellora had no idea how much time had passed since they got Oriel into that room. She was, however, extremely aware of Hunter's presence beside her, and she was aware of every sound that came from inside that room.

It was only when Rainclarke appeared at the door that time started to move again for Ellora. His cheeks were streaked and stained, and his eyes were tired.

"She's alive," he said, leaning against the doorframe. He looked as much of a sight as Hunter, with his blood-stained white shirt and hands. There were also smears on his face where he must have wiped his face with his bloody hands.

Ellora and Hunter simultaneously exhaled in relief but made no move to do anything else, waiting for him to continue.

"Genevieve, Thomas, my apologies for the disruption. Please," he gestured for them to enter the infirmary, a polite way to ask them to leave them alone. Mrs and Mr Sotto, having caught the hint, nodded solemnly and entered the room, closing the door behind them.

Another few minutes passed in silence before Rainclarke spoke again. "I'm sure the two of you know, Oriel had a... a *dagger* in her abdomen." His face paled even further as he spoke. "Somehow, Oriel must have managed to get back to you without moving the dagger, luckily, since it stopped her from losing any more blood and didn't pierce any vital organs. Oriel being Oriel, she also managed to cast a healing enchantment on herself to replenish some of her blood. If she hadn't done so, she would have been dead already." He swallowed.

"Healer Amare has removed the dagger and healed the wound as well as her broken ankle, bruised ribs, concussion and some other external wounds that needed to be treated."

"So she's okay?" Ellora asked, jumping to her feet.

"No."

Ellora felt her heart stop.

"Why?" it was Hunter who spoke this time, standing next to Ellora.

"She won't wake up." His voice shook as he spoke, but he forced the words out, nonetheless. "Healer Amare says there is nothing wrong with her, as far as she can tell. She's not in a coma; she's no longer injured. There is no reason why she wouldn't be waking up."

At that moment, Belle appeared from the door. "You can go back in with her, Master Rainclarke," she said softly, putting a hand on his shoulder and holding the door open for him. He slumped inside, his eyes down and his shoulders hunched, and only when the door was closed behind him did Belle turn to Hunter and Ellora. "There's something seriously wrong," she said in a hushed voice.

"We know," answered Ellora. "She should be awake."

"Not just that. We only noticed after Rainclarke left, but Oriel has this weird rash on her back. It's like a purple glow under her skin."

"You think this could all be because of Aura?" Hunter asked.

"Yes," answered Belle. "Although I have no idea how an Aurum could do something like this; it's unheard of."

Suddenly, Ellora remembered the conversation she and Oriel had just one day before. "Magi Aura," she said in a whisper. "It must be Magi Aura."

"I thought that was just a myth," Belle said, her face carved into a frown.

"No, Oriel was telling me about it yesterday; it's all real."

Hunter looked between the two of them before taking a deep breath. Just as he opened his mouth to speak, a loud laughing voice drifted down the corridor, and it was then that the three of them remembered that students had begun to arrive back at the Madori School of Aura. "We'd better talk in private," he said.

They decided to meet in Oriel's office, giving Hunter time to change out of his blood-stained clothes and shower and for Ellora to wash the trails of blood from her hands.

"Are you okay?" Belle asked her when she emerged from the bathroom. "Silly question, I know," she continued, "but I mean... are you?"

"No better than any of us," Ellora replied, shaking the excess water from her hands. "But we just need to figure out who did this, especially considering what Kristen told us yesterday."

"You saw Kris yesterday?" Belle asked, confused.

Ellora nodded. "She came to a dinner party. But that's not the important part. There's something going on here, Bee. Something worse than any single attack or attempted attack. Something big." She explained what Kristen told her about the attempted break-in, or break-*out*, as was likely more appropriate, before the two of them headed down to Oriel's office.

Ellora knew where Oriel kept the herbs for her Lavender tea as well as the teapot and mugs, so she automatically went about making the tea, using her Aura to fill and boil the teapot, as Oriel taught her to do. It felt bizarre for her to be in here, making her tea, without Oriel. She had to bite her lip to prevent a sob from choking out, but she was determined to find whoever did this to Oriel and to fix it. She knew crying wouldn't help.

Hunter entered only a couple of minutes after Ellora finished making the tea, sitting down silently with his eyes fixed on the table.

"We need to *do* something," Ellora said, eager to get on with figuring out what they could do.

"But what *can* we do?" asked Belle.

"We could ask Asyra," Ellora stated.

"No," Hunter replied, snapping his eyes up to her. "You're not doing that."

"But she could—"

"Artemer, it's out of the question. You know why."

"Why...?" Belle began to ask, frowning at the two of them, before Ellora cut her off with a quick shake of her head. It wasn't safe to tell Belle at the moment. Not when she didn't know how to prevent Asyra from being able to read her thoughts. "Okay, fine, so what can we do?"

"We could ask Kristen?" suggested Hunter.

"That's a great idea!" Belle agreed eagerly. "We'll have to tell the entirety of the Upper Council anyway, so maybe we could call a meeting and ask for their help?"

"No!" Ellora and Hunter disagreed at the same time. Belle frowned at the two of them.

"He meant... *just* Kristen." Again, this was something that they shouldn't have been discussing in the school.

"Okay... well, in that case, I think Asyra might be our best option," Belle said, looking cautiously over at Hunter.

"No," he grumbled, his voice heavy with reluctance. "We just... *can't*."

"Hunter," Ellora said in a quiet voice, "we might not have a choice." She knew as well as he did that speaking to Asyra at the moment was risky, but what other choice did they have?

She could see the concern etched in Hunter's eyes as he searched for an alternative, for a way out.

"Fine," he said at last, with a sigh of resignation. "But you're not going alone."

Ellora felt a flicker of frustration. "Hunter, I have to. You know I do."

"No, Artemer, I don't actually," he replied stubbornly. His tone was firm, but she could see the fear in his eyes,

"You remember what happened last time; it'll be easier if I go alone."

"What happened *last time* is exactly why you *can't* go alone!"

"Hunter, don't be silly. We already established that I'm in no danger. For the moment, at least."

"But we don't know how long that moment will last, do we, Ellora? How could you think I would even take a chance like that?"

"But Hunter—"

"If you two are done quarrelling," Belle interrupted, "could somebody please fill me in?"

Ellora looked over at her best friend and felt embarrassed at the scene they had just created. She also had no idea how to tell Belle about what was going on without Asyra finding out what they knew; Hunter and Ellora knew how to block her out, but Belle hadn't needed to learn before.

"I'm so sorry, Bee, we can't tell you just yet. You're just going to have to trust us for the moment until we can find the right *time and place*," she said, hoping Belle would understand her meaning.

Whether she did or didn't understand, she at least left the topic alone. "Well, I suppose we'll have to compromise, then. Elle, you'll go and see Asyra, Hunter, you'll go too, but you won't speak to her."

Ellora thought about arguing, but she knew it wouldn't make a difference. There was only one way this was going to work, and the other two wouldn't be happy about it.

The three of them went to the infirmary as soon as they were able. The sight of the strict and powerful Master Rainclarke hunched over in a plastic chair, his eyes vacant and hopeless as he stared at his injured wife, was more than devastating. Ellora could only thank the Spirits that no other students would see him in this state.

It should have been more difficult to see Oriel as she was, lying in that bed and all but waiting for death. Instead, she looked strangely serene. Her face was peaceful and tension-free, and she simply looked as though she was asleep. It was a relieving change from the sight of her with a dagger protruding from her and covered in blood, that was certain.

For some bizarre reason, this sight of Oriel so motionless and relaxed made determination pump through Ellora's veins. It was only one day ago that she was talking about her time at the Madori School of Aura, that she was so excited to see her best friend, that she was as determined to find out what was going on in this Realm and to fix it. It hadn't even been a day since she left, leaving Ellora with more questions than answers, promising everything would be okay.

And now nothing was okay. The only person who could help the realm was in an Aura-induced coma. And Ellora was going to heal her, no matter what it took.

"Master Rainclarke," she said softly, placing a hand on his shoulder so as not to startle him.

"Hmm?" He looked up at her and blinked, his eyes blank and his gaze distant, looking heartbreakingly similar to her mother after the loss of Ellora's younger sister, Ophelia.

"We've had an idea," she continued in a gentle voice. He needed to know what was going on, no matter his state. "Healer Amare told you about the rash, right?" He nodded but didn't speak. "Well, we think it might be Aura-induced, and we think our best option is to ask Asyra if she knows anything about what's going on or how we could stop it and bring Oriel back."

It was almost as if Oriel's name brought his attention back to her. He frowned, his forehead etching into a deep crease as he examined her face. "that's the only idea I've come up with, too," he spoke for the first time. His voice was hesitant, his eyes flickering between fear and desperation. Finally, he released a resigned sigh. "Just be careful." He looked her in the eye. "She always has an ulterior motive."

Ellora glanced worriedly over her shoulder at Belle and Hunter, who were waiting near the entrance to the infirmary, not wanting to overwhelm Master Rainclarke. Hunter raised an eyebrow at her, and Ellora shot him a tight-lipped smile in an attempt at reassurance.

But she had already made up her mind. She was going to visit the Madori Spirit.

Belle and Ellora decided to stay in Ellora's room that night. Getting up before sunrise was the only way they could visit Asyra while the courtyard was empty, and they needed to do so without waking Belle's roommate Violet had already returned.

It was only around 2 am that Ellora was finally sure that Belle had fallen asleep, her loud snores rumbling through the room, even frightening Lucifer awake from his small, makeshift bed on Ellora's bedside table.

As silently as possible, Ellora slipped out of bed and tiptoed across the room, grabbing the first pair of trainers she saw and leaving the room barefoot so as not to make a noise.

She shut the door quietly behind her, shoved on her shoes and wasted no time in getting downstairs to the West Courtyard. Her stomach was a pit of guilt at going behind Hunter's and Belle's backs, but she knew there was no way she would get the information she needed if Hunter came with her. She took a steadying breath before opening the door to Asyra's lake, willing the nausea bubbling inside her to *stay* inside.

If Hunter was right, if Oriel and Rainclarke were worried for her because of Asyra, this was a huge risk. But it was a risk she needed to take.

"Asyra?" she called softly, trying her best to keep her mental shields up enough to hide her fear but low enough for her to communicate with Asyra.

"Ellora, how lovely to see you again so soon," Asyra's voice echoed in her head. Her voice sounded too sweet, almost rich, and Ellora knew she had made a mistake in coming alone.

"You too, Asyra," she said, trying to keep her voice even. Asyra still hadn't revealed herself; she could have been anywhere. So Ellora stayed close to the door, refusing to get any closer to the lake than she needed to.

"I assume your visit means you've discovered the information I asked you for?"

Ellora had completely forgotten about that; Asyra had wanted to know where Julia was being kept, and Ellora and Hunter had both agreed that that information should stay out of Asyra's hands, no matter what. But now, she might not have a choice.

"Not exactly," Ellora lied.

"What exactly do you mean by that, Ellora?" Asyra hissed in her head. Ellora heard a splash to the left side of the lake and turned to see Asyra had emerged from the water and was staring at her with icy eyes towering over her. "I thought we established how important it was for me to find out."

"I know, I know! Believe me," Ellora said, shuffling back even further until her back touched the wall. "It's just that... Oriel left before I could ask her. I didn't have the chance, but now she's hurt. She's not waking up."

"And *why* do you think I would give a Mistfall about that?" Asyra seethed, still growing taller. Her eyes were fixed on Ellora, and they didn't have the protective energy that Hunter noticed last time. Instead, they oozed with disgust.

Ellora gulped. Asyra *didn't* care about Oriel being on the brink of death? She had to think quickly. "There's no way I can get that information while she's in this state!"

Asyra narrowed her eyes, considering Ellora's words, but remaining raised out of the water.

"She has a strange rash on her back – a purple glow under her skin," Ellora continued, taking the silence for interest.

Asyra's eyes widened in an emotion one could have easily mistaken for fear if they didn't know Asyra. "A purple rash?" Asyra's voice sounded dangerously low in her head.

"Yes," Ellora whispered, pressing herself even flat against the wall. She swallowed hard when Asyra turned away, considering if it would be a good idea to try and run out of there now.

"They're back." Asyra's voice was a whisper now, and there was no mistaking the dear in her voice. "I didn't believe it..."

"Who? Who are back?" Ellora asked.

As if Asyra suddenly remembered Ellora was there, she turned sharply to stare at her. Her skin was paler than usual, something Ellora had thought impossible since she was already translucent, and her eyes were sparkling with warning. "Listen to me, Ellora, and listen *well*. What you need to do is speak to Arellia."

"Arellia?" Ellora gasped. "But she's—"

"Dead. Yes, she is. You'll need to go to The Under to speak with her. Tell her about the glow; she is the only one who will know how to fix it. You need to wake Oriel immediately, so she can tell us who did this to her. Is that clear?"

Ellora nodded quickly.

"And Ellora?" added Asyra. "If you fail, it'll be the entire Realm in danger, not just your precious Madori Mistress."

"What in the Realms were you thinking?!" Belle hissed at Ellora, dragging her by the wrist into Oriel's office, where Hunter was already waiting. He didn't even look at her and instead glared at the table in front of him. Ellora felt guilty enough as it was for going behind their backs without his ignoring her. It would somehow have been better if he just yelled at her, or insulted or, or just generally showed and directed his anger towards her.***

Apparently, Belle woke up not long after Ellora left and found her missing and woke up Hunter in a panic before realising that she had likely gone to see Asyra without them; Hunter waited in Oriel's office while Belle went to find her.

It was true that Ellora tricked the two of them, but it was the only option they had to save Oriel. She felt even more certain of that after the visit she just had; she didn't want to imagine how Asyra would have reacted if Hunter had been with them.

"I'm sorry I lied to you," she began, but Belle wouldn't let her finish.

"Lied? We couldn't give a leitock about the lying, Ellora. You could have been seriously hurt. Or worse. You don't know what a Spirit is capable of! I have no idea why Hunter didn't want you to go alone, but I'll be willing to bet he had a reason behind it, and your little plan was completely foolish."

Still, Hunter said nothing, remaining motionless in his seat, his teeth clenched and his shoulders stiff and tense.

"I know, Bee, Hunter. And I'm sorry. But it worked; isn't that all that matters?"

Belle sighed deeply, sinking into Oriel's chair and placing her head in her hand, rubbing the bridge of her nose with her fingers. "What's done is done," she said, finally. She didn't look any less angry at Ellora, her fists were still in tight balls, but at least she was finally ready to hear what Asyra had to say.

"Asyra looked really scared when I told her about the purple glow," Ellora began. At that, she finally received a reaction from Hunter. His head shot up to look at her, and his eyebrows wrinkled into an intense frown. Ellora could hardly blame him; nobody had heard of an Aura Spirit being frightened before. "She said that Arellia, the School's founder, would be able to tell us how to cure Oriel and wake her up."

"But Arellia—"

"Is dead, I know. But Asyra was adamant that we need to talk to her, that we need to go to The Under." Belle looked unconvinced, but the fact that Asyra was worried frightened them all. "She said 'they're back'," continued Ellora, "and looked really spooked. I don't know about you, Hunter, but I've never seen Asyra show an emotion that was anything like scared. It's not a good sign." Hunter remained silent, grinding his jaw. " She also told me that the entire Realm would be in danger unless we woke up Oriel immediately and found out who did this to her," she added finally.

Belle swallowed while Hunter returned his gaze to the wooden desk before him.

There was a beat of silence amongst them as the three of them attempted to absorb this information before Hunter spoke, breaking the thick quiet. "Once."

Ellora raised an eyebrow and glanced at Belle, but she seemed just as confused. "Once what?" she encouraged.

Hunter exhaled. "Only once have I ever seen Asyra afraid." He looked away, keeping his eyes fixed on the wall now rather than the table. "When I was younger, there was an incident. I was here at the time, at the Madori School of Aura, with my grandfather.

"It was just a regular day, as far as I can remember, until the other Upper Council Members came storming in. I was taken out of the room, so I don't know what exactly happened, but I had never seen my grandfather look so pale as he did that day when he came out of that meeting.

"There had been a death, that much I know. Who had died and how, I do not. My grandfather refused to leave me alone and brought me with him to see Asyra. Again, I was young and wasn't paying much attention; I didn't like visiting Asyra very much because she made it very clear she didn't like me, so I stayed as far away as I could. Having an Aura Spirit dislike is much more substantial than a mere playground spat.

"What I do remember is my grandfather mentioning a rash."

"A purple, glowing rash?" whispered Belle.

Hunter nodded silently.

"What happened?" asked Ellora.

Hunter shrugged. "Nothing. Everybody was on edge for a few days, weeks, even, but nothing else happened. I once overheard my grandfather and Oriel discussing it; they said it was some sort of false alarm, that upon closer examination, the rash was actually an allergic reaction to a poisonous plant that turned somebody's skin blue. As soon as that was discovered, everything went back to normal. Well, almost. Not long after, my grandfather retired, and Oriel took over as the Madori Mistress. But I always thought his early retirement was something to do with that day, to do with the rash."

Ellora swallowed.

"I guess we have no choice, then," said Belle finally, a slight tremble in her voice that Ellora wouldn't have recognised had she not known her for so long. "We'll have to go."

"Go?" asked Ellora.

Belle nodded. "To the Under."

"How do you suppose we get there?" Hunter panned.

"I'm the Madori Mistress in training," said Belle. "I can take us almost anywhere Oriel could, and that includes the Realm of the dead."

"We'd better clear it with Rainclarke," Hunter murmured. "He deserves to know what we're doing." Ellora couldn't help but think his tone was slightly pointed.

The infirmary was silent – a thick and tense silence that was unusual for the middle of the day.

"Master Rainclark,e?" Belle asked him as they approached Oriel's private bed in the far corner of the room. "We've spoken to Asyra." They decided it would be best to exclude the part where Ellora had gone alone; Rainclarke had enough to worry about right now.

"What did she say?" Rainclarke asked. He seemed to be more present and aware this time, even if the bags under his eyes were worse and his face was as pale as Asyra's.

"She told us we need to speak with Arellia in The Under, and she would be able to tell us what to do."

Rainclarke looked at the three of them for a moment, the thoughts churning through his mind and flashing across his eyes. "If I had any other options, I wouldn't let you go. But without Oriel, not only is the School in danger, so is the Kingdom and the Realm." He massaged his head with his hand. "I really want to say no. But I don't know if we have any other choices."

"We don't," Hunter replied calmly.

"One of the main issues is the Gate, I suppose. As far as I am aware, only an Upper Council Member can open the Gate to The Under," he said, the exhaustion obvious in his voice.

"We could ask Kris?" proposed Belle.

Rainclarke shook his head. "There have been a few issues in her own Kingdom. We can't ask her to leave them without an Incendi Mistress for that long."

"What about if we take the jewel?" suggested Hunter.

"Will that help?" Ellora asked him.

"When I was a young boy, I remember there was an emergency and Oriel, as the Madori Mistress in training, had to go without my grandfather. Because she was recognised by the Madori Orb, she took it with her, and the Gate let her through. Obviously, we can't leave the Kingdom without the Orb *or* a Madori Mistress to protect it, but we could take the jewel." His words were directed to them as a group rather than as a reply to Ellora.

Rainclarke thought carefully for a couple of minutes before finally speaking again. "That could work. And if you stay away from Mistfall, it should be a fairly simple journey for you all."

"We'll go as soon as we can, Master Rainclarke," Belle assured. "We'll go today so we can get Oriel up again. She'll be alright."

"Just be careful. And *stay away from Mistfall*."

All of a sudden, a loud cry came from outside of the privacy curtains around Oriel's bed. Hunter threw the curtains open, only to reveal Mrs Sotto running towards them.

"Mrs Sotto, is everything okay?" he asked.

"It is Melody!" she cried. "She is awake!"

CHAPTER ELEVEN

The Nameless One

E llora was the first to run directly to Melody's bed. Upon turning the corner, she saw Melody sitting up and staring at her father with concern while he sobbed next to her. A surge of relief coursed through her at seeing her awake again.

"What is going on?" Melody asked, her voice scratchy and weak.

"How are you feeling?" asked Ellora, coming closer to perch on the edge of Melody's bed and trying to keep her voice steady.

"I am fine, but what is going on?" Melody asked once again.

Belle arrived, holding a cup of water with a straw in it for Melody, helping her sit up and gesturing for her to drink while she performed some of the basic healing enchantments she knew to make sure Melody really was okay. "You've been in a coma, Melody," she said after completing and analysing the results of her enchantments.

"A coma?" Melody exclaimed, her voice sounding slightly smoother now that she had drunk a few small sips of water. "I do not remember anyzhing."

"Well, you're alright now," Ellora told her warmly. She squeezed Melody's hand gently. "We've missed you."

Mrs Sotto came running back again, this time with Healer Amare in tow, and wrapped her arms around Melody.

"Maman!" Melody cried, her voice muffled because her face was squished. "You are squashing me!"

"Je suis desolée, ma petite puce," she said, letting go of Melody and smoothing her hair down with her hands. "'Ow are you feeling?"

"She appears fine as far as my basic examinations can tell," Healer Amara said, pleased with this turn of events.

"And I *feel* fine, zhank you, 'Ealer Amare."

"Mr and Mrs Sotto, why don't we let Melody's friends fill her in on what's been happening while I discuss the medical side with you?" Healer Amare asked, leading them off to her office. The relief was clear on Melody's face as she exhaled in relief.

"We do have a few things to fill you in on," Hunter, who stayed back until now, finally contributed. "It's nice to see you're feeling better, Melody," he said.

"Zhank you, 'Unter. So come on, fill me in!"

By the time Healer Amare appeared again at the end of the room with Melody's parents, who were a lot calmer by now, Ellora, Bella and Hunter had finally managed to fill Melody in about almost everything. Of course, Ellora and Hunter were still unable to share what they learnt about Asyra and about what Kristen told them about the Upper Council and the breach from The Under without the risk of Asyra listening to Melody's or Belle's thoughts.

"I'm coming with you," Melody insisted.

"Absolutely not!" Ellora and Belle said simultaneously.

"You've just come out of a coma, for Spirits' sake!" Ellora exclaimed. "There is no way that we can take you with us to The Under."

"Besides, we shouldn't be too long," Hunter added. He was silent throughout the discussion, and Ellora noticed he was still avoiding looking at her or talking to her. "We should be back by the end of the day."

"You are going today?" Melody asked.

Belle nodded. "We need to get back as soon as possible so that we can wake Oriel up again. If the Realm is in danger, we haven't got any time to lose."

"I'm worried about leaving Master Rainclarke alone, though," Ellora said. "He's really struggling. I'm not sure he's even eaten anything today."

"Well, if you are not going to let me come wizh you, zhen I suppose I can stay wizh 'im. I will make sure 'e is eating and looking after 'imself," Melody said, her shoulders slumped at the realisation there was no way anybody would let her join them, but perking up at the thought of having a reason to stay behind.

"You're sure?" confirmed Belle.

"Oui."

"In that case," Ellora said, reaching into her pocket, "I would appreciate you looking after my little guy, too." She handed Lucifer over to Melody, who immediately began to coo over him.

"And Clara should be back at some point today," Belle added, smiling at the sheer happiness on both Melody's *and* Lucifer's faces upon seeing each other. "If you could fill her in while we're gone, that would be helpful."

"Absolument," Melody agreed, now much more upbeat.

It was then that Healer Amare and the Sottos returned, allowing Ellora, Belle and Hunter to leave, promising her they would visit as soon as they were back.

Ellora and Hunter headed directly to the kitchens to gather supplies to take with them while Belle went to grab some backpacks and the Madori Jewel.

"These could be useful," Ellora commented, opening the fridge to reveal rows and rows of energy drinks, pulling out three of each type. Hunter didn't even acknowledge that she'd spoken. "And these," she opened a cupboard filled with the blue sugary sweets Oriel had given Belle last year when she accidentally used up and drained all of her Aura. Still, Hunter didn't react, looking through the rest of the kitchen instead.

Ellora sighed. There was no way they could survive a trip to the Realm of the Dead if Hunter was refusing to even look at her. "You know, you'll have to speak to me at some point." No response. "Hunter, are you for real? You're behaving like a child."

All of a sudden, Ellora found herself pinned against the large metal fridge. Hunter twirled and forced her back until she could go no further. "Like a child, am I?" he rumbled in a low voice. "Says the one who *lied* and could have gotten herself killed? And for what? If anybody has behaved like a child, it sure as Mistfall has been *you*."

Ellora gulped. Even as Hunter moved back and stepped away from her, she felt her limbs shaking. She cleared her throat, ignoring the strange and unfamiliar fluttering that began in her stomach and took a breath.

"I didn't mean to lie."

"Yes, well, you did lie. Whether you meant to or not."

"You wouldn't let me go alone, and—"

"Didn't you ever stop to consider *why*?" Hunter asked, his tone calm and even once again, all emotions vanished as though he hadn't just suddenly pinned her against a fridge in anger. "Just because you're careless with your own life doesn't mean we all wish for you to get yourself killed, you know."

"I'm not careless!"

"Oh? Who was it, then, that decided it was a good idea to chase after a crazy sociopath who endangered the entire Kingdom and our Madori Mistress last year without waiting for Oriel to help you? Or what about sneaking out in the middle of the night to a courtyard and opening a creepy, glowing door without having *any* idea what was behind it? Does any of this ring a bell?"

She couldn't argue with him on that. But those events were taken out of context. She opened her mouth to counter, but he sighed before she had the opportunity. "I can't be bothered to argue with you, Ellora. You'll do what you want to, anyway."

Ellora lowered her eyes. She didn't realise she had upset Hunter so much by going to see Asyra without him. She hadn't thought it would be *that* big of an issue.

"Are we ready to go?" Belle asked, appearing in the kitchen and dumping the bags onto a counter. She was the only one other than Oriel to know where the Madori jewel was being kept, so she had gone alone.

"Ready," said Hunter, grabbing two bags and shoving in the supplies.

"Ready," Ellora said, a little less confidently, filling the third bag.

The trio arrived at the Gate Room reasonably quickly; it was time for breakfast, and most of the students who had already returned were eating in a dining room, so there was no need to avoid anybody on their way. Ellora hadn't returned the Gate key, instead having wrapped the delicate necklace around her own neck for safe-keeping. Especially after what Kristen told her, she didn't want to leave it lying around for anybody to find.

"Are we certain this is a good idea?" asked Belle again.

"It's our only option," Ellora replied.

"We'd better get on with it, then," stated Hunter.

Part of Belle's training to become a Madori Mistress was to learn about the different Gates and how they work, so Belle knew and told them that there was only one Gate to The Under, rather than separate Gates for Paradise and Mistfall. She also said that after going through the Gate, they would be able to find their way easily.

The moment they stepped into the Gate room, it was clear which Gate led to The Under.

The Gate to London was made up of a pale blue, rock-like substance, the rocks all glowing a bright blue hue; the Gate to the Incendi Kingdom was a fiery red; the Gate to the Glassi Kingdom was a crystal white.

The Gate to The Under, however, was dull, dark, and grey. It didn't glow. In fact, although there were shadows reaching out and around it, it looked rather static. Ellora lifted the key, holding the necklace up with a trembling hand. All of a sudden, the stones covering the interior of the arch-shaped Gate dissolved away, revealing a dark, jet-black tunnel.

Hunter looked over at Ellora and Belle, who were staring, frozen and wide-eyed, into the void. "I'll go first," he said reassuringly, making his way past the two of them.

"Wait," Belle called, holding out an arm to stop him. "That's nice of you, Hunter, but I've got the jewel. It should be myself who goes first. Just in case," she said before walking into the pitch-black space.

The faint blue glow of the Madori Jewel that Belle was holding up was their only guide in this endless tunnel, helping them forward. As far as Ellora could tell, it was a direct tunnel, straight with no twists, turns, corners, or other passages. Even so, she couldn't wait to get through to the other side and out of this cold and dark place. None of the other Gates she had been through turned into tunnels like this one; instead, they simply transported her from one place to the next, almost as simple as walking through a door to another room.

But this one, of course, was different.

The Gate to The Under, to the Realm of the dead, led down to the pits of the world, which living beings would never *dream* of visiting accidentally, let alone willingly.

Hunter entered after Belle, leaving Ellora to enter last and close the Gate behind her, but she didn't let him get too far ahead. She was careful to remain close enough that she could feel the fabric of his jacket brush against her arm as they walked, not willing to get lost in an inky place like this; she would never be found.

Under their feet, the floor was rocky and jagged, making it hard to keep their balance. And from above, the slow drips of some cold, silver liquid dropped down, each droplet that landed on them forcing a shiver to rush through them.

Ellora looked to the left, and suddenly, a pair of white irises blinked open, glowing against the darkness and staring at them as they walked. She yelped and jumped forward, bumping into Hunter, who instinctively turned and grabbed her shoulders to steady her. "What happened?" he asked, his voice deep and predatorial.

Ellora swallowed and turned back to where she had seen the eyes, but there was only black. "I... I could have sworn—"

Hunter released her before she could say anymore and turned back to the front, marching forward once more. In the frosty dome that was this tunnel, Ellora felt the loss of his contact like a brick. "Sorry," she whispered.

It felt like hours must have passed before, finally, the three of them emerged into a large, open stone cavern. The tunnel behind them that they had come through immediately turned into the solid, black, rocky substance that filled the Gate on the other side.

There was no way back.

There were two twin tunnels leading in opposite directions; one to the left and one to the right.

"This feels wrong," muttered Hunter.

"It *is* wrong," Belle answered. "Oriel told me about what it's supposed to be like down here; this is not what she told me the entrances to Mistfall and Paradise look like." She held the Jewel up higher, coming closer to each of the tunnels, trying to light the way and peer inside.

"She said the entrance to Paradise was filled with sweet-scented flowers blooming from the arch like it was the first day of Spring, that a warm and bright beam of sunlight shone through it from the other side, and you could hear the sounds of happy chatter and laughter and the peaceful sound of birds and water. She said if you stood in front of it, you could feel a warm breeze being carried through all the way from Paradise.

"She also told me that the entrance to Mistfall was dark and cold. Icy, even. She said you could hear dark, taunting whispers from the other side, telling you your darkest fears. She said it gave off a negative energy, while the entrance to Paradise just radiated happiness."

But from both of the tunnels, there was nothing.

"So Hunter was right," commented Ellora. "Something is going on here."

"Well, we can't go back now," said Belle, turning to look at the blocked-up tunnel behind them. "That Gate only led in; we need to get to Paradise to find the Gate out."

"Um, while we have a moment," Ellora began, "it would probably be a good idea to tell you what Kristen told us, Belle, now that we're out of the castle."

Hunter nodded his agreement, and the two of them briefly told Belle about what was going on. Ellora could practically see the fear and shock flittering across Belle's face as Hunter spoke.

"It must all be connected, then," Belle stated. "I mean... these weird changes in the Kingdoms; the attacks; what happened to Oriel; the arches; somebody trying to *come back from the dead*. There's no way these could all be coincidental, could they?"

"When you put it like that," said Ellora, "I suppose not."

"What about what happened with Julia?" asked Hunter. "That could very well be related—didn't she say there were more people she was working with?"

"Spirits," muttered Belle. "You're right."

"I guess we'll just have to hope Arellia has an answer," Hunter stated.

"We'd better get a move on then," added Ellora. "Which way do we go?"

"We'll have to make a guess," replied Hunter. "We have no other option."

It wasn't quite an easy decision.

One entrance would lead them down a dangerous path, with all of the deadliest Aurum souls, either imprisoned or deceased, in the entirety of the Realm. They were dangerous, they were desperate, and they wouldn't give a leitock about harming three students to get what they wanted.

"Look," Belle whispered all of a sudden, lifting the jewel and holding it in front of the left arch. Almost instantly, the jewel began to glow brighter, emitting a strange blue glow that was more disconcerting than it was comforting. She moved the jewel again, holding it in front of the arch on the right side this time. The glow immediately dimmed so it could barely be seen. She repeated the movements, shifting the jewel between the left and right arches, only to find the jewel glowing brighter, dim, brighter, and dim once again.

"I guess we know which way we're going," murmured Ellora, examining the jewel with curious eyes.

"Are we sure?" Belle was hesitant.

"I'm not sure we have any other choice but to follow it," Hunter replied.

Belle took a deep breath but nodded in resignation. "I'll go first."

Once again, she led the way into the dark, Hunter following behind her and Ellora at the back. With every step they took into the tunnel, the Madori jewel glowed brighter but still not bright enough to light up what lay ahead of them, but bright enough to see each other at least.

Almost immediately after Ellora stepped through the archway, the hole closed up behind her. So, now there really was no turning back.

They had only been walking for a few seconds when they began to hear the sounds from the other end of the tunnel.

Happy giggling, a light and airy voice singing to them, calling to them, the gentle sounds of water. As soon as she heard them, Ellora felt relief course through her; they had chosen the right path, the path to Paradise. They would make it through, they would find Arellia, and they would save Oriel *and* the Realm.

But only a split second later, her heart filled with dread.

The joyful giggles turned into menacing laughs. The warm singing turned into cold, icy whispers. The gentle water turned into violent storms. The pleasant breeze turned into blazing, fiery gusts that made them choke as the oxygen lodged in their throats. Ellora dropped to her knees, the burning air making it impossible to breathe.

"Not... Far..." Belle croaked, using the walls to drag herself along, forcing her legs to continue moving forwards. "Need... To... Get... Out."

A sharp, burning sensation exploded in Ellora's chest as she pulled herself across the floor. There was light ahead. It was so close. But her eyes were closing. Her limbs were no longer responding, and her brain was fogged up, clouded by the heat and lack of air.

"Come... On... Artemer..." Hunter grumbled from beside her. The sound of his voice snapped Ellora's eyes open. She forced herself forward. One inch forward, then two. From the corner of her eye, she could see Hunter's dark head of hair moving beside her.

In front of them, Belle emerged from the tunnel and gasped, gulping in the breathable air greedily, doubled over with her hands on her knees. She looked back at them, so close to the end but not close enough.

Just as Ellora's eyes began to close once again, she felt a hand wrap around her wrist.

"Oh no, you don't," Belle grumbled, her voice thick again now she was back in the tunnel.

She felt herself being dragged, the rough stone of the floor scratching through her clothes. But then, she could breathe. She inhaled deeply and coughed but inhaled once again, desperately absorbing all the oxygen her body could possibly take as she lay on her back.

"We did it," Belle panted, collapsing on the floor in between Ellora and Hunter, who was slowly inhaling and exhaling like Ellora. "We did it," Belle repeated.

"Thank you, Belle," Hunter choked, his voice scratchy and rough.

She flicked a hand up in the air to wave him off. "Can you see that?" Belle asked, still breathing heavily as she pointed to the floor.

"See what?" asked Ellora, forcing herself to sit up, a rush of dizziness swarming her head with the movement.

"When we used this jewel to find the Madori Orb, I could see a glowing, blue trail along the floor."

"I remember; nobody else could see it," Ellora responded.

"I can see it again." Belle pointed to a hill not far from where they were resting. "It trails that way."

"Where do you think it leads?" asked Hunter.

A loud growl came from behind them, and Ellora jumped up. "I have no idea, but I have a feeling wherever it is, it'll be better than standing here like sitting ducks," she whispered.

Belle and Hunter followed her lead, hopping onto their feet. They climbed the slight slope of deep, red sand Belle gestured to, and Ellora motioned for her to lead their way forward.

Hunter's jaw tensed, and Ellora followed his gaze to the other side of the hill was a small, deserted town in the middle of nowhere. It seemed empty, with no visible signs of anybody living or *not living* around.

She glanced at Belle and Hunter, who were looking down sceptically; Belle's eyes narrowed as she traced the rest of the trail while Hunter carefully scanned the area. His eyes landed on a large building that looked like it could have been a dark-coloured mansion, or perhaps a hotel, that looked as though it was falling apart, with smashed and boarded up windows and missing panels from the walls. Behind it, a large body of dark and angry water crashed violently onto a small stretch of land before it.

"I don't suppose the trail leads *away* from that place, does it?" Ellora asked Belle.

"Unfortunately not."

The town was just as deserted up close as it looked from afar. A door belonging to a run-down, dingy building on the right was flapping loudly on its hinges, creaking in the wind, the inside dark and empty.

"Where in the Realms are we?" whispered Belle.

"Mistfall," said Hunter, staring in front of him, where one single, darkly-dressed person stood in the middle of the dilapidated path, staring straight at them. Its face was disfigured and drooping, while its limbs were long and skinny under its cloak.

Slowly, the stiff and cloaked figure began to move, cracking its arms outwards, snapping its neck to the side and slowly crunching its legs, stumbling towards them.

Belle took a step forward in front of Hunter and Ellora and tucked the Madori Jewel into her pocket. She took a deep breath and summoned a small gush of water into each hand, her Aura ready to leap into action. Ellora followed suit, creating a somewhat smaller ball of water between her two hands; she was nowhere near as powerful or as talented as Belle, but she could certainly hold her own. Hunter conjured a tiny flame in his right hand while preparing his left to summon or control any wind if needed.

The figure walked slowly towards them, its legs moving in jolted, unstable motions while it kept its yellow, wide eyes fixed firmly on Belle in the middle.

"Mistress Belle," the figure croaked, coming to a stop a couple of metres away from them, its back hunched over and its arms dangling downwards, as if it had no control over them. "How may I serve you?" The figure crashed down to one knee and bowed down to Belle.

Ellora and Hunter both turned to look at Belle, confused, but Belle looked just as surprised as they did.

"Um... what is your name?" she asked the human-like creature.

"I am a Nameless One, Mistress Belle. Here only to guide your journey into and through Mistfall."

"Does it mean it only exists because you're here?" asked Ellora in a hushed whisper.

"Elle, how in the Realms would I know?" Belle hissed back.

"Very well, Nameless One," Hunter spoke, his voice strong and commanding. "Could you tell us how to get to Paradise?"

The Nameless One shot its head up towards Hunter, its yellow eyes narrowed, before letting out a loud and angry roar. The creature flew at Hunter in the blink of an eye, capturing him with its sharp, claw-like hands. "The Nameless One serves *only* the Madori Mistress," it growled, in a voice so grotesque and unearthly, it made Ellora shiver.

"Let him go," Belle ordered quickly. And it did. Ellora exhaled in relief. "While we are here, you are under strict instructions *not* to harm either of my friends."

The nameless one looked at Ellora, first, and then Hunter, in disgust but bowed its head again. "No Nameless One will hurt your friends during your journey, Mistress Belle," it said in that disturbing voice.

"Thank you." She cleared her throat. "Like Hunter asked, could you tell us how to get to Paradise?"

"Only one way from Mistfall to Paradise, Mistress Belle." And just as Ellora hoped it wouldn't, it pointed towards the water. "River of Death."

"Of course they couldn't have decided on a more pleasant name," Ellora muttered.

"And how exactly do we get across?" asked Belle, ignoring Ellora and keeping her focus on the Nameless One.

"Mistress Belle must speak to Gatekeeper, ask for boat."

"Where can we find the Gatekeeper?" demanded Hunter.

The nameless one pointed to the abandoned, dilapidated mansion.

"Perfect," muttered Ellora.

"Please, take us to the Gatekeeper," Belle asked the grotesque creature.

"Yes, Mistress." It smiled.

CHAPTER TWELVE

The Prisoner

T he mansion was even worse inside than it looked from the outside. The door was barely holding onto its hinges, the staircase was all but crumbling apart, the chandelier wouldn't work and was swinging from one corner, and the wallpaper was almost completely peeling off the walls.

"Where are all of the Aurums?" pondered Hunter, looking around cautiously.

"Breakfast," replied the Nameless One. The three of them exchanged a glance, but none of them were brave enough to ask any more; they felt lucky enough as it was to have avoided any Aurums already.

The Nameless One led them up the stairs and down a long, gloomy corridor and into a dark room, in which a person with long, grey hair was sitting at a window, watching the ground below them. As Ellora approached, she felt the hairs on her arms prickle as a shiver coursed through her bones. Below them, hundreds, if not thousands, of pale, shadowy figures all sat at a large, long table, all sitting in silence. If it weren't for the fact that they were all inhaling some sort of red gas from the middle of the tables, Ellora could have easily mistaken them for statues. It was chilling how mechanically they were moving and the way this Aurum at the top was just *watching* them, a wide grin plastered across their face.

"Madori Mistress," the Gatekeeper said, their voice calm and quiet but with a hint of a smile in their tone.

"You are the Gatekeeper?" Belle asked, stepping forward.

"And you search for a way to Paradise," the Gatekeeper replied.

"Er... yes, the Nameless One told us you would be able to help us with that," Belle replied.

"Us?" asked the Gatekeeper, finally looking away from the window and turning towards them. They seemed like a normal Aurum, as far as Ellora could tell. So, what had they done to be stuck in a place like this? "Yes, I see. One Madori Mistress – almost," they said, analysing Belle with their eyes, "one broken prince," they stared at Hunter, "and one... *well,* aren't you interesting?" they asked, looking amusedly at Ellora. "One... *half* of a pair."

Ellora had no idea what they meant by 'broken prince' or 'half of a pair' but wasn't entirely sure if it mattered all too much. All she wanted right now was to get out of there.

"So, could we use the boat?" Hunter asked abruptly.

The Gatekeeper's amused gaze shifted into one of annoyance aimed at Hunter. Ellora swallowed, recognising the similarity between their expression towards Hunter and Asyra's. "Patience, prince," they snarled in a sing-song tone.

"He didn't mean to offend you," Ellora apologised quickly on his behalf. If this Aurum was their only way out, they needed them to be willing to help. "We're just in a little bit of a hurry; you see, somebody we care about is seriously hurt, and we were hoping someone in Paradise would be able to help us."

The Gatekeeper snapped their eyes back to Ellora, softening their gaze again.

"I see," the Gatekeeper said mysteriously. "Well, not that I want to keep you waiting at all, but unless you want to walk through them," he pointed down where the dead Aurums were eating, "and I must say, you *do not,* you'll all have to wait."

"Okay," Belle said before Ellora or Hunter could say anymore. "We'll wait, then."

Ellora noticed the Madori Jewel hanging on the edge of Belle's pocket was about to fall out. She grabbed it as quickly as she could before it hit the floor. She wasn't sure if something like that could break, but she certainly didn't want to risk it.

And for the first time, she saw a glowing blue trail along the floor, leading out of the room.

"Belle," she whispered as soon as the Gatekeeper turned around again to watch the Aurums through the window.

"What is it?"

"I can see something," replied Ellora. "There's a blue trail leading out of the room. I think the jewel wants to take me somewhere."

"Where in Mistfall would it want to take you? Literally!"

"I don't know," Ellora replied. "But I need to find out."

"I'm not sure this is a good idea; the jewel has brought us here of all places, after all. Maybe we shouldn't be following it."

"I know it seems like that, but it must have a reason for bringing us here, Bee."

"But what if it doesn't want to help us? What if, like Asyra, it doesn't care about what happened to oriel?"

"It has to. Asyra doesn't care about Oriel because she wants control over the Kingdom and the Madori Master or Mistress; she doesn't care *who* that Master or Mistress is. The jewel, on the other hand, like the orb, has a connection with Oriel. And Oriel would never want to hurt us."

Belle sighed and ran her hand through her hair. Finally, she looked up at Ellora with a stern face. "You can't go alone," she hissed urgently. "This place is dangerous. We don't know what could happen."

"I don't think I have a choice, Bee. You can't get away, and I can't leave you here alone without Hunter. Besides, he's not talking to me; it'll be useless to bring him with me."

"I'm really not okay with you going alone, Elle."

"Then send the Nameless One with me; just order it not to harm me and to do whatever it takes to help me." Ellora didn't like the idea of that *thing* coming with her, but if that was what it would take to follow the jewel, that was what would have to happen.

Belle, albeit very reluctantly, gave in and gave the orders to the Nameless One, who escorted Ellora out of the room.

The jewel didn't lead her very far; out of the room, down a corridor and down a flight of stairs. It took Ellora uncomfortably close to the red-coloured area, where the spirits were eating or absorbing or whatever it was that they were doing, and she jumped back in fright when she glanced out of a window to see one of them staring directly at her.

She quickly looked away and moved out of sight of the window, determined not to look out there again. Finally, the trail took her outside to what looked like some form of a garden. She followed it even further to a small row of short, worn-out wooden sheds.

It led her past the first one, but Ellora peaked in to see that it was empty of any Aurums, living or dead, with only a metal table placed in the middle of the room.

It also took her past a second shed, this one closed with the door locked, so Ellora couldn't try to look inside even if she wanted to.

Finally, the trail ended at the third shed, this one more worn than the others, the dark paint faded and the wood splintering. There were dents in the walls, and from what Ellora could see, the tiles on the roof were all but completely gone, leaving behind a rough concrete foundation.

The door was slightly ajar, with a faint light coming from within. The Nameless One stopped outside of the shed. "The Nameless Ones must wait here," it said, somehow knowing this was where the trail led. Ellora looked curiously at it. Why wouldn't it come in with her?

"Aren't you supposed to come with me to protect me?"

It shook its head. "The Nameless One cannot enter."

She knew this was a bad sign, and she could just turn around right now, go back to Belle and Hunter, and never look back. But she also knew she *couldn't*; the jewel wanted to bring her here for a reason, and she needed to know what it was.

Gently, she pressed her cold fingers against the scrap of wood that acted as a door and pushed it, taking a deep breath as it creaked open ever so slowly. She peered through the small gap the door created, but it was too dark inside to see. She nudged it again, and this time a small stream of light pierced through the room, showing her the same wooden table that Ellora had seen in the first shed. Finally gathering her courage, she pushed the door open all the way and allowed the room to be flooded with the red glow that came from the sky.

She stuck her head inside first and gasped when she saw the interior. At the back of the room was a cage big enough to contain a grown Aurum. In the corner of the metal enclosure stood a tallish figure with long hair facing the wall. The figure's shoulders were hunched, and its head was slumped down. Ellora took a step inside, and a floorboard groaned loudly underneath her.

At the sound, the figure snapped into movement, lifting its head and turning around to stare at Ellora.

"Ellora?" the figure asked, their voice croaky and hoarse. "Ellora, is that you?" the figure spoke in a voice that Ellora recognised.

That voice had haunted her thoughts over the past few months. It had cursed her dreams.

"Julia?" she exhaled.

Of course, she had forgotten that Julia was detained here in Mistfall.

Julia took one step forward, stumbling on her weak legs, then another. Finally, she reached the bars that were keeping her trapped and grabbed desperately onto them, gripping them with dirty and bleeding hands.

"What are you doing down here?" she hissed, her eyes filled with warning and her strained voice with thunderous urgency. "You need to get out."

"You don't think I already know I need to get out of here?" Ellora demanded. "The Madori Jewel led me to you."

Julia's eyebrows furrowed. "Why?"

"I wouldn't know. That's why I followed it," Ellora barked, feeling anger bubble in her stomach at the sight of Julia, at the sight of the person who betrayed all of them, who tried to *kill* Oriel and Belle.

"Well, I don't know why," Julia responded, not even reacting to the malicious tone in Ellora's voice. "Ellora, this place is awful. Every day, five times a day, I hear noises. Noises from outside of this shed." Her fists tightened fearfully around the bars as she spoke. "I don't want to find out what happens out there, and you shouldn't either. You need to get out of here soon, before they finish *eating*. Whatever happens when they finish eating Ellora, it's not pretty." For a split second, Ellora felt sorry for Julia, scared for her, at the pure terror in her eyes as she looked desperately at her.

At that moment, a large grumbling sound came from outside of the shed. Julia looked at her frantically. "Please don't tell me you're here by yourself."

"Of course not," started Ellora. "Belle and Hunter are upstairs with the Gatekeeper."

"Good. Good," said Julia, sounding breathless. "Get back to them; get the gatekeeper to let you out."

"Why do you care, Julia?" asked Ellora. "You were the one who tried to destroy the entire kingdom and kill Oriel. And you admitted that you would try to kill Belle."

"Seriously, Ellora!" Julia groaned. "You're not so naive as to *still* think I did all of that *just* to harm Oriel, hurt Belle and destroy the Kingdom, are you?" asked Julia.

"I have no reason to believe otherwise," Ellora hissed. "Give me a reason, then; tell me. What was your motive? What was your reasoning behind it all?"

"I... I can't tell you," said Julia. "But you have to trust me. Whatever it is that's going on, it's not because of me. There's something seriously *wrong*. In the realm, I mean. I was just trying to stop it!"

"No, Julia, I really *don't* have to trust you. Why should I? You tell me." There was a brief moment of silence before Ellora spoke again. "I'll tell you – there's absolutely no reason."

"Ellora, I'm telling you. Nothing is as it seems in that Realm. Or in this one, for that matter. I know you think I'm evil and greedy, or whatever it is you think of me, but it was all for the greater good. It still is. You'll see what I mean someday. Someday soon. You don't have to trust me. But please, if nothing else, *please* do listen to me when I say you *have* to get out of here."

Another rumbling sound came from outside, and Ellora started to panic. There was shifting outside and loud, crunching noises, like the sound of metal scraping against metal.

Ellora didn't need to be told twice; she hurried out of the shed, looking back one last time to see Julia watching with tears streaming down her face, and told the Nameless One to take her back. Out of the corner of her eye, she saw a slow-moving figure moving across the garden. Its limbs cluttered along like bones.

"We need to hurry," she said, and the two of them moved faster, running past the window once again on her way up the stairs, only to see that the place below them was empty.

They had finished eating.

CHAPTER THIRTEEN

To Paradise

Ellora ran back into the room where Belle and Hunter were impatiently and anxiously waiting for her.

"It took you long enough," grumbled Hunter, shooting her a glare.

"I told you he wouldn't be happy about you going off alone," said Belle.

"We need to get out of here," said Ellora. "Right now."

"*Now* what have you done?" Hunter grumbled.

"Nothing!" Ellora exclaimed defensively. "The jewel took me to Julia," she said.

"Julia?!" exclaimed Belle.

"Why in the Realms would you go alone?" Hunter demanded. He stepped closer, his dark eyes staring dangerously at her.

"What in the Realms did she have to say?" asked Belle. "And why would the jewel take you there?"

"Right now isn't the time, guys," Ellora hissed, taking a step away from Hunter on trembling legs. "We need to get out here!"

"Well," said the Gatekeeper, "it looks like my prisoners have finished their meal."

"Great, now, we can get out of here?" Ellora asked.

"Not quite," laughed the Gatekeeper, leaning casually back against the window and folding his arms over his chest.

"You said we wouldn't want to go through them while they were eating," said Hunter.

"I did, didn't I?" The Gatekeeper smiled a wide, creepy smile that stretched across his face and caused a shiver to travel through Ellora, feeling cold to the bone. "But when did I say I would let you out?"

"You... you're bound to help me," stated Belle, holding up the jewel. "I'm here on behalf of Madori Mistress and Upper Council member Oriel, and I have the Madori Jewel!"

"Yes, you said," the Gatekeeper waved their hand dismissively. "But I know your precious Oriel can't have sent you down here herself."

"What's that supposed to mean?" asked Ellora.

"Oriel knows that I would never help you." They turned to face the window.

Ellora looked in fear at Belle, who furrowed her eyebrows in confusion. Hunter, who was standing ever so slightly in front of them, put his hands behind his back, creating a flame with one and a small tornado in the other like he did when they first arrived. Belle and Ellora followed suit, preparing themselves for a fight that, with one party being backed by an entire army of dead Aurums, was not in their favour.

"I'll tell you what," the Gatekeeper said, turning around to face them again with a wide grin plastered across their face. "My fight is only with certain members of the Upper Council, not any of you. I'll let you *try* to get yourselves out of here. If you make it across the River of Death, good for yourselves. Once you reach the shore on the other side, I give you my word that nobody from this land will harm you or follow you.

"*But...* if any of you touch the river, or if any of my prisoners draw blood, all three of you will remain here. For eternity. I've been getting a little bored with nobody but the dead and the damned here to keep me company."

Ellora looked up at them in fear. "That hardly seems like a fair—"

"Will you at least provide us with a boat?" Belle asked.

The Gatekeeper looked at her in surprise, eyebrows raised high on their head. "If you accept, I will provide the boat."

Collectively, the three of them looked out at the River. Its jet-black water bubbled, daring them to accept the challenge. Belle looked over at the two of them, silently asking for confirmation, not that they had any other choice.

"We accept."

When Ellora, Belle and Hunter first arrived in Mistfall, it had been an eerie ghost town, and all three of them wished they were somewhere else, anywhere else, as long as it was somewhere less creepy. They regretted that wish.

The trio found themselves in the garden where Ellora had been earlier, only this time, they were trying to lug a boat out of an old, worn-out barn and lug it to the River of Death. Ellora, while she knew she shouldn't have, looked over at the house they had just left to see one of the prisoners staring at her through the window.

She had never felt such intense fear coursing through her body as she did at that moment. He looked even more frightening than he did when he was eating. His eyes were empty and soulless, and his mouth curved upwards into a predatory grin. His skin was pale, but black, shadowy figures surrounded him. As she watched, more and more of the prisoners slowly gathered in the windows, each with the same dark grin, watching them.

"Snap out of it, Artemer!" Hunter shook her by the shoulders.

Ellora looked up at him with wide eyes and gulped. She was hardly the bravest person, but the image of those *creatures* staring at them, watching them like a lion would watch its prey, like they were playing a deadly and awful game, shook her to her core.

"They—" she pointed up at the windows, trying to explain to Belle and Hunter what was about to happen, but when she glanced back up, they were all gone. All of the windows, from the very top to the very bottom of the house, were empty. "We need to go. *Now*," she demanded.

The three of them worked even harder and faster, pulling at the boat. It was a heavy thing made of splintering wood, and Ellora wasn't entirely convinced it would float, but it was their only chance.

Suddenly, a loud screeching sound echoed from behind them. They turned slowly to see the door to the mansion exploding open, and one of the prisoners crouched on all fours, staring at them as though she was about to pounce.

"Hurry!" shouted Belle, letting go of the boat. "You two get it into the water; I'll cover us."

They must have been only a couple of hundred metres away from the water by now, but the 200 metres trek with the heavy boat felt like an eternity. Ellora could hear the sound of splashing behind her, the sounds of Belle using her Aura against the prisoners. Another louder splash resulted in Ellora and Hunter being hit by droplets of water, some of them stinging their skin as if they were tiny needles.

"Please hurry!" Belle grunted, creating whirlpools and large waves to try and push the prisoners back and keep them away. "There are so many!"

Ellora risked a glance behind her and was met with a terrifying sight. Hoards of the dead were closing in on them, crawling, running and leaping with a single-minded purpose. Belle was unleashing wave after wave of water, throwing groups back and knocking them over, but they seemed never-ending. Just as she pushed one group back with a powerful surge of water, the next was even closer, and then the next, and then the next, each one more relentless than the last. The ground was slick with the water and the blood, making it difficult to keep their footing. The smell of decay and rot was overpowering, making it hard to breathe.

"Help her!" Ellora screamed to Hunter, over the sounds of the water and the growls of the prisoners, combined with the sounds of them dragging their bodies across the stone and gravel floors. She knew that she would be next to no help, whereas Hunter was much more skilled than she was, even if she didn't like to admit it and even if his abilities were nowhere near Belle's level.

Hunter looked between the boat and the River of Death, judging the remaining distance. He then looked back at Belle fighting against the prisoners. He nodded at Ellora before running off in Belle's direction.

Ellora took a deep breath and continued to force the boat forward, trying her best to ignore the sounds coming from behind her. All of Belle's and Hunter's work would be for nothing if she couldn't get this Spirits-forsaken boat into the river.

She was so close. The boat was practically touching the water. They would be able to get out of there alive, get to Arellia and save Oriel. Just a couple of metres left, and she would have done it.

But that was when things started to go wrong for Ellora. The boat suddenly stopped moving. Ellora shoved it, but still, it wouldn't budge. "No!" she called, slamming her fist on top. "No, come on. Come on, come on, you stupid thing, move!"

She ran around to the other side of the boat to find a rocky ledge where the boat was trapped, and her heart sank. There was no way she would be able to lift this heavy boat that high. Even if she, Belle and Hunter tried together, she wasn't sure they would be able to lift it.

She looked around in despair, desperate for anything that would help her. She caught sight of movement in the house above them and saw the Gatekeeper watching them in amusement. They waved at her, and she paled. They had known from the start that the three of them wouldn't make it; they just wanted entertainment.

"Artemer, we can't hold them off for much longer; there's too many of them," Hunter called out, his voice barely audible over the sounds of stampeding feet, bursts of flames, gusts of wind and explosions of water. As soon as he spoke, a blast of fire shot towards them. Ellora's eyes widened. That fire did not come from Hunter; it came from the prisoners.

"Spirits!" Hunter shouted. "We *really* can't hold them off, Artemer!"

"I can't move it!" Ellora cried. "The boat is stuck."

"Use your Aura, Elle!" called Belle, her voice strained. "You can do it."

Ellora couldn't believe she didn't consider it sooner. She closed her eyes and felt herself conjure a stream of water, pushing it against the boat to lift it up into the river. She deposited it gently in the water and ran over to keep a hold of it before it got too far.

"It worked!" she called. "Get in." She held the boat steady as Hunter and Belle walked back towards her, still pushing back against the prisoners. If they weren't fighting for their lives, Ellora would have commented on the beauty of Hunter's and Belle's auras. While Belle was creating magnificent whirlpools with one hand and tidal waves with the other, controlled to perfection with the most delicate of movements, Hunter was simply flicking his hand to blast away large groups of the dead with large gusts of air, while using his other hand to create small, but powerful, fireballs and aim them at specific prisoners who were approaching too quickly.

Slowly and still sending crashes of water as she did so, Belle stepped into the boat, followed by Hunter, and Ellora climbed in after them. All three of them were panting and covered in a thin layer of sweat but stopped moving when the dead Aurums crowded together at the edge of the water to watch them.

Hunter used his Caeli Aura to create a wind against the sail, while Belle used her Madori Aura to create larger waves, making the boat move away, as far from them as they could possibly get.

"We did it," Ellora breathed when they were finally too far enough for the prisoners to get onto the boat. "I can't believe we did it."

"If I never see one of those *things* again, it will be too soon," Hunter gasped, leaning against the side of the boat as Belle continued to push it along with precise waves, keeping them too small to crash upon them but large enough to move them fast.

The Aurums were still gathered on the shore, watching them eagerly, and Ellora looked up at the Gatekeeper only to see them still grinning down at them. Why in the Realms were they smiling? They had done it. They had gotten away.

"Ellora," Belle said calmly. "Ellora, step towards us." A small tremor vibrated through her voice as she held out a hand for Ellora.

Ellora turned towards Belle and Hunter, who were both looking behind her with wide eyes fixed over her shoulder, and did as they said, making her way over to them. Just as she was about to reach out and grab Belle's hand, the boat began to shake, and mid-step, Ellora lost her balance. She tumbled to the bottom of the boat, falling onto the cold, wet wood below. A strong arm lifted her up from where she had been, perilously close to the edge of the boat and falling into the River of Death, which would have trapped her soul in this place for eternity.

Hunter effortlessly hoisted her up and over to where he and Belle were gripping tightly onto the mast in the middle of the boat, keeping one hand on the mast and one arm around her until she was able to grab onto the mast for herself. For the first time, Ellora was able to look at the other side of the boat and instantly realised why the Gatekeeper had still been smiling.

In front of them, an enormous serpent had emerged from the ink water below them, its mouth lined with multiple rows of sharp, pointed teeth. The large creature was a dark blue-grey colour that blended into the River of Death and stood out like dark ink against the red, glowing sky above it. Its scales were large and sharp, and the creature had spiky thorns protruding from its head that looked large enough to impale a person.

"Mistfall," she whispered. As soon as she did, the serpent released a wet, sickening, gut-wrenching roar that forced the boat backwards through the water. It turned to stare at them, each of its glowing red eyes bigger than Ellora's head. It watched silently as Belle, Hunter, and Ellora prepared themselves to fight but moved no closer towards them. The three of them exchanged glances, but nobody dared to speak or move.

Slowly, the creature sank down, submerging its long and slithering snake-like body into the depths of the water, keeping only its head above, turning its head frantically, its ears pricked up.

"What—" Ellora began in a hushed voice but didn't have the opportunity to finish her thought. The creature dove towards them, its head mere metres away from the boat. Hunter quickly clamped his hand over her mouth.

Once again, the giant snake's head turned, and its ears pricked up as it sank into the water.

Belle slowly lifted one hand and wiggled her fingers, creating a current that drifted them ever so slowly away. "It's blind," she whispered in a breath so quiet it almost could have been mistaken for the wind. She kept the current going, but they were barely moving, Belle unable to create a stronger current for risk of the creature hearing it.

When they moved further away, Hunter tapped them both on the shoulder. He spread out his hands, gesturing for them to wait where they were and made fanning motions before pointing at the sail.

Ellora nodded eagerly. If Hunter was able to use his Aura to create a wind against the sail, they would be able to get out of there quickly *and* silently.

But when Hunter shifted on his feet, a wooden board creaked loudly under him. The serpent immediately released a screeching noise and raised itself from the water, towering over all of them as it continued to grow and grow. Suddenly, it dove in Hunter's direction, its toothy jaws snapping eagerly at him.

Just in time, Hunter ducked but remained flat on his stomach at the bottom of the boat, not risking the chance that the boat would creak once again. Ellora made to move towards him, but Belle grabbed her by the wrist and shook her head. The creature was too close to miss now; if any one of them made a sound, that would be it.

They were stuck.

Ellora looked around her, looking around the boat for anything she might be able to use as a distraction, but there was nothing. Until an idea struck.

She flicked her fingers in the direction of the water behind the serpent, far enough away from them for it to sense them, and a small wave bubbled. The creature twitched in that direction, its ears pricking up. Belle widened her eyes and waved her hands in a circling motion, urging her to keep going. Again, Ellora flicked her hands, this time causing a larger wave to crash upon the water.

The serpent dove this time in the direction of the wave, and Hunter took the opportunity to stand. Belle created a wave to carry the boat, and Hunter created a small yet strong breeze to push against the sail. Ellora flicked a finger again, creating a wave closer to the shore where the Gatekeeper was watching with wide and angry eyes. A twist of her wrist created more waves for the serpent to follow.

It growled, moving violently in the same direction, chasing the waves as they went.

The boat moved faster, drifting along the River of Death with the help of Belle's waves and Hunter's breeze.

"Almost there!" exclaimed Belle, raising her arms in a sweeping motion, strengthening the waves and moving them faster, as fast as they could go without the water splashing onto them.

The serpent roared, jumping out of the water and stretching up to the sky, torn between the gentle splashing noises before it and the crashing of the boat. Its ruby eyes glowered at them and dove into the water, travelling like a torpedo through the river towards them.

"Faster!" Belle demanded, lifting her arms in wider arches. They were so close, only a few hundred metres away. Ellora gave up on the distractions, putting her efforts into helping Belle push the boat. Her Aura only made a small impact, but it was an impact nonetheless.

The white, sandy stretch of land was in sight, but the serpent was getting closer. It surged out of the water just as the boat hit the sand, and before she could think, Ellora ran into Belle and Hunter with full force, tackling them out of the boat and tumbling across the sand.

The serpent stopped at the boat, snatched it into its sharp teeth and sank back into the river. They made it.

CHAPTER FOURTEEN

Arellia

Ellora sighed with relief, flopping down onto her side on the sand and gratefully allowing the pleasant sun above to warm her face after the icy cold breeze of the river. "Thank the Spirits," she breathed.

"Yes, thank the Spirits," said Belle, lifting herself up to lean against a large rock. Hunter turned to lie on his back, still panting and covered in a thin layer of sweat.

"I think now's a good time for a refuel," suggested Belle. She heaved up her backpack and dug around, handing a blue bottle to each of them.

"And here," said Ellora, pulling out the blue fizzy sweets she packed and distributing them.

She took a large swig of the drink Belle chucked to her before popping one of the sweets in her mouth, feeling the effects in her Aura and her energy almost instantly as she became more and more aware of her surroundings.

In Mistfall, the sky was red and blazing above them, the air dusty and difficult to inhale and the breeze icy cold. Here, the sun was warm, and there was no trace of the bloody red in the clear blue sky. A pleasant breeze drifted across them, tickling their faces and providing them with clear air to breathe.

Finally feeling steady enough, Ellora got up from where she was lying, a slight wobble still present in her legs, and actually looked around her.

There was no sign of Mistfall to be seen; the clear, blue ocean in front of them was just that, an ocean with gentle waves coming to meet them. There was no inky river, or enormous serpent, or abandoned mansion with vicious creatures staring at them. There was no rickety old boat or Gatekeeper watching them as if they were some sort of entertainment show. There was just... ocean.

But that was it.

"Paradise doesn't seem like much, does it?" she asked, her voice heavy with disappointment.

They had landed on a small island, covered in nothing but sand and the occasional rock and lined with foliage. There was a small clump of trees towards the right side of the island, but otherwise, it seemed completely deserted.

"This can't be it," said Belle, frowning and looking around. "Surely this can't be paradise."

"Maybe not," murmured Hunter, "but it could be the *entrance* to paradise. After all, if it was this easy to get in, anybody could."

"Easy?" scoffed Ellora. "What part about that, "she gestured to the large body of water that used to be the River of Death, "was easy for you?"

"You know what I mean," said Hunter, his tone just as bland as before. "If we did it, anybody could. They have to have precautions in place."

"Well, we'd better get a move on then," said Belle. "I have a feeling that whoever it is that's trying to destroy the realm will not wait for us to save it first."

Exhausted but finally feeling steady enough to walk, the three of them trudged towards the patch of trees. In comparison to the other trees on this strange little island, this patch was different. It was brighter, the different shades of green more vibrant and colourful.

"Can you two feel that?" asked Belle, stopping abruptly in front of them.

There was a feeling of familiarity about those trees that Ellora sensed more with every step she took until she came to stand beside Belle.

"I can feel it," agreed Hunter.

"What is that?" Ellora asked. They edged closer, and a soft humming sound filled their ears, a faint shimmering surrounding the leaves hanging from the tallest trees ahead. "It looks like... a Gate."

"I guess that's the way," stated Belle, still hanging back and clutching tightly onto her bag.

Hunter glanced at her and stiffened his shoulders, jogging ahead to the Gate and poking his head inside, through the shimmering gap between the trees. Only moments later did he remove his head again and turn to look at them. "Yup, definitely the way," he said, gesturing for them to join him in going through the Gate.

The very moment Ellora stepped through, she felt a change inside her. She felt... lighter, almost. Free. The exhaustion that was sitting on her shoulders eased. There was no doubt about it; this was Paradise.

In front of them stood a pair of tall steel gates and behind them was the liveliest town Ellora had ever seen. Large crowds of Aurums bustled about, their laughter and chatter filling the air. Children raced and played along the picturesque cobblestone paths, which were lined with vibrant lanterns, their giggles and squeals of delight adding to the festive atmosphere. In the heart of the town stood a grand square where musicians played lively tunes, Aurums sang along, and others danced to the music, their feet moving gracefully to the rhythm. The square was alive with energy and joy, a celebration of life and community. The lanterns cast a warm glow on the faces of the people, and the cobblestones were worn smooth from years of use. The music and laughter were a symphony that blended together, creating a harmonious atmosphere.

Bright and colourful buildings lined the streets, each one looking brand new, with fresh coats of paint and beautifully decorated doors. One door was a cheerful yellow, while the next was adorned with paintings of cats. It was a stark contrast to the gloomy and dilapidated streets of Mistfall.

Colour was everywhere. On every corner, the streets were a riot of hues. The pavement was brightly paved with stones in a variety of colours, ice cream stands in vibrant shades, and lush flower beds bursting with a variety of blooms—roses, lilies, daffodils, chrysanthemums and every other flower one could think of. The vibrant colours and designs were a feast for the eyes, and the smell of flowers mixed with the sweet scent of ice cream, creating a truly magical atmosphere. It was hard to believe that this place existed so close to the drab and dreary Mistfall.

"Wow," whispered Belle.

"Spirits," breathed Hunter.

"Excuse me!" exclaimed a loud voice. A large metal trident swung in front of them, blocking their path. "Where do you think you're going?"

Standing in front of them was a large, tall, stone creature carrying the huge trident.

"Who are you?" asked Ellora.

"Who are *you*?" asked the stone giant.

"My name is Belle," Belle interrupted. "I come on behalf of Madori Mistress Oriel, head of the Upper Council." She held up the Madori jewel.

"What's going on 'ere?" Another stone creature arrived, carrying its own trident. "Who are you?"

"We've already been through this," Hunter sighed in frustration.

"So," the first stone creature said to the second, "these lot are claiming to be here on behalf of Oriel."

"Not possible!" the second one said, "Oriel always comes for herself."

"Exactly what I was thinking, Fred," said the first one.

"I'm sure that usually, Oriel would come for herself," Ellora said, quickly, "but she's hurt. We need to speak with somebody here to help her."

"Have you got any proof?" the second one, Fred, asked.

"I already showed you the jewel," said Belle.

"Well, either way, it doesn't matter," said the second one.

"What do you mean, Fred?" the first one asked.

"You're both called Fred?" asked Hunter.

"Because the reason why I came over here in the first place was to let you know about the new decree that just came through. Nobody in *or* out of Paradise," Fred number 2 replied, ignoring Hunter.

"Oh no," whispered Belle.

"Where did that rule come from?" Ellora asked. Oriel was at the very top of the Realm, as the head of the Upper Council, and she didn't give that order, so who did?

"That is on a need-to-know basis," said the second Fred.

"You're probably only saying that because you don't even know yourself," said Hunter. Ellora looked at him, bewildered as to why in the Realms he was taunting the only people who could let them into Paradise.

"I'll have you know, I am the one who gets all the information 'round 'ere!" Fred number 2 growled.

"Is that so?" asked Ellora, hoping she had figured out what it was that Hunter was doing. "So, are you saying that Fred is not important enough to know where these orders came from?" she gestured to Fred number 1.

"Yeah, Fred, is that what you're saying?" asked Fred number 1.

Belle interrupted before the second Fred could answer. "Oh no, Fred, I'm sure that isn't what Fred means at all, is it Fred? No, no, I think what Fred is *actually* trying to say, is that you're simply not good enough at keeping secrets to know. Otherwise, of *course* he would have told you!"

"I'll have you know, Fred," growled Fred number 1, "that I am *amazing* at keeping secrets."

"No, you're not, Fred! You were the one who told my girlfriend that time when I was out instead of at home, sick, like I said I was!" Fred number 2 said angrily.

"Well... *you* were the one who told my ex boyfriend that I was going to break up with him before I had the chance to do it!" Fred number 1 replied just as angrily, dropping his trident to the ground and facing Fred number 2.

"That was only because you ate my sandwich the day before!" Fred number 2 replied, dropping his trident, too.

"Because you ate my cake!" Fred number 1 cried.

"I think the Freds have some things to work out," whispered Belle. "Let's go."

The three of them slipped quietly around the Freds, although it probably wouldn't have mattered much even if they all ran around screaming; the Freds were too engrossed in their own argument. They slipped open the Gate and snuck through, closing it behind them.

"Finally," Belle whispered. They were here. In Paradise.

The moment Ellora stepped through the gates, she felt herself relax even further; a tension in her eyebrows that she was unaware even existed eased away as she felt her body relax. Her jaw unclenched, and her shoulders sank down further with every breath. It was clear the others were also having a similar reaction; Belle's eyes looked brighter, and Hunter's posture less rigid.

"Where do you think we'll find her?" asked Ellora.

"Maybe near water?" Belle suggested.

They scoured the area, looking for any sort of body of water other than the one they came from.

"There," Hunter pointed at a sunny, sandy area with a scattering of palm trees and what looked like a lovely blue sea to swim in. "That's perfect."

The three of them walked over, basking in the warmth that they sorely missed while in Mistfall. It was as if Mistfall drained them of their colour, energy, and spirit, and just *being* here was restoring it all.

Surrounding the glittering blue body were many Aurums. Some were simply lying by it, absorbing the warmth, while others were chatting, dancing, or playing games in the sand.

Sat in the middle of the beachy area, in the middle of all the different groups in the area, Ellora spotted one face that she would never forget. The bright, twinkling eyes belonging to Arellia shone brightly, reflecting the water in front of her.

She moved her arms effortlessly, her hands making a huge arc motion in the air, lifting the water up and swirling it around, creating beautiful displays in the air with the water. A group of children that were playing in the sand nearby giggled excitedly as they watched her work.

"Again, again!" one of them cried eagerly, jumping up and down in the air in anticipation. Arellia laughed, melodically and sweetly, and happily obliged.

Once again, she lifted her arm in a huge, sweeping motion, lifting the water up in a thin stream before making a quick fist with her hand. In an instant, the water turned into tiny droplets, softly drifting down on the children, looking like sparkling glitter floating through the air. The children looked up in awe, their mouths open in wonder.

"That will be her," said Belle, pointing. Even she watched the display in amazement. As a Madori mistress in training, Belle knew there was almost no limit as to what she would be able to do. But for now, she was just beginning and while Ellora knew some of the wonders that Belle would be able to show when she improved in her Aura training and mastered Madori Aura, it was really intriguing for her to see what it was that her powers would be able to achieve one day.

"You guys head over," said Hunter, looking over at a small building opposite the beach-like area. "I'll catch up."

Ellora and Belle looked at him curiously as he walked away towards a building, but headed over without him nonetheless. By this time, Arellia had stopped her display as the children all ran off. She was sitting on a little bridge over the water, her feet dangling over and making soft wiggling motions with her fingertips, creating little waves and ripples in the water.

"Um, excuse me," Belle said a little timidly when they walked over.

"Yes, can I help you?" Arellia asked, looking up from the water at them. She looked even more Goddess-like in person than her statues did back at the Madori School of Aura.

"My name is Belle. I'm the current Madori mistress in training."

Arellia's eyebrows shot up in surprise. "What in the Realms are you doing down here?" she asked, alarmed.

"Well, you see, the Madori mistress is hurt," said Belle. "She's been injured, and we were sent down here to find you." She motioned towards Ellora, who was standing a step behind Belle, allowing her to do the talking.

But, now, Belle motioned for her to come forward. "Yes," Ellora said, "Asyra said that you could help."

"Asyra?" Arellia jumped up to her feet at the mention of the Madori Spirit. She scoffed. "She must be desperate, then." After a moment of consideration, she asked: "Who is your Madori Mistress? Time runs differently down here, and it's easy to lose track."

"It's Oriel," answered Belle.

"I like Oriel," said Arellia, "she's very kind." She looked at the two of them suspiciously through narrowed eyes. "Before giving you any information, I will need to know if you have the same... *beliefs* as Oriel."

"If you're talking about whatever it is that's going on with the Upper Council, then yes," said Ellora.

"We're not *entirely* sure what's going on, but we're absolutely on Oriel's side," added Belle.

"Good," said Arellia. "Well, in that case, how can I help?"

Ellora stepped forward once again. "Well, it's a little bit of a long story, but something happened in the Realm, and Oriel went to find some information. She returned injured, so we took her to the healer, who did as much as she could, but for some reason, she still wouldn't wake up. After examining a little further, we discovered a purple glow on her back."

At the mention of the glow, Arellia inhaled sharply. "Like a glowing rash on her back?" she asked. "Under her skin?"

"You're familiar with it, then?" asked Ellora.

"Spirits," Arellia muttered under her breath. "Unfortunately, I know what it is that has happened to Oriel, and I will not keep you for long, for you have no time to lose. You need to help her. You must listen to me carefully. Oriel has been harmed, and not by any old Aurum, but a Magi Aurum.

"The first thing you will need to find to help her is a scythe enchanted by a Magi Aurum. Any other scythe will reverse the healing properties and effects of the herb you will need during harvest. Instead of helping Oriel, the herb will poison her instead. Unless you use a Magi-enchanted scythe.

"You will also need a Redmer stone in a metal-gage amulet. The concoction you will have to create is very powerful and contains a huge amount of energy; she will need this necklace to protect her when you apply the tincture.

"And, most importantly, you will need the Herb of Asphodel. This herb is found only in barren lands where the soil was once rich and filled with nutrients. You will find, in places like this, once the soil is dead, the herb will grow.

"Finally, you will need to grind three stars of this herb together with exactly seven drops of the Waters of Paradise.

"Where in the Realms will we be able to find all of those things?" asked Ellora.

"That I can't help you with; The Aura Realm has changed greatly since I was there, and you will have to navigate for yourselves. There is one thing I can help you with," she said, gesturing to the water in front of her.

Quickly, Belle opened her bag and pulled out an empty bottle of the drink she had finished. She gave it to Arellia, who filled the bottle and handed it back.

"I wish you great luck on your journey, but you have no time to waste. Please, help Oriel."

"Wait!" Ellora called. Belle looked at her in curiosity, but this was something she needed to know. "Before we go, there's something I need to ask you. Have you seen a girl around here? She was eleven years old. Her name was Ophelia. Ophelia Artemer."

"I'm sorry, I'm afraid I haven't. However, that doesn't necessarily mean she isn't down here."

Ellora frowned. "Thank you anyway."

She couldn't hide her disappointment. But either way, they needed to get back. The two of them headed back to the area they parted from Hunter.

"Where did you run off to?" Belle asked as Hunter stalked back over to them. His cheeks were pink.

"I needed to see someone while we were down here. Did she give us all of the information we needed?"

"She did," answered Ellora. "Now, we just need to find our way out of here."

"I've taken care of that already," Hunter answered. "This way." He led them to a tall mountain after the little town, past all of the buildings, the beach, the lake and all of the Aurums.

As they walked, Ellora and Belle filled Hunter in, telling him exactly what Arellia said, although Ellora chose to leave out the part about her sister.

At the bottom of the mountain was a cave entrance. "It's in here," said Hunter, leading the way inside.

And sure enough, there was a Gate. By now, Ellora couldn't mistake the humming sound or the shimmering radiating from the portal.

"Are we ready?" asked Belle.

They all nodded, and Ellora held up the Gate key.

CHAPTER FIFTEEN

Drako

"Where in the Realms do we start with something like this?" asked Ellora as they walked through the Gate from Paradise to the Gate Room in the Madori School of Aura, watching the Gate disappearing behind them, vanishing into thin air.

"Where can we even find all those things?" asked Hunter. "It feels like we're being sent on a wild goose chase."

"I don't think so," Ellora replied. "Arellia seemed really spooked about the whole situation. She definitely wanted to help Oriel."

"Well, I think first things first," said Belle. "Before doing anything else, we need to go and update Master Rainclarke and Melody. They're probably waiting for us; we have no idea how long we've been gone."

"You're right," said Ellora. "And maybe one of them will have some ideas on where we might be able to find some of these things."

The three of them headed straight for the infirmary. They had no idea how long they had been gone, but judging by the number of students walking through the corridors, some carrying suitcases and big bags, they knew it couldn't have been too long. Arellia was right; time did get confusing down in The Under, but they at least knew they hadn't been away for too many days.

As they walked through the corridors, they spotted some familiar faces walking past them, chatting with their friends without a care, not even aware that there was anything wrong apart from the fact that they had been asked to return to school. It was strange to come back to this environment after having spent time in Mistfall and Paradise and discovering some of the horrible things that had been happening in The Realm.

Henry Fischer smiled at them as he walked past, albeit with a curious glint in his eye, as did some of the other people from their form. But most people just sent them odd glances. Not that Ellora could blame them; they looked fairly rough, with dirty and ripped clothes and torn, scorched rucksacks on their backs. They also hadn't showered in a while, so Ellora couldn't imagine they smelt like daisies.

As they approached the infirmary, they heard voices talking; it had to be more than just Melody and Rainclarke. When they walked through the entrance, they saw a group of people huddled outside of Oriel's private ward at the back of the room, which was shielded by a curtain.

"Dan!" cried Belle, running over to him and jumping into a hug.

"Clara, you're back!" called Ellora as she and Hunter walked over to the trio.

"Spirits," said Dan, "I was worried sick about you!" he said, putting Belle back down on the ground. "About all of you!" He turned to look at Ellora and Hunter, too. "Melody told us that the three of you took it upon yourself to go down to The Under."

"What were you thinking?!" exclaimed Clara.

"We didn't have a choice," Belle explained.

"She's right," agreed Hunter. "And we had no time to waste."

"At least you had each other, I suppose," Dan sighed.

"Well, was it at least a successful trip?" probed Melody.

"Eventful," said Ellora, thinking about what happened in Mistfall, "but definitely successful. It's nice to see you up and walking around too, Melody."

"We need to fill you all in," said Belle. "Where's Master Rainclarke?"

Rainclarke appeared through the curtain with a cup of tea that had probably been forced into his hands by Melody. "I'm relieved to see you all back; I was starting to worry, but I know time worked differently down in The Under."

"How long were we gone?" Hunter questioned, staying at the back of the group.

"Three days," answered Melody.

"And how is she doing?" asked Ellora, nodding her head to the curtains where Oriel was lying still in the bed.

"The same," answered Master Rainclarke.

"And how are *you* doing?" Ellora asked him.

"The same," he repeated. "Listen, Belle, Hunter and Ellora—I am so incredibly sorry I let the three of you go down there. And alone, too. I wasn't thinking properly; I should have never sent you off like that."

"Please, Master Rainclarke, we weren't asking you permission; you could have said no, and we still would have gone," Belle said.

"Well, even so, I should have known better than to send the three of you off on a dangerous journey like that. It's not as though you went to the Ferri Kingdom. No, you went all the way to the realm of the dead. You have barely been here a full year."

"None of this is your fault," Ellora said sincerely. "Besides, you need to stay with Oriel; she would want you here. We can take care of ourselves."

"We've proved that before," added Belle.

"I suppose you're right," Rainclarke chuckled softly.

"And Belle's not the Madori Mistress in training for nothing!" said Clara.

"You've got a point there," Rainclarke said. "Well, as long as you are okay, I suppose. Please, tell me the trip wasn't for nothing."

"Certainly not," said Ellora.

At that moment, Healer Amare arrived. "Sorry, but I'm going to have to kick you all out for the next hour or so; I need to perform some diagnostic enchantments and make sure she's stable," she said. "Noah," she said, turning to look at Master Rainclarke, "you should take this time to get something to eat. Please, she needs you to look after yourself. "

Master Rainclarke looked as though he might have been about to argue but surprisingly sighed and nodded his head defeatedly.

"Well, in that case," said Belle, "why don't we all go down to the dining room and have a cup of coffee? I could definitely do with one."

They agreed and headed downstairs together. Thankfully, as Rainclarke told them, it was only 11 o'clock in the morning, so although everyone was finished with breakfast, nobody had started with lunch yet and the dining room was empty.

"First things first," said Belle as they sat around a table. "Arellia *did* give us a way to heal Oriel."

"Thank the Spirits," said Rainclarke, sighing in relief. "What do we need to do?"

"Well, that's the problem," answered Ellora. "There are a few items we need, and we're not quite sure where to find them."

"We've got this for a start," said Belle, pulling out the bottle filled with the Waters of Paradise. "According to Arellia, we'll need to mix this water with the Herb of Asphodel to turn it into a paste, which we'll then spread over Oriel's rash."

"The Herb of Asphodel?" asked Clara. "My father is a Healer who specialises in Botany, and he's mentioned it before. It can be found in the Obscuri Kingdom nowadays, since the war. He's never been able to find the right one, though. Every time he's gone there and harvested some, the herb he brought back has turned out to be poisonous. Are you sure that's the herb we need?"

"Well, that leads us on to the next thing," answered Ellora. "A Magi-enchanted Scythe."

"A *what*?" asked Dan.

"A scythe enchanted by a Magi Aurum," confirmed Belle.

"Zhe Magi?" whispered Melody. "I zhought zhey were only legends. Are you meaning to say zhat zhey are real?"

"Apparently so," replied Hunter.

"Where in the Realms are we going to find something that is so rare and, well, might not even be real?" asked Clara.

"We have to find a way to get one; Arellia told us that if the Herb of Asphodel was harvested with anything other than a Magi-enchanted scythe, the healing properties of the herb would be reversed, and instead of healing her, it would poison and kill Oriel," stated Belle.

Master Rainclarke cleared his throat and everyone turned to look at him. "I have heard rumours," he said. "There have always been whispers of the Magi enchantments across the entirety of the Realm. Some people aren't even aware that the Magi Aurums existed, thinking them to be just a legend. But they were. One thing is for sure, though—most of the Magi-enchantments were destroyed, so if the rumours of the Magi-enchanted scythe are true, there is only one left. And I have no idea where it could be."

"Do you think Asyra might know?" Ellora asked.

"No," stated Hunter, with a sharp glare at Ellora. "She won't know, and even if she did, you know it wouldn't be a good idea to go back again!"

"Fine," sighed Ellora, not wanting to cause another argument when he was finally speaking with her, even if it was just barely. And if she was being truly honest, she was worried about going to see Asyra, too.

"What about Kristen?" asked Dan, suddenly cutting through the silence and forcing Hunter to break his stare as he turned to look at Dan.

"What *about* Kristen?" asked Belle.

"Well, do you think she might know where the scythe might be?" Dan asked.

"That's a good point," said Rainclarke. "I'm not sure if Oriel knew, but if she did, then there's a good chance that Kristen also knew."

"Looks like we'll be going to the Incendi Kingdom, then," said Ellora with a small smile at Belle.

"Was zhere anyzhing else we needed?" asked Melody.

"Yes, a couple of things," said Belle. "We need a Redmer Stone, for one."

"The one I got for you was from the Terrari Market," said Dan. "That's where Julia bought it, at least."

Ellora frowned at the mention of Julia; she hadn't told them yet about her encounter with her, but there was something about it that she just couldn't shake off.

"Perfect," said Hunter. "That's another one, then."

"Do you think we could find a metal-gage amulet there as well?" asked Ellora

"I actually think that's the *only* place you'll find a metal-gage amulet," answered Rainclarke. "That's a very rare metal."

"Two birds with one stone, then," said Hunter.

"Our first stop will be to see Kristen then," said Belle. "What are we waiting for?"

"Master Rainclarke, I assume you don't need the Gate key?" asked Ellora.

"Not for the moment," he replied.

"We'll have to take it with us then," said Ellora.

"Obviously we can't all go," Hunter stated bluntly. "I'll stay here and research the Obscuri Kingdom so we know the best way to get there and where to find the herb."

"I'll help," added Clara. "I've been there once before with my father, even though it was years ago. Maybe I'll remember something useful."

"And I can begin gathering supplies," suggested Melody."

"You'll need another pair of hands; I'll stay, too," volunteered Dan.

"Oh, are you all sure?" Belle asked. "It will be a relatively short trip."

The others nodded and Ellora smiled at Belle. "I think it would be a good idea if I came with you; Kristen needs to be told about everything that's been going on."

"You're right," agreed Belle.

"It's settled then said," said Dan.

"We'll leave immediately," said Belle to Ellora.

"Wait," Ellora said. "Can we shower first? We kind of smell."

"You're not wrong. Half an hour, then," Belle chuckled.

"Agreed."

Their journey was fast, and Kristen quickly let them through the other side, into the Incendi School of Aura. "What are you doing here?" she asked happily, a wide smile on her face as she pulled her sister into a warm hug. "It's so early in the morning!" She pulled Ellora into a hug, too.

Ellora had forgotten the time difference – the Incendi kingdom was five hours behind the Madori Kingdom.

"Come, let's go to my office," Kristen suggested, opening the door and gesturing for them to follow her out. "I'll make us something to drink. I definitely need a coffee. Did you manage to speak to Oriel?" she asked Ellora as she led the two of them down the corridors.

"Something's happened," said Ellora. Kristen's expression immediately flipped, and she frowned, waiting for Ellora to continue. "Oriel's been hurt," she said, her thoughts tumbling out of her almost as fast as she could produce them. "I spoke to Asyra, and she said I had to go and find Arellia in Paradise in The Under."

"Spirits!" Kristen exclaimed, looking at the two of them worriedly. "When do you need to go?" she asked, as they reached her office and she unlocked the door. The office looked gorgeous, with matching, dark wooden furniture making the space warm and inviting.

"Oh... actually, we've already been," said Ellora as they settled into the seats.

Kristen stared at the two of them for a moment, blinking slowly and silently. "You went to The Under?" she demanded, still staring. Belle nodded nervously. "What?!" Kristen exclaimed. "How? When? Why didn't you tell me?! Did you come back alright? Are you safe? Was anybody hurt?"

"We're fine, Kris," Belle reassured her. "Ellora, Hunter and I went together, and came back earlier today."

Kristen didn't look very happy with them, and opened her mouth to speak, but apparently, she decided now wasn't the time to lecture them. She sighed heavily, slumping back into her chair. "Well, did you at least get any useful information from Arellia?" she asked.

"Yes," Belle replied. But there is one item that we need to collect, and we have no idea where we can find it. Master Rainclarke thought you might have an idea."

"What is it that you need?" Kristen asked.

"A Magi-enchanted scythe," replied Ellora.

Kristen's eyebrows shot up. She looked between the two of them. "You need the scythe?"

"Arellia told us that, without the site, the herb we need for the medicine will end up poisoning Oriel rather than healing her," Ellora insisted.

"But surely—"

"No, Kristen," Belle interrupted. "We asked; there's no other way."

Kristen sighed once again and looked at the two of them in silence. Finally, she spoke. "Getting the scythe, if it's even real, is going to be no easy feat, girls."

"We're not expecting it to be easy, Kristen," Ellora said, "but we don't have a choice. You, of all people, know what will happen if we don't heal Oriel."

"You're right," said Kristen. "Okay, listen, most of the Magi enchantments were destroyed, but there are stories of a few remaining. One of those stories is about the scythe. I can't tell you whether or not it's true. But if it is, and the rumours are anything to go on, you'll find it in the Caeli School of Aura."

"Well, that's great, isn't it?" muttered Belle. "Couldn't we just ask the Caeli Master for it?"

Kristen shook her head. "The Caeli Master will do nothing to help Oriel. In fact, if he can get away with it, he'll probably go out of his way to *stop* you from helping her, too, if he finds out. Nobody can find out that she is in this state. Nobody."

"He must be one of the ones the Gatekeeper was referring to," Ellora murmured.

"The Gatekeeper?" repeated Kristen with a grave expression. "What happened with the Gatekeeper? You didn't tell me about the Gatekeeper."

"They said they weren't happy with Oriel right now," Belle replied. "In fact, they said if it was Oriel down there, they would've kept her there and not let her leave Mistfall. They only let us leave because we weren't with her. Well... 'let us' is a bit generous, I suppose. It was pure luck we made it out of there alive."

"Spirits," whispered Kristen in a tense voice. "Things are becoming so much worse than I ever imagined they could be if people are starting to pick sides and make alliances. And powerful alliances, at that."

"If it helps, Fred and Fred in front of Paradise are definitely on Oriel's team," Belle added.

Kristen gave a small smile. "They *are* very loyal. The entirety of the metal guard are, so at least we have them on our sides. They're certainly very powerful allies."

"So, what can we do about the scythe?" asked Ellora. "If the Caeli Master won't help us..."

"We'll have to take it," Belle finished determinedly.

"Yes, actually, that's exactly what you'll have to do," Kristen sighed. She didn't look happy about any of this but obviously realised there was no other option. "I won't be able to come with you to help."

"Nobody is asking you to, Kristen," Belle said gently. They could tell how anxious Kristen was feeling. "I know you're my big sister, but I'm the Madori Mistress in training now, Kris. We've, quite literally, been to Mistfall and back. As difficult as it must be, you need to know that we can do this."

"We'll need your help, of course," Ellora said with a smile, "but you need to take care of other things, too."

Kristen smiled. "You're right, both of you. And if I'm honest, I do think that between the two of you—"

All of a sudden, she froze.

Kristen's eyes glazed over as her face went slack, and she stared into thin air.

"Kristen?" Belle asked urgently, running around the table to shake her sister by the shoulders. "Kristen, are you okay?!"

"What's going on?" Ellora asked urgently, jumping to her feet.

"I have no idea," Belle replied, looking up with wide, panicked eyes as she continued to try to shake Kristen into awareness.

"Should we get someone?" asked Ellora, rushing over to the door, ready to run out and call for help. But before Belle could say anything or Ellora could go any further, Kristen gasped and blinked rapidly, looking between them, alert again.

"Spirits, Kristen!" Belle exclaimed. "You scared the Aura out of me. Are you alright?"

"What just happened?!" asked Ellora.

"I'm okay," Kristen said quickly, standing and hurrying to the door. "But the two of you need to come with me." She looked back at the two of them with a dark expression on her face. "Something's very wrong."

Ellora and Belle exchanged a worried look as they followed Kristen through the empty corridors of the castle. Despite their questions and confusion, Kristen remained silent, focusing solely on leading them to their destination.

Finally, they came to a seemingly dead end in a corridor with pristine white walls. Kristen walked over to a small, circular table and turned to face the wall on the left of the table.

"Kristen, what's going on?" questioned Belle, trying to get her sister's attention now that they had stopped, her breathing slightly heavier from running across the castle.

Kristen whispered a few words under her breath and lifted her hand, her palm facing the wall. To Ellora's surprise, when Kristen's hand touched the wall, a panel slid open, revealing a dark, stone stairway leading down into inky blackness.

"A secret door?" Ellora whispered nervously, her heart pounding in her chest. Belle, on the other hand, looked excited at the discovery, as if this was the coolest thing in the realm, apparently having completely forgotten about her question.

"Quickly," Kristen urged them. "We need to hurry."

Without hesitation, the three of them descended the shadowy staircase.

As they climbed down the stone stairwell, Ellora couldn't help but feel a sense of unease wash over her. The steps were not steep, but they seemed to go on forever, and the cold air of the underground passage chilled her to the bone. Despite the dim lighting, Ellora could see Belle shivering beside her, and she wrapped her arms around herself in a futile attempt to stay warm.

The further they went, the darker it got and the colder the air became. Ellora couldn't help but wonder what could be at the bottom of this seemingly never-ending staircase. Finally, after what felt like hours of climbing, they reached the bottom.

Ellora glanced behind her and groaned at the endless stairs leading upwards, already feeling exhausted at the thought of climbing them again. But as she turned to face the cavern in front of her, she tripped over a loose stone and grabbed the wall to balance herself. And as she looked up, her eyes widened in shock at the sight before her.

A deep, dark, bottomless cavern stretched out before her, dropping into depths even colder and darker than the stairwell they had just climbed. Above them, the rising sun shone through a gaping hole in the sky, the colours of the dawn painting the rocks around them in shades of pink, orange, and yellow. Ellora couldn't believe what she was seeing. It was as if they stumbled upon a hidden world, hidden deep beneath the surface of the Incendi Kingdom.

"Drako!" Kristen called, her voice echoing through the vast chamber as she approached the edge of the huge hole in front of them. "I came as quickly as I could. I had to bring my guests with me," she added hesitantly, her voice edged in a mixture of nerves and concern.

Belle turned to Kristen, a look of confusion on her face. "Who are you talking to?" she asked in a whisper.

There was a deep rumbling sound emanating from below them, and the sound of something large and heavy being dragged along stone echoed around the cavern. Another rumble sounded, even louder this time, bouncing off the rocky walls and causing the ground to tremble beneath their feet.

"I was not aware of your guests when I called you, Kristen," spoke a loud, deep voice that seemed to come from everywhere at once. "Who are they?"

"This is my sister, Belle," Kristen explained, "and her best friend, Ellora. Belle is the Madori Mistress in training, and both of them are on our side."

The loud voice growled once again, creating another quake beneath them, but said nothing further. Kristen shifted awkwardly before clearing her throat. "Oriel has been hurt," she said, her voice laced with concern. "That's why they have come."

Apparently, that struck a nerve. A loud, flapping sound surrounded them, and Belle and Ellora ducked to the ground, looking up warily for anything flying towards them. From what must have been the very depths of the deep cave in front of them emerged a magnificent creature, flying fast and high into the skies above them before diving down once again and landing, perched, on the rocks.

Belle and Ellora stood still, gazing ahead, shocked into silence.

"You...," stammered Belle, "you're...."

"The Incendi Spirit," finished Ellora in a whisper, her eyes wide with wonder.

The burning sunlight of the dawn glistened over the great, red scales on the magnificent creature in front of them, making his skin sparkle brightly. His wings were spectacular, larger than Ellora herself, and his bright eyes were the colour of wild, blazing fire. He was a sight to behold, and Belle and Ellora couldn't believe they were seeing him with their own eyes.

A dragon.

"What ails Oriel?" the Spirit asked, and unlike Asyra, Drako actually spoke aloud rather than communicating telepathically. His voice was sincere, and he leaned closer to them, lowering his face so that his eyes were on a similar level to theirs. Unlike Asyra, he wasn't attempting to intimidate or threaten them into giving him answers.

"That's why we're here," Ellora replied, stepping closer to him until she was a few steps away from the edge. Drako hummed, staring down at them with his great eyes. "She needs a remedy, but to create it, we need a Magi-enchanted Scythe."

Drako's eyes widened in surprise at Ellora's words, and he let out a curious grumble. "I have not heard of the Magi in many years."

Ellora nodded, her lips pressed tightly together. "I know. Nobody has. In fact, most of us thought they were merely a myth."

Drako shifted on his rocky perch at that, straightening up. "Ellora," he growled, his deep voice strong and commanding. "Step forward."

Ellora glanced back at Belle, who was still staring at Drako with wide eyes, then at Kristen, who merely shrugged and nodded her confirmation.

Taking a deep breath, Ellora took a small step forward. "We will find the scythe," she declared, her voice slightly wavering but filled with determination. "We will wake Oriel. She will be fine soon."

Drako nodded. "I have no doubt you will," Drako told her in a low voice, taking flight and landing directly in front of her. She stumbled backwards, falling onto her hands as she looked up at the great creature before her.

She gulped.

He narrowed his big eyes at her before moving his massive head in what looked to be an attempt at a nod before flying back to his perch. "You must wake her," he said. "And soon. There is a grave problem, Kristen," Drako continued, speaking as though he had completely forgotten about Oriel already. "I have sensed great unsettle in the Realm of the dead."

Ellora scrambled to her feet and exchanged a concerned glance with Belle.

"How do you know?" asked Ellora, her head cocked to the side.

The dragon shifted his large head to look at her, and surprisingly, Ellora didn't feel uncomfortable at all under his gaze. "As the Spirit of Indendi, I have a strong connection with fire," Drako replied. "The fire has told me."

Ellora had never met Drako before, but if the fact that the Incendi Spirit was worried enough to Summon Kristen so early in the morning was anything to go by, this was not a good sign. They had to act fast if they hoped to save Oriel and restore balance to the Realm of the dead.

"What does this mean?" Belle asked, looking at Kristen with wide eyes and a furrowed forehead for clarification.

"It means, sister of Kristen," began Draco, his voice serious and grave, booming across the cavern, "that something is afoot, and we must act quickly."

"Understood, Drako," Kristen replied. "We'll move quickly. I shall have to secure the Gate, and so I shall send Belle and Ellora back to help Oriel. Please do let me know if you hear anything else."

Drako bowed his head to Kristen in agreement before lifting his wings in preparation to leap into the sky. Before he took off, he turned back to Belle and Ellora, a look of concern in his eyes.

"Please help Oriel," he said, his voice urgent. And with that, he soared upwards, disappearing through the gap at the top as Belle, Ellora, and Kristen watched.

"Sorry, girls," Kristen said once Drako left. "It seems that's the end of your trip."

CHAPTER SIXTEEN

An Unwanted Assistant

"**W**e need to make a move already," said Belle anxiously as she and Ellora walked back into Oriel's office, where Hunter, Dan, Melody and Clara were already waiting, supplies laid out in front of them.

"'Ow did it go?" asked Melody, her voice laced with concern. "Does Kristen know anyzhing about zhe scyzhe?"

"She did," Ellora answered.

"Well, did she tell us how to get it?" Clara asked impatiently.

"Kristen told us that if it's going to be anywhere, it will be in the Caeli School of Aura," Belle answered. "With the Caeli Master."

"Well, that's good news, isn't it?" questioned Dan.

Ellora and Belle exchanged looks before Ellora took a deep breath and began to explain what Kristen had told them. "Unfortunately, the Caeli Master is not on our side. He doesn't have Oriel's best interests at heart, and we can't ask him for help."

Hunter frowned, likely already having an inkling of what they were going to tell him. But as Ellora looked around at the others, she saw the confusion and fear on their faces, and it all began to feel too real. Finding the scythe and saving Oriel was going to be a much more difficult task than they originally thought.

"Why?" asked Clara, her brow furrowed.

Belle cleared her throat. "That's not important for the moment. Right now, we just need to focus on the scythe." Her deliberate, and not subtle at all, tone of voice let them all know that neither Ellora nor Belle felt comfortable talking about it while Asyra had the opportunity to listen in.

"So, 'ow are we going to get it?" Melody asked, following Belle's lead and steering the conversation back to the task at hand.

Ellora sighed and frowned at Melody, knowing she would be upset with her for what she was about to suggest. "I'm still not sure you should come with us, Melody," she said apologetically. "I don't want to put you in danger."

"What?!" Melody exclaimed, her eyes clouded with hurt. "'Ow dare you even zhink I could stay 'ere while you all went wizhout me?!"

"Melody, of course I want you there, but... you just got out of a *coma,* for the Spirits' sake!" Ellora replied. There was no way she would be able to live with herself if any more harm came to Melody. Her voice softened. "We don't know what we'll face on this journey, and I couldn't bear it if something happened to you."

Melody sighed heavily and placed a hand on Ellora's shoulder. "I understand you are worried for me, Elle, and I appreciate it. But 'Ealer Amare gave me zhe all clear. My body 'as rested up, and technically, I am in better shape zhan any of you. Please. You know I would not be able to 'andle staying 'ere while you were all out zhere like zhat. I already 'ad to stay while you went to zhe Under."

"Melody's right," surprisingly, it was Hunter who cut in. "We need her."

Ellora frowned but nodded. They were both right.

"Well, now that that's all cleared up, how are we going to get the scythe?" asked Clara, getting back to the conversation at hand.

"We'll need to sneak in, then," Ellora said, chewing on her bottom lip as she paced the room.

"Ilisha," Hunter said suddenly.

Ellora snapped her head to look at him with her eyebrows raised.

"What?" Belle was equally as confused.

"She used to attend the Caeli School of Aura," Hunter replied as if it were obvious. "She can help us."

"Absolutely not!" Ellora answered quickly. It was no secret that she didn't like Ilisha, and the *friendship* she had with Hunter, but this was about more than that. There was no way she was going to allow Ilisha to ruin their chances of helping Oriel. No matter what anybody else said, there was something about her that Ellora simply did not trust.

"I know you don't like her," began Belle in a calm voice.

"No," said Ellora, cutting her off before Belle could say anymore. "I don't. But this isn't about that. She's not coming with us."

"You're being ridiculous," Hunter said, rolling his eyes at her.

She wasn't sure why, but his response and eye roll particularly annoyed Ellora. "*You're* being ridiculous," she replied angrily. "How can you know whether or not she's even on our side? What has she done to earn our trust?"

"She doesn't *need* to earn our trust, Artemer," Hunter argued. "Can't you just take my word for it? Can't you just trust *me* for once?"

Ellora hesitated then. Did she trust Hunter? She was sure she did, but then why was she so against Ilisha coming with them? "This isn't about that, Hunter. We just can't risk it. Not for something as important as this."

She could see the anger flash across Hunter's face, and she was sure there was hurt mixed in there, too, but she just couldn't let anybody get in the way of them saving Oriel, not when she knew how serious this could become.

"Ellora, wait," said Melody with a frown. "'E 'as a point."

Ellora immediately turned to look at Melody in shock. "You're taking his side?"

"Nobody's taking any sides," sighed Belle. "Hunter, you have a point, but Ellora, you're right; we need to think about this carefully." She sighed again, leaning her hands against the table, her head hung down in thought.

"Hunter," she said, looking up at him after sending Ellora an apologetic glance. "Talk to Ilisha and see if she would be willing to help us. We'll need all the help that we can get if we're to do this."

Ellora took a deep breath, staring down at the table in silence.

Hunter nodded silently and got up, heading straight out of the library without a single glance back.

"Ellora, we need all the help we can get," Belle said apologetically.

"I know that," said Ellora, "but that doesn't mean I need to be happy about it." She felt slightly guilty at having snapped at Belle like that, but she couldn't shake the feeling that they were making a mistake in inviting Ilisha. And she was almost certain that her relationship with Hunter had almost nothing to do with it.

There was a brief stretch of silence between the others in the room, but Ellora didn't want to dwell upon what happened, especially if there was nothing she could do about it and if the awkwardness was going to get in the way of helping Oriel.

"Did you manage to find any information that will help us at all?" she directed the question at Melody and Clara, trying her best to keep her tone light so the others knew she would get over it. The last thing she wanted was to cause any unnecessary tension.

"Actually, yes!" said Melody. "We did some research on zhe Obscuri Kingdom and discovered zhat it is best to cross zhe sea from zhe Terrari Kingdom."

"Which is perfect," added Clara, "because we can go to the Obscuri Kingdom straight from the market. All we'll need to do is find a boat."

"Great!" said Belle. "So from here, we'll go directly to the Caeli Kingdom, then the Terrari Kingdom and then we'll go straight to the Obscuri Kingdom and come back."

"And hunter and I managed to find some supplies for our journey," added Dan, dragging a sack of rubies, the Aura Realm currency, onto the table. "This should get us the Redmer *and* the amulet with some left over."

"Perfect," said Ellora. "Well then, I suppose all we need to do now is wait for Hunter to come back with Ilisha."

With another silent stretch, Ellora looked around to see everyone looking at her nervously.

"Listen," she said, addressing the four of them, who were looking at her as though they were worried she would sprout wings, turn into a pickatoo and bite their heads off. "I know you all think that I have something against Ilisha because of her apparent relationship with Hunter, but the truth is I don't," she insisted. "If she's willing to help us and she's on our side... if she's coming on this journey with us to help Oriel and, possibly, the rest of the Realm, and I'll be very, *very* grateful. But all I'm saying is that I don't trust her. My instincts tell me something is off with that girl, so all I ask is that all of you *please* just stay on your guard."

It wasn't long before Hunter walked back into the room, with Ilisha following closely behind, her silky hair bouncing gracefully over her shoulder as her eyes twinkled. Ellora couldn't help but feel a twinge of disappointment in her stomach that she agreed to help them, but she couldn't pretend she expected otherwise. Of *course* Ilisha would drop everything to help Hunter.

"It's nice to have you on board," Ellora said, to everyone's surprise.

"Thank you, Ellora," Ilisha replied, and Ellora fought the urge to scowl; the surprise in Ilisha's voice meant that Hunter had probably already warned her that Ellora wasn't too keen on her joining them.

So Ilisha, Hunter's probably already filled you in, but we need a way to get into the Caeli School of Aura and get the Magi-enchanted scythe," Said Belle, breaking the tense silence.

"Hunter told me," Ilisha replied with a smile. "And I think I have just the way."

CHAPTER SEVENTEEN

A Harsh Betrayal

"**D**o we all know the plan?" Ellora asked, looking around at the group of seven gathered inside the Gate Room. The castle was finally in full swing with everyone having returned, and students were roaming the corridors, so they knew they needed to get a move on before anybody asked any questions. Before anything, Belle went to inform Master Rainclarke of the plan, and although he wasn't happy about it, he knew it was the only option.

They all nodded.

"Are we sure this is going to work?" asked Dan, chewing on his bottom lip with furrowed brows. It surprised Ellora to see Dan so anxious; she had never seen him like this before.

"It's our best chance," answered Ilisha.

"Let's get on with it then," said Belle, a faint tremor ever so slightly present in her words. "We've got no time to lose."

Ellora held up the key to the portal that was glowing a bright, light orange colour. Almost immediately, the stone cleared away, leaving behind an orange shimmer for them to walk through. Belle turned one last time to give them an encouraging glance before she and Ilisha stepped into the glow and into the Caeli Kingdom.

Their plan was for Belle and Ilisha to get through to the Caeli Kingdom and, in the process, make the Caeli Master open the Gate. When it was open, Belle would signal to the others that they were through to the other side and the Gate was open so that Clara could use her Terrari Aura to create some stone to wedge into the Gate, temporarily tricking it into thinking there were people passing through the Gate. Then, when Belle sent a second signal to let them know the coast was clear, the rest of them would go through and find the scythe while Ilisha and Belle kept the Caelie Master distracted.

A few moments after Belle and Ilisha crossed through the Gate, the glowing blue light of the Madori Jewel flashed back through to them.

"That's it!" whispered Ellora. "That's the signal."

Immediately, Clara got to work. With her hands outstretched and her face narrowed in concentration, she lifted her arms in slow, strenuous motions, crafting two stone pillars that somewhat resembled legs and balancing them inside the Gate. With any luck, Belle and Ilisha would keep the Caeli Master distracted enough not to notice the Gate wasn't fully closed.

It was only a few minutes later that the faint blue glow came through the red once again, and it was time to go through.

When Ellora Hunter, Dan, Clara and Melody walked through, into a room that looked remarkably similar to the Gate room in the Madori School of Aura, they found themselves entirely alone.

Ellora exhaled in relief. So far, everything was going according to plan.

"Right," Said Ellora, knowing there was no time to lose, "Hunter and Melody, are you okay with going to the bedroom? Dan, Clara and I will head to the office."

Ellora wasn't a huge fan of the fact that everything they were doing now was reliant on Ilisha's tip that if there was any place in the Caeli Kingdom that the Caeli Master would have kept the scythe, it would have to be either his office or his own bedroom. Their entire plan was based on her opinion, but it wasn't as though they had any other choice.

Ellora also wasn't a fan of the idea of splitting up, but without knowing which room the Caeli Master kept the scythe in, there was no other way.

Hunter and Melody nodded, determination clear on Melody's face, while Hunter's face was as blank and stoic as usual.

"Good luck," Melody whispered before heading down the corridor on the right with Hunter.

With no time to lose, Ellora, Dan and Clara headed down the corridor on the left, following Clara's directions in silence. While Oriel requested all of the students return to the Madori School of Aura, it appeared the Caeli Master didn't feel the same need, as the corridors were still empty.

"I think it's this door," Clara whispered, pointing to a locked, wooden door.

"What are we going to do now?" hissed Dan. It wasn't as though they had a key.

"Time to show you what I've learnt," Clara replied with a smug smile.

She lifted her arm in the air, making a fist with her hand and twisting it. As she did so, some sort of plant tendril emerged from the floor, growing and leaning its way towards the locked door. Slowly and in a strangely calculated manner that Ellora was unaware was possible for a plant, the tendril made its way into the lock, twisted, and all of a sudden sprung out and slithered away again, back into the floor.

As soon as the bright green appendage was gone, Clara twisted the door handle, and the door swung open inwards.

"You did it!" Ellora whispered excitedly to Clara.

"That was so cool," added Dan.

Clara shrugged modestly. "When Ilisha mentioned this door would have a lock, whereas the Master's bedroom would have an Aura lock, I knew I would be able to open it."

The three of them entered quietly and closed the door behind them, plunging them into darkness.

Almost instantly, Dan created a tiny palm in his hand that was barely big enough to let them see each other. It was true that nobody in their group was as talented as Belle when it came to their Aura; even Hunter, who worked harder than almost anybody Ellora knew, could barely hold a light to Belle and her power.

"Dan, is there any way you can make that flame a little bigger?" Ellora whispered.

"We probably shouldn't risk lighting the room in case anybody walks past, but we need to be able to see," added Clara.

Dan's eyebrows furrowed in concentration as he glared down at his palm and the flame. After a short moment of intense focus, the flame grew bigger and bright enough to allow them to see their surroundings.

"Perfect. Thanks, Dan," said Ellora.

This office was very bare and minimalistic, unlike Oriel's or Kristen's. While Oriel's office felt comforting and warm, as though someone actually spent their time there, this one felt cold and empty, as if it was for show rather than in actual use. There was a pristine white desk in the middle of the large room with a large and intimidating white leather chair placed perfectly behind it. Even the desk was empty, with no pencils or paper, not even a mug. Similarly, the harsh white walls were completely clear of any sort of decoration. The only other piece of furniture in the room were the two small and uncomfortable-looking plastic seats on the other side of the desk that were the exact same shade of white.

"Is it just me, or does this look more like a robot's office than it does a person's?" mused Dan, nervously examining his surroundings.

"There's no way he's keeping it here," said Clara after they did a scan of the desk. "There would be nowhere for him to even keep it."

"Unless he's got some sort of hidden compartments somewhere, maybe?" proposed Ellora, although even she was unconvinced. Even so, she tentatively placed one hand on the wall, feeling along the length of the room for some sort of button or trigger or *anything,* but turned up empty.

"It must be in his bedroom, then," said Dan.

"I remember the directions Ilisha told us; maybe we can go and help Hunter and Melody go through the room faster."

Dan extinguished the flame, and they closed the door behind them.

Just as they were about to turn the corner out of the corridor, Ellora heard the distant sound of voices. She immediately grabbed Dan and Clara by their arms, just about fast enough to stop them from being seen, and yanked them back towards her. She opened the door to the closest room behind them and shoved them inside, throwing herself in too and leaving the door open just a crack.

She watched through the thin gap as whoever it was they heard turned the corner, and although she didn't manage to see any faces, she did catch a glimpse of pink fabric. She held her finger up to her lips and looked at Cara and Dan, urging them to be quiet.

The voices in the corridor became louder as whoever it was moved past until slowly, they became quiet and distant once again. Finally, a few moments later, the voices were completely gone, and Ellora sighed in relief, opening the door just wide enough to peek outside and make sure the coast was clear. "Thank the Spirits," she whispered. "We almost got caught."

"Who was it?" asked Dan, still speaking in a low voice as they emerged from the closet they were stuffed into.

"No idea," answered Ellora. "All I saw was some pink."

"Maybe the Ferri Mistress, then?" suggested Clara.

"Spirits, that's not a good sign," Ellora muttered.

"Come on," said Clara, leading them forward again, "we're not far from the others."

Eventually, the trio came to a corridor that was almost completely empty, not only of people and furniture, but also of doors. At the end of the corridor, they turned once more to find a single door looming at the end.

"This must be it," said Ellora as she twisted the handle, pleased to find that it twisted open easily. She walked in to find herself entirely submerged in darkness, and immediately her heart sunk into her stomach. Why in the Realms would Hunter and Melody be in the dark like this?

"Melody, Hunter, it's us," she hissed.

"What's going on?" Clara spoke softly from outside.

"Are they in there?" whispered Dan.

Before Ellora could respond, the large overhead light snapped on, dousing the room in a harsh bright light that stung Ellora's eyes as she squinted.

But the light was the least of her worries; in front of her, Melody and Hunter sat back to back in two wooden chairs, bound tightly down with rope that was digging into the sensitive skin on their wrists and ankles. They both had strips of cloth in their mouths that prevented them from crying out.

Ellora froze in panic.

Melody's eyes were wide in alarm, only a muffled, unintelligible sound coming from her mouth through the cloth. She wiggled her arms, trying to escape. Hunter, on the other hand, looked vacant and disappointed. Immediately, Ellora snapped out of it and hurried over to them. She couldn't believe this was the moment Hunter was choosing to let his ego be damaged.

She instantly started on Melody's rope, trying to get the girl free, and when Dan and Clara saw what was going on, they rushed in after her.

"What in the Realms..." Dan muttered, trying to undo Hunter's binds.

But in trying to release her, Melody's movements became even more frantic, widening her eyes at Ellora.

"Just hang on a sec, Melody. Then you can say what you're trying to tell us," Ellora said, still working on the rope.

The door slammed loudly behind them. "I think what she's trying to tell you is that you should turn around."

The three of them span around in unison, coming face to face with the three faces that shook them to the very core.

"You stupid children," laughed the Caeli Master, standing next to a smug-looking Ilisha and holding a teary, horrified Belle tightly by the arms, a bronze knife to her throat. "Did you truly believe you could get in here undetected?" He smirked.

"Ilisha?" asked Clara in a shaky voice. "What are you doing?"

Ellora realised at that moment that the disappointment on Hunter's face wasn't because of his wounded pride but because he was angry with *himself*. He was, after all, the one to insist they trust Ilisha.

"Let her go," demanded Ellora.

She looked at Belle in sheer terror. This was a crazy Aurum who could easily hurt—*kill*—Belle, and she had no idea what she could do to stop it.

But Belle looked strangely calm in this situation. Her eyes widened as Ellora met them, her gaze travelling down to the ground. She was clearly trying to tell her something, but what, Ellora couldn't figure out.

"Please," begged Dan, his wavering voice etched in distress. "Please let her go."

"Why in the Realms do you think I would do that?" asked the Caeli Master. Ilisha didn't even flinch, folding her arms in refusal. "Ilisha here tells me that you lot were trying to take my Scythe. How any of you were gullible enough to think I would keep something like that in my *bedroom*, I will never understand. But hey, it got you here, so how could I complain?"

"It *was* far too easy, Master Nick," Ilisha responded eagerly and sweetly, like a puppy dog begging for a treat. She looked maliciously at Hunter. "Fool one, and you fool them all."

For reasons unknown to Ellora, it was this comment, not the fact that she betrayed them, that made her want to lunge at the girl and grab her by the throat. She looked behind her at Hunter and felt her heart twinge at the sight of him sinking into his chair, unwilling to meet any of their eyes with his own, which were blank and void of emotion. As somebody who so rarely made friends, he must have been deeply hurt to have trusted someone who didn't deserve it. If one thing was for sure, it was that she wouldn't be saying 'I told you so' today.

Belle blinked her eyes faster and more urgently at Ellora, who still couldn't piece together what Belle wanted to say. But for whatever reason, she didn't look nearly as worried as she should have. She flicked her eyes to the side as if to look behind herself, and all of a sudden, everything clicked into place.

"You're right," she blurted out to the Caeli Master, who frowned at her in the same way one would frown at an irritating child. "Thinking back, I can't believe we ever thought you would keep something so precious in a place that was so easy to find."

"Precisely," replied the Caeli Master. "Especially when I have somewhere like Fiona's Garden within easy access."

"Exactly. In fact, it was silly of us not to have guessed it was in Fiona's Garden in the first place," Ellora continued.

"Not that it matters now," said the Caeli Master. "Although I can't help but wonder why Oriel sent the six of you instead of coming herself."

At that, Ellora felt herself tense. Under no circumstances could he know of Oriel's state, and she thanked the Spirits nobody told Ilisha about it.

"She didn't think she needed to," Clara said quickly. "She thought we were good enough to outsmart you."

The Caeli Master's face became redder than Ellora had ever seen anybody become before. "*How dare she?*" he seethed.

"It doesn't matter, Master Nick," Ilisha scoffed. "They *didn't* outsmart us."

The Caeli Master looked thoughtful for a moment, considering them with hot anger in his eyes. "Fine, you're right," he said finally.

It was at this moment, seeing the pure fury in his eyes, only because of a slight insult to his ego, that Ellora realised they needed to act quickly. He could easily change his mind in a split second.

She knew Dan and Clara were behind her and thanked the Spirits that even if she was not as skilled or as powerful as Belle, she could still do some handy stuff with her Aura. She put her hands slowly behind her back, continuing to look at the Caeli Master as he ranted about being underestimated. She focused all of her energy on conjuring a good amount of water and holding it in the shape of a flame, hoping that would cause Dan and Hunter to understand that she wanted them to burn the ropes to break them. She couldn't look behind her to see if they understood without alerting the Caeli Master that something was going on; she could only keep up the fire shape and hope.

It was simply lucky that Hunter hadn't yet had the opportunity to tell Ilisha about his newly discovered affinity for Incendi Aura.

"Ilisha," barked the Caeli Master, "I'm going to check on the scythe. And I'm taking this one with me," his grip on Belle tightened slightly, and she winced. "I'm sure you can handle this lot; two of them are already tied up for you. Just lock them in and guard the door."

"Yes, Master Nick," Ilisha agreed quickly, eager to please.

The Caeli Master left, dragging Belle behind him, and it took everything for Ellora to stay calm and not go straight for Ilisha.

"Ilisha, how could you do this?" she asked, purposefully making her voice sound betrayed and hurt. She had to bide time for Hunter and Melody to get out of those binds; if Ilisha locked them in first, it would be twice as difficult to get to Belle.

"Please, Ellora, don't insult my intelligence *or* yours," Ilisha scoffed disbelievingly. "You didn't like me from the very first day I met you. Even though I did nothing wrong."

"Well, as it turns out, I did have a good reason not to like you," Ellora replied, gesturing to the situation around them.

"You know, we don't want to hurt anyone," Ilisha continued as though Ellora had never spoken. She looked up at Ellora with a slight vulnerability in her eyes. "It's Oriel who isn't thinking straight. If she were, she would have sorted all of this out already."

"Your Caeli Master just dragged my best friend away while holding a knife to her throat, and you say Oriel's the one who needs a reality check?"

Ilisha shook her head sadly. "You'll see in the end. All of you," she glanced briefly at Hunter. "We're doing this for the greater good."

"What's that supposed to mean?" countered Ellora. It seemed like everyone had a noble excuse for their horrifying actions these days.

"You think we're in the wrong, but the truth is that you're all blind. You're sheltered away, and you have no idea what's really going on in the Realm. You should feel grateful for that, really. It's a great burden to carry. And the Caeli Master and I, and all of the others, we're just trying to fix it. You'll see in the end."

Ellora wasn't sure how she was supposed to react to that, but she didn't have a chance in the end, as it was. A sudden gust of wind swept by her, grazing her gently in almost a light tickle. But when the wind reached Ilisha, it was not so gentle anymore. The light breeze turned into a harsh vortex of air, trapping Ilisha in a constricting prison.

"Spirits," she whispered, partly in awe and partly in shock. That Aura was manifesting itself so aggressively that it was obviously being fueled solely by Hunter's raw and unadulterated anger.

"Be careful, Hunter," Dan said, watching him closely. "We need to trap her, get her to talk and tell us where Belle was taken, not kill her."

"Where is Fiona's Garden?" Hunter asked through gritted teeth, completely ignoring Dan and squeezing the vortex tighter.

Ilisha simply stared up at him, mouth gaping open, her entire face painted in horror. Hunter forced the tornado tighter once again, but still, she continued to stare back in silence.

That was Hunter's breaking point.

He stood slowly, dangerously, and stalked towards her. He crunched his fists even tighter, squeezing the air around Ilisha even further. Tighter and tighter, he went.

"Hunter!" Dan hissed. "She needs to tell us where Belle has been taken!"

"I will ask you *one. More. Time,*" Hunter said in a voice that was so frighteningly deep and low it was barely audible. "*Where is Fiona's Garden?*"

"The orchard," Ilisha finally cracked, barely able to choke out the words. He loosened the tornado, and she repeated herself, able to breathe this time, "the cherry orchard."

The moment she gave her answer, the tornado vanished, and she doubled over, gasping her throat and panting. Hunter gave her no time to recover, grabbing her by the wrist and dragging her over to the chairs he and Melody had been tied to. She shoved her down and tied the ropes tighter than they had been on him, placing another piece of rope in her mouth and marching out of the room.

"Hunter," Ellora began as she ran out after him, putting a hand on his shoulder hesitantly. She had no idea what she could say to him at that moment and, after that display, had the unnerving feeling that she should be scared of him, but instead felt an overwhelming urge to reassure him that this was not his fault.

"What are we waiting for?" Hunter asked in a gruff voice, shrugging off her hand before she could say anything more. "We need to get to the cherry orchard as soon as possible."

CHAPTER EIGHTEEN

Fiona's Garden

I t didn't take them long to locate the cherry orchard. Belle, thinking and working one step ahead as usual, had left them a trail of water droplets to follow.

Only a few minutes later, they were within hearing distance of the Caeli Master once again.

"You'll never get away with this," Belle uttered calmly, with a matter-of-fact tone to her voice that was barely audible under the heavy crunching of leaves. "Oriel won't let you, and you know it."

"Will you be quiet, you irritating child," the Caeli Master spat at Belle, frustrated. "Your precious Oriel isn't as powerful as you think. There's nothing she can do around here, especially not against all of us."

"You're wrong," Belle stated flatly.

"Insolent girl!" the Caeli Master huffed. "If I'm so wrong, where's your Madori Mistress? Why isn't she here, saving the day like the superhero you seem to think she is? Yes, that's what I thought."

There were a few minutes of silence as the Caeli Master continued on, dragging a defenceless Belle with him, and the others trailed carefully behind at a distance far enough to remain unnoticed yet close enough to listen in. "What do you even need the scythe for?" asked Belle eventually.

The crunching sound of the Caeli Master and Belle treading along the leaves suddenly stopped, and Ellora immediately threw her hand out, gesturing for Clara, Melody, Dan and Hunter to stop moving and stay quiet behind her. Without the sound of the Caeli Master ahead of them, he would easily be able to hear them walking behind, no matter how quietly they moved.

"The scythe can be used for many things," said the Caeli Master. "Although, although I cannot help but wonder exactly what it is that *you* need it for." Ellora's heart sank. Coupled with the fact that Oriel had not come with them, it wouldn't take much for the Caeli master to figure out what was happening. "It's filled with powerful Magi Aura, it's true, but most Aurums don't even know of the existence of Magi Aura. What in the Realms could mere Second Formers want with such a thing?"

"It hardly matters anymore," Belle quickly uttered in an attempted nonchalance. "You've made it clear that we're not going to get it anyway."

"I suppose not," the Caeli Master chuckled. "But it *would* be useful to know what Oriel is planning." There was a groaning sound, the eerie creaking of wood. "It's always good to be at least one step ahead. That's why I sent Ilisha in."

Their voices started to become distant again, so Ellora poked her head around the corner. All she caught was a glimpse of Belle's panicked eyes with the Caeli Master dragging her away before two thinner and bare cherry trees groaned and twisted themselves, covering up the path they had gone down and hiding them from Ellora's view.

"We have to hurry," Ellora said, her voice barely above a whisper as she peeked around the tree she was hiding behind to ensure the Caeli Master truly had gone.

"Where has he taken her?" Dan asked, panicked as he looked around the empty orchard. There was no sign that anybody had been there at all.

"From what I saw, those two trees are covering some sort of a hidden path," Ellora replied, hurrying over to the trees and trying to force them apart. "All we need to do is figure out how to reveal the entrance." Dan jogged over to join her, adding his own strength to the effort.

But Melody shook her head. "Surely 'e would not be willing to risk anybody being able to access 'is secret area."

"You're right, Melody," added Clara. "Hunter, you have Caeli Aura, so why don't you try opening it? Use your Aura."

Hunter didn't even respond, already having stepped up to the trees and analysing them. Without a word, he stood and lifted a hand in front of himself. With a few twisting motions of his fingers, a mini tornado the size of a plum formed in his hand, small but strong as it attracted the leaves from the surrounding trees. Slowly, in a calculated manner, he swung his arm back and forward, sending the gusts of wind towards the crooked trees. Almost instantly, they let out the same groaning and creaking sound Ellora had heard earlier as they twisted themselves upwards and curled themselves back, bending to reveal an entire orchard of cherry trees behind it.

"Woah," Melody whispered as she approached and stuck her head between the giant wooden beings.

Ellora stepped through first, looking anxiously around the orchard for any sign of Belle. "Which way do we go now?" asked Clara, the last to step through.

With a grinding sound, the trees closed up behind them and began to shrink, getting smaller and smaller until they were completely gone.

There was a distant yelp, and Ellora turned. "Belle," she whispered. She felt relief course through her veins instantly, followed by a pang of dread.

They followed the sounds of the voices quietly, marvelling at their surroundings as they did so. It felt as though they were walking in never-ending circles, the trees all around them infused with different shades of pink.

But then there was a shift.

The energy was different, more vibrant, more electric. The trees were taller, and the leaves were bigger and brighter. The blossoms were generally pinker and fluffier, while the cherries themselves were rich and juicy. Everything just seemed *better*.

"Now," said the Caeli Master, stopping before an enormous oak tree with a never-ending amount of thick branches, "be a good little Madori Mistress in training and stay still, would you?" He let go of Belle but, despite his words, conjured almost solid handcuffs made of wind to contain her wrists before she had a chance to move. The handcuffs were tight and were constantly moving, like a tornado to trap Belle's hands. And from the look on her face, they were as painful and biting as they looked. This was much more advanced than anything Ellora had ever seen before in terms of Caeli Aura, and even though it shouldn't have been surprising, as a Caeli Master, he did it without even blinking.

As if things couldn't get worse, the Caeli Master flicked his fingers half-heartedly in Belle's directly, and she shot up into the air, hovering high enough above the ground that if the Caeli Master decided to drop her, she would definitely need something below to cushion the fall.

The five of them watched from behind a group of trees anxiously as he waved his hand in a circular motion over the enormous tree trunk. With every turn of his hand, something was emerging from the wood; a large, round thing.

A door handle.

He walked through the door that emerged and made a 'come along' gesture towards Belle, who floated along behind him, trying her best to escape the wind prison he trapped her in.

"What in the Realms is going on?" Dan asked in a hushed whisper as they hurried to catch up before the door closed. Clara shot out a hand, and one of the branches of the tree folded downwards, keeping the door propped open for them.

"Zhat must be Fiona's Garden," whispered Melody before entering. "Wow."

They found themselves in a beautifully colourful garden area filled with lush trees and a never-ending supply of perfectly ripe fruit. Only everything was absolutely tiny. The tallest trees barely grazed Ellora's shoulders, and the tiny flowers looked to them like colourful sprinkles scattered all over the area. A patch of sunflowers grew all the way up to Ellora's hips, but most of the rest of the garden was too small for them even to pick up.

"What is this place?" whispered Clara in awe, bending down to pluck a miniature apple from one of the trees. As a Terrari Aurum, it was only natural she was curious about this garden.

"I guess we will 'ave to find out," answered Melody.

Ellora was relieved to see that the trail of glistening water droplets Belle had been leaving them still continued; that meant she still had some Aura left in her, even if the little puddles were getting smaller and smaller. They needed to hurry.

The trail ended soon afterwards, but luckily Belle was not too much further ahead.

They came to an enormous lake, big even by their usual standards, and so it must have been the equivalent of an ocean compared to the tiny garden around them, which Belle was hovering above, her face twisted in pain.

The Caeli Master was standing in front of the lake and appeared to be talking to somebody in front of him, but Ellora couldn't see anybody there. Melody gasped and pointed to the Caeli Master's hands. It was the scythe.

It looked like such a small ordinary thing, a tiny wooden handle with a metal blade attached, that Ellora could scarcely believe this was the item that had caused so much trouble.

They wasted no time.

Clara immediately shot her arms out in front of her, and long vine-like roots emerged from the ground around the Caeli Master. One vine tapped his shoulder on the right while the other snaked around the other side to grab hold of the scythe, wrapping itself around it and quickly bringing it towards them.

As soon as the Caeli Master noticed, he made a chopping motion of his hand, and a sharp gust of wind cut the root, dropping the scythe at his feet, which he made quick work of lifting with another gust of wind. "How in the *Realm*—" the look of shock on his face was unrivalled.

Of course, they did not let him finish. The five of them were relentless towards the Caeli Master. Ellora summoned a huge wave from the large body of water behind him to crash over him, knocking him off his feet while Melody made a flock of birds dive low at him in distraction. Hunter used his Caeli Aura to carry the scythe to Clara, who grabbed hold of it with a vine, using another vine to wrap around and bind the Caeli Master.

Dan immediately ran over to Belle and attempted to pull her down. Belle cried out in agony, her face contorted into expressions that conveyed just how much pain she was in.

"Stop!" Ellora called. "She's in pain." Dan immediately froze.

"We need him to drop his hold on her," Hunter murmured, running over.

"No!" cried Clara from behind them. They all turned to see the Caeli Master on his feet once again, moving slowly but surely towards her, each flick of his wrists sending sharp, angry gusts of wind towards her.

Ellora took a deep breath. She put both of her hands in front of her and imagined she was submerged in the cool water ahead. She moved her hands in a spinning motion, moving them faster and faster until a whirlpool formed, which she lifted and dropped straight onto the Caeli Master. Ellora instantly felt her body start to tremble from a lack of aura. That had drained more of it than she would have liked. If she used anymore, she would surely lose consciousness.

The Caeli Master was dragged around and beaten, but only for a few moments before he stretched out his arms and made slicing motions, cutting through the water around him and turning it into still little puddles. He turned towards her with a dark glint in his eyes and lifted his arms, taking in deep breaths. Ellora had seen what he could do just by flicking his fingers; she didn't want to know what he could do to her if he really used his Aura.

Ellora didn't get a chance to blink twice, let alone move out of the way, before an enormous, powerful tornado flew towards her. Her life flashed in her eyes as she watched the whirlwind of air march towards her as if it was in slow motion. She knew that thing would kill her.

But just as it was about to touch her, the entire tornado stopped, the air still and motionless around her. Ellora, who had been holding her breath, breathed out in surprise, looking around her. The Caeli Master seemed as shocked as she was.

Her eyes landed on a dark figure standing near her with their head down and their shaky arms outstretched. Hunter.

His head shot up to look at the Caeli Master, and in his eyes, Ellora saw a darkness, an anger she had never seen in him before. He quickly drew his arms back to his body once again before making a pushing motion towards the Caeli Master. The Caeli

Master's eyes widened in shock before he was thrown back by an invisible but clearly powerful wind.

Hunter continued. He pushed his arms out again and again as the Caeli Master was thrown around like a doll by the unseen force that was Hunter's Aura.

"Belle!" Dan yelled behind her, and Ellora turned to see that Belle was on the ground, her face no longer contorted and her eyes closed. She looked unconscious.

"Hunter, that's enough," Ellora said in a hoarse voice. She tried to shout, but her energy levels were almost completely depleted.

Hunter continued. He conjured another tornado, just like the one the Caeli Master managed, and sent it forward.

"Hunter, no!" Ellora tried again, her voice a little stronger this time. She wanted to walk to him, to make him stop, to tell him that was enough. But she was tired, and it was too bright. She couldn't see.

Out of nowhere, a huge shadow passed over them in the sky. There he was. Hunter was right in front of her. She moved forward again, slowly but steadily. If Hunter didn't stop now, he would kill the Caeli Master. And no matter what he deserved, Hunter shouldn't have to have that on his conscience; none of them should.

Finally, and agonisingly slowly, she made it. She put her hand on his shoulder, and the tornado vanished as Hunter collapsed onto the floor. Ellora dropped down with him.

Please don't let it be too late.

"Get on!" a voice called from above.

It was Kristen with Drako.

She felt a long vine wrap around her and Hunter and start to lift them up. She decided then that it was finally alright to close her eyes. They were safe.

***

Ellora woke up with a gasp as her stomach lurched. Everywhere she looked, clouds were rushing past them. A cold, but gentle breeze caressed her skin, whirling her hair back and out of from her face.

"Oh good, you are awake!" voice said from behind her.

"Melody!" Ellora sighed with relief. "What's going on?"

"Kristen and Drako saved us, zhank the Spirits," Melody said with a reassuring smile as she sat down next to her.

Slowly, the memories trickled back into Ellora's mind. "Belle?" she asked worriedly.

"Is fine," Melody responded. "She woke up a little while ago, and 'er Aura is a little bit drained, but ozherwise she is alright."

"And Hunter?"

"Is sleeping. 'E is in a bit of a worse state, but Kristen checked, and she zhinks 'e will be alright."

"Good, good," Ellora whispered in relief. "What about the scythe?" she asked nervously. She had lost track of it when the Caeli Master had been coming for her, and the thought of them all having to go through all of that for no reason made her feel nauseous.

"Clara got it." Melody beamed. "We did it."

"We did it," Ellora replied in a whisper.

"'Ere," Melody said, jumping up and holding out a hand to help Ellora up, too. "Zhe ozhers will want to know you are okay, and we should really get some sugar into your system."

Ellora followed Melody along Drako's back a couple of metres to where the others were sitting with their backpacks. From the ground, you really couldn't tell just *how* big Drako was. Ellora's stomach lurched again as Drako swooped down a little, but she steadied herself quickly.

"Ellora!" Belle cried, running to hug her friend. "Thank the Spirits. You're alright. You're not used to using that much Aura, Elle. You need to be more careful!"

"Yes, mum," Ellora murmured jokingly.

"Here," Dan said, holding out a purple energy drink. "You could do with some sugar." She accepted it from him with a 'thank you'.

It seemed that everyone's energy was pretty depleted, and Ellora didn't like the sight of Hunter lying alone, limp. "I think I'll stay with him until he wakes up."

Clara raised her eyebrows, and Melody smiled cheekily at her.

"We're all a bit worried about him," Belle said with a frown.

Ellora, feeling somewhat better, having had a rest and having downed the purple drink, hauled up one of the backpacks and took it with her to Hunter.

CHAPTER NINETEEN

The Terrari Market

"He worked hard out there," Kristen said, looking back at Ellora and Hunter, who she had shifted slightly. Ellora now sat on the ground with his head in her lap, solely to prevent his waking up with a crick in his neck, using the pack as a backrest.

"He did," Ellora said with a worried frown. "I've never seen anybody who wasn't an Upper Council Member use that much Aura. Come to think of it, I don't even think I've seen an Upper Council Member use that much Aura before."

"It was definitely... *something*," Kristen said, narrowing her eyes at Hunter in curiosity.

"Thank you for saving us," Ellora said earnestly. "I don't know what we would have done without you."

Kristen waved her off in an easygoing flutter of her hand. "Don't mention it. I said I couldn't come in with you. I didn't say I couldn't help you get out."

Ellora chuckled. She looked down at Hunter and immediately stopped laughing. He looked so awfully pale, even more than usual. "How long have we been in the air?"

"About 30 minutes? We're not far now."

So Hunter had already been unconscious for 30 minutes. That was it; she was not letting him lie here like this any longer.

"Hunter," she whispered gently, rubbing his shoulder. "Hunter, come on." She retrieved a piece of chocolate, water and a red sugar drink from her bag. Hunter barely cracked his eyes open, but it was good enough for Ellora.

She eased him into a semi-upright seated position against her shoulder and unwrapped the chocolate. "You need to eat." It took a while, but he finally managed to chew the chocolate and swallow it. "Water," she said, holding the bottle to his lips. He drank slowly but obediently and did the same with the energy drink. When Ellora was satisfied he had a little more colour in his face, she let him lie down again and fall asleep. Although, whether he was actually awake or not, she wasn't sure.

"You did well out there too, Ellora," Kristen said once Ellora settled Hunter back in and got comfortable.

"Oh. Right," Ellora said in an attempt at nonchalance. The fact that her aura drained so completely and so quickly made her almost entirely useless to them all, and it was playing on her mind. But she didn't need Kristen to know that.

"I'm serious," Kristen said enthusiastically, clearly not convinced. "Your Aura drained quickly, but that whirlpool was brilliant! I think with a bit of endurance training, you could get your Aura depletion a bit steadier. It tends to happen when you haven't had much practice. I remember Belle mentioning your Aura was blocked. So you haven't been using it for as long as your classmates?"

"Yeah, I guess not." Ellora appreciated Kristen trying, but nothing was going to stop her from feeling a bit like Mistfall about it all at the moment.

Thankfully, the conversation didn't need to last much longer. "We're here!" Kristen called out over her shoulder, loud enough for all of them to be able to hear her. "Maybe try to get him up and functioning again," she said more quietly to Ellora, nodding her head towards Hunter.

Ellora got Hunter up and gave him some more chocolate, which seemed to perk him up a little bit more. Slowly, she could see the colour returning to his face until she was no longer so worried about him.

"Be careful, then, will you?" Kristen asked as she leapt down from Drako, pulling Ellora into a hug.

"Promise," she responded.

"And don't overdo it," Kristen added, looking pointedly at Hunter.

Hunter, who was now steady on his feet and looking much more stable, nodded, his hands stuffed into his pockets.

Kristen said her goodbyes before pulling her sister into a warm hug. "Here, before I forget," she said, pulling a small gold ring out of her pocket. On the top was a shining rock that she flicked open to reveal a smooth, flat stone surface with a swirled marking engraved in. "All you need to do is touch this marking, and Drako and I will be on our way. We can track you with the jewel on top." She held it out to Belle.

"Here's hoping I won't have to use it," Belle said jokingly, putting it on her middle finger.

Kristen smiled and gave her another hug before jumping back onto Drako. "The Terrari Market isn't far from here; just follow the sunflowers. Good luck!" she called as they flew away.

"I guess it's that way then," said Melody, pointing towards a path lined with bright, towering sunflowers on either side.

Belle led the way with Dan by her side. Melody and Clara followed closely behind them at the back of the group, and Ellora walked with Hunter.

By now, Hunter had begun to regain the colour in his face and looked much steadier than he did only minutes ago.

Even so, Ellora couldn't help herself from glancing over at him every few steps, just to make sure he really was okay.

"Will you stop that, Artemer?" grumbled Hunter finally, glaring at her after her tenth glance.

"Stop what?" she asked innocently, snapping her eyes away from him.

"I drained my Aura, Artemer. That doesn't make me an idiot."

Ellora continued to look forward. "I was just making sure you were okay," she mumbled eventually. They walked in silence for a few moments before Ellora decided to try again. "Do you want to talk about what happened?"

"What happened?" Hunter asked in a stiff tone.

Ellora sighed. "You really are insufferable sometimes, you know," she grumbled.

Though Hunter did not respond, Ellora could have sworn she saw his lips twitch with a smile through the corner of her eye.

"I meant," Ellora spoke again, "do you want to talk about Ilisha?"

Any trace of the tiny smile on Hunter's face vanished in an instant. "What's there to talk about? You were right. I was wrong. There's no need to gloat."

Ellora stopped walking. "Hunter." She grabbed his elbow to stop him from continuing on without her. "Are you *serious*?" she exclaimed, bewildered. "Do you really think after all that what I wanted to do was to gloat?!"

Hunter looked down at her hand, which was still gripping his elbow tightly, and back up to her face. There was an intensity in the way he was looking at her, which made Ellora's breath catch in her throat. She felt, all of a sudden, entrapped by his eyes, unable to move or look away.

All of a sudden, the feeling was gone, and he shook her off, yanking his arm away from her.

"I just wanted to check if you were okay," Ellora whispered, holding her hands together to hide their trembling as she began to walk ahead once again.

Hunter cleared his throat and caught up to her quickly, his long legs resulting in a quick stride. "Why wouldn't I be? Am I annoyed? Yes. But we got away safely in the end, didn't we?" A beat of silence. "Am I annoyed at myself for putting us all in danger and risking all of your lives?" he continued.

"It's not your fault Hunter," Ellora interrupted gently before he could continue.

"But that's where you're wrong, isn't it, Ellora?" asked Hunter. "It *is* my fault. She chose *me* to befriend. Out of everyone, she chose *me*. She saw me as the weakest member of the group, and in the end, she was right. I'm the one who let us all down."

Ellora scoffed.

"Oh, I'm sorry, is that funny to you, Artemer?"

"The idea that you could be the weakest of all of us? Yes, of course that's funny. It's funny because it's ridiculous."

Hunter stared at Ellora with a look on his face that could only be described as a mix between confusion and anger."

"There is no way in Mistfall that you are weak in any way, Hunter. Ilisha didn't choose to befriend you because of that. She saw that you were a kind person and that you would welcome her in and be a good friend. And she was right. You *are* a kind person. And none of this is your fault.

"Besides, the reason why I was asking if you were alright was because you were friends, not because I think it's your fault."

It was Hunter's turn to scoff. "We were hardly friends," he replied, sounding more like himself. "We said 'hi' in the corridors, and that was about it."

"Well, it looked like more than that to me," Ellora muttered under her breath.

Hunter looked over at her with raised eyebrows, the corners of his mouth twitching. "What was that?" he asked, an amused tone colouring his words.

"Nothing," Ellora replied a little too quickly.

Hunter's lips immediately spread into a wide grin he couldn't control.

"What?" asked Ellora, but Hunter merely shook his head and continued to smile, clearly trying his hardest not to laugh. "What is it?" she demanded. "Do I have something on my face? "Oh no, is there a bug on me? Where?!" She leapt up, trying to shake the bug off, wherever it was.

"There's no bug," Hunter chuckled. "I'm laughing because you're jealous."

"What?!" Ellora exclaimed. "I'm not jealous, thank you very much, Hunter Nash."

"If you say so, Artemer."

Ellora felt heat rise in her cheeks and turned quickly away from him so he couldn't see. "You know what, Hunter—" She began.

"I think that's it!" Belle called from the front of their group, pointing ahead of them. Ellora's jaw dropped.

The Terrari Market.

"Okay," said Belle in a hushed voice as the group gathered around at the entrance, "so we need the Redmer Stone and a metal gauge amulet."

"Perhaps we should split up?" asked Melody.

"I think that's a good idea," added Clara. "This place is massive."

It was true. Ellora had never been to the Terrari Kingdom before but had briefly heard mention of the Terrari Market. Even so, she had expected only a few stalls, or perhaps a few rows of stalls, but nothing quite like this. There were lines of never-ending vendors, some selling food or fresh ingredients, spices, drinks, antiques, and jewellery—absolutely everything.

A few rows over in the market, Ellora spotted an older lady selling cups of hot spiced tea, while behind her was a stall filled with toys and stuffed bears surrounded by children.

"Okay, great. So Dan, maybe you and I can go this way?" asked Belle, pointing towards a less busy area of the market on the far right.

"Clara and I can go this way," Melody added, pointing to the left where there seemed to be more antiquarian items.

"I guess that leaves the two of us, Artemer," Hunter spoke. "We'll go straight on," he said, addressing the group.

"Kris said the metal gauge amulet and the Redmer stone are rare enough that it's likely only one vendor here will be selling each of them, so if you find one, grab it," Belle said as Clara equally divided up the coins. "Half an hour. We'll meet back here, at the entrance, in half an hour."

As the others walked in their respective directions, Ellora could not help but gravitate towards the old lady making homemade tea. The scent of fresh apples and cinnamon floated through the air, and Ellora was convinced.

"Good morning," she said with a friendly smile.

"Good morning, dear," the older lady replied. "Would you like to try a cup of my homemade apple spiced tea?"

"No, thank you," Hunter responded from behind her before Ellora had a chance to reply.

She turned to glare at him before smiling back at the lady. "I would love a cup, thank you. It smells delicious."

"Why thank you, dear," the old lady said happily, filling a fresh cup with the steaming drink and handing it over to Ellora, who paid quickly and wished her a nice day.

Ellora let the tea warm her hands before she blew on it, using her aura to cool the drink down ever so slightly so that it wouldn't burn her.

"Mmm," she hummed happily, taking a sip. The tea tasted sweet, with a hint of honey, a subtle dash of spice, and the perfect touch of apple. "Do you want some?" She held out the cup for Hunter, who made a face at her. "It's only tea, Hunter," she sighed.

"We don't have time to stop for tea, Artemer. Besides, you don't know what's in it."

Ellora scoffed. "If it were poisoned, I'm sure somebody else would have noticed and shut her down. I'm sure I'll be fine."

"Whatever. We only have half an hour. A Redmer stone might be somewhat easier to find, but the metal gauge amulet is going to be a tricky task," Hunter said as they walked through the food stalls, the smells of spices and chillies enveloping them.

"Well, I don't see the harm in stopping to buy a cup of tea," Ellora replied stubbornly, draining the last of her drink and throwing the cup into a bin.

"Over there," said Hunter, ignoring her. He was pointing towards a stall tucked away in the corner with no customers. How it was so clear, Ellora didn't know; it was covered in glowing gems and shiny rocks. It was exactly the kind of place one would find a rare stone.

"Look at that one." She pointed to a red rock that looked exactly like the one Dan gifted Belle with the year before.

"Perfect," Hunter whispered just loudly enough for Ellora to hear him.

"Hello, how may I help you today?" the vendor, an older man with a grey beard, asked.

"Actually, you might be able to help us," replied Hunter. "We're after a Redmer stone like that one." He pointed it out.

"Well, actually, this one is not avai—"

"My fiancé and I are so happy you were able to procure one!" Ellora blurted out, interrupting the vendor and grabbing onto Hunter's arm.

As soon as she spoke the words, her eyes widened. Why did she say that?

Hunter turned to look at her in horror.

"Oh of course! Your fiancé!" the old man exclaimed happily. "Are you the gentleman I spoke to about reserving this stone?"

The two of them exchanged a quick glance. "Yes," Ellora replied quickly before Hunter could disagree. "It's him. He reserved the stone."

Hunter shot her a trying look but didn't contradict her. A couple had reserved the Redmer stone, and they were taking it from them, but this was a matter of life and death; surely they could find another stone?

"How lovely," the vendor said happily. "I'll get it all ready for you then."

"What did you do?" asked Hunter in a hushed voice.

"I don't know!" Ellora replied, just as confused as he was. "It just came out!"

"So when is the special date?" asked the old man excitedly.

"Oh, we haven't—"

"Next month," Ellora blurted out, interrupting Hunter. Why did she say that?

"Oh yes, of course," the vendor said. "Actually I do remember you mentioning that on the phone." He nodded at Hunter, who forced an awkward smile in response.

The old man frowned strangely at the look on Hunter's face, and Ellora felt the urge to smack her face into her palm. She snaked an arm around Hunter's arm and, when the old man turned around, grabbed his hand and put it around her waist. When the vendor turned back, she put her head on Hunter's shoulder and smiled sweetly up at him. Hunter was glaring at her so intensely that Ellora had to bite her lip to prevent herself from laughing.

"Although, I thought you wanted it to be a surprise at your wedding," he said to Hunter, his eyebrows etched in a frown.

"Yes, he did," Ellora replied quickly, moving even closer to Hunter and snuggling into his side, intertwining her fingers with his on her waist. This was hardly the ideal situation for them to be in, but Hunter's discomfort was at least making it somewhat entertaining. "But I got it out of him," she continued. "You can never keep secrets from me, can you?" she giggled cutely, hugging his side.

"Nope," Hunter replied between gritted teeth. "I can't keep anything from you, *darling.*"

"Okay, well, here is your Redmer stone, all ready for you," the vendor held out a small velvet pouch for them. "That will be three hundred gold coins."

Spirits. They only had two hundred. Again, Ellora felt the strange but urgent need to speak.

"Oh, I thought you said you agreed on two hundred?" she said to Hunter in a sweet voice.

Hunter said nothing but raised an eyebrow at the vendor, who flushed pink. "Oh yes, of course, it slipped my mind. Two hundred coins we agreed on."

Ellora disentangled herself from Hunter, and he handed over the money, taking the stone.

"Let's go before the real soon-to-be-married couple turns up," she whispered.

They hurried through the stalls towards where they agreed to meet the others again. It took them long enough to find the stone, and they were almost late already.

"What was all that about?" demanded Hunter.

"No idea," Ellora replied. "I had this weird... urge inside of me to talk, and one moment I was thinking about the stone, and the next I'd spoken without even realising what I said."

"An urge?"

"Yeah, like something inside of me just... spoke for me, I suppose. I was doing the speaking, but I wasn't in control." Hunter looked at her with furrowed brows. "Strange, right?" She asked.

"It must have been the tea."

"What tea?"

"The apple tea you bought from that old lady?" prompted Hunter. "It must have been some sort of lucky elixir or something like that."

"Really? I've never heard of such a thing," said Ellora in wonder. "See? And you didn't want me to buy the tea!"

"Whatever, Artemer. I stand by what I said about consuming food and drink from strangers."

"Whatever, Winnashire," Ellora countered. "We should go back and get some more."

"We don't have time to—"

"Hunter, if you're right and that tea was a lucky elixir, it could come in handy!"

"I suppose—"

"I'm going, with or without you," Ellora interrupted. If he wasted any more time arguing with her, they definitely *would* be late.

"You're infuriating, Artemer," Hunter grumbled, but he followed her all the same. "I hope you know that."

"I may be infuriating, Winnashire, but I got us that stone, didn't I?"

"This is where the old lady was," Hunter said, swiftly changing the subject and pointing to an empty space.

"But there's nobody here."

"What a deduction you have made today Artemer."

Ellora smacked him sharply on the arm. "Is this snarkiness your way of re-establishing balance after pretending to be my fiancé for all of ten minutes?" But he was right. The toy stall was still there, along with the children playing around it—just no sign of the old lady and her tea stand.

"We need to go."

"Fine, come on then." Ellora marched ahead without waiting for him.

"Thank the Spirits," exhaled Belle as they arrived back at the entrance a few minutes late. "We were starting to worry. What took you both so long?"

Hunter scowled at Ellora but said nothing, leaving Ellora to explain. "We'll explain later."

"Okay, well, we managed to get the metal gauge amulet," Dan said, holding the item up by the chain.

"Great, because we managed to get the Redmer Stone," replied Hunter, shooting Ellora another look.

"Zhat's good because even zhough Clara and I did not find zhose, we arranged our journey."

"Come on, follow us," said Clara, ushering them towards the left side of the market. They moved behind all of the stalls until they came to a small dock surrounded by glistening blue waters. Wooden boards squeaked under them as Clara led them along a row of large and beautiful boats.

"Here it is." Ellora's mouth dropped when Clara showed them to a rickety, rotting piece of wood barely floating in the water.

"It's..." Dan said, his mouth open.

"It's certainly a boat," Belle finished for him.

"I know it is not ideal," Melody said apologetically, "but in order to 'ire a bigger boat, we would 'ave 'ad to return it."

"None of the sailors were *confident*, shall we say, that we would be able to give the boat back to them after going to the Obscuri Kingdom," Clara added, wringing her hands.

"Why is that?" questioned Hunter, his eyebrows etching into a frown.

Melody and Clara exchanged an uneasy look before Clara answered. "Apparently it's not the safest of journeys."

"It used to be more commonly used," Melody explained, "but apparently, since zhe war, zhe waters became too rough for anybody to get zhrough and return safely afterwards."

Ellora groaned internally. She was foolish to have expected a smooth journey at any point in this expedition.

"Well, it'll have to do anyway," said Belle, heaving her bag onto the boat. "If we have no other options, at least we have something."

"Thank you for managing to get it," Ellora said, following Belle and getting settled into the boat. "If it were up to *his* persuasive skills," she nodded in Hunter's direction, "we would have nothing." Melody chuckled as Hunter shot her an annoyed glance.

"Besides," continued Dan, "we have the Madori Mistress in training with us. Navigating water shouldn't be too difficult."

CHAPTER TWENTY

A Stormy Sea

"**S**pirits!" exclaimed Ellora. "I think you jinxed us, Hunter."

"I did no such thing," Hunter grumbled over the splashing waves.

Only twenty minutes into their journey, the six of them were already drenched. The rickety old boat couldn't cope very well with the harsh waves, either, and despite Belle's best efforts, she couldn't stop them. The water would not stop throwing them about.

"There's something wrong here, guys!" Belle cried over the thunderous roaring of the sea. "This isn't normal water!"

"What in the Realms do you mean, Bee?!" Ellora shouted.

"It's resisting my Aura!" Belle screamed over the sounds of the water splashing over them and onto the creaky wood. "It's like it's... I don't know, alive!"

"'Ow is zhat even possible?!" called Melody, using a bucket to try and remove some of the water pooling around their feet.

"No idea!" replied Belle.

"Let's focus on getting through this!" called Dan. "We still have quite a journey to go!"

He was right; they had barely begun their journey to the Obscuri Kingdom.

"Hold on tight!" Belle called suddenly, and Ellora grabbed onto the side of the boat just in time as they hit an enormous wave that flung them across the surface. It was as if, all of a sudden, the rough water became treacherous.

"Spirits!" Clara cried, one hand gripping the boat as tightly as possible and the other pointing ahead to warn the others of the danger. A cluster of deep grey clouds loomed over the sea before them, dark and swelling with storm. Bright flashes struck out of the clouds, striking the inky water ahead. Thunder grumbled all around them, coming from every direction as the flashes got brighter and brighter the closer they got to the storm.

And they were headed straight into it.

An especially strong wave bombarded into the side of the boat, throwing Melody onto her back. "Melody!" cried Ellora from the other side of the vessel. Hunter immediately jumped into action, grabbing the smaller girl by the hand and pulling her back up onto the bench, holding onto her tightly.

Another wave smashed into the side of the boat almost immediately, and the vessel began to fill up even faster, sloshing them side to side. Not that it made any more of a difference; they were already soaked through.

But things were only going to get worse. With every moment that passed, the sea became rougher, the water got darker, and the storm grew closer.

The moment they hit the vicinity of the cluster of angry clouds, the boat was submerged entirely under a violent wave. Ellora hung tightly to the side of the crumbling wood for as long as she could, barely escaping without being hauled away by the strong current. When they surfaced again, she wanted to collapse on the floor in exhaustion, but already another wave was on its way.

Dan and Belle huddled together at the front of the boat, gasping for breath and clinging to the edge, while Melody, Hunter and Clara sat in a clump, Hunter keeping his arms around the two of them as they fought to stay together.

There was room among the three of them for her to join them, and Ellora knew it was her only chance of making it through this horrifying journey. Together, the chances of them being thrown over were smaller. She just had to get the timing right.

No wonder nobody ever returned from Obscuri.

Ellora waited for the next wave to crash into them, this one strong but not large enough to submerge them again, and she held tightly onto the side. Then, just as the wave passed, she leapt from her position on the other side of the boat to get over to the bench.

She felt a spray of water hit her face and saw Hunter's expression turn into one of horror as she moved. But it was too late.

All of a sudden, a strong and painful force hit Ellora and dragged her over the side of the boat. She moved her arms and legs in a fury, trying to force her way through to the surface, but it was no use. She was being thrown around by the current like a doll being chewed up and spat out by a dog. She had no idea which was up or down, and through the darkness of the inky black water, she couldn't even see the boat anymore. For all she knew, the boat was long gone.

She worked her limbs harder, forcing them to move, forcing them to save her and find her air, but she couldn't. She felt a sharp sting in her lungs and began to panic. She flailed her arms desperately and clawed the water around her, trying to feel something, anything.

Ellora had always considered herself a decent swimmer, but despite her best efforts, she couldn't seem to break through to the surface. She had no control over where she was going. The water was in charge here.

In vain, she attempted to use her Aura with the little energy she had to give herself a boost from the darkness, but Belle had been right. The water here was not water. It didn't respond.

Her lungs tightened the longer she was underwater, burning.

This was it.

All of a sudden, she felt something brush against her leg. Instinctively, she tried to scream, opening her mouth and inhaling a gulp of icy water. She had no idea what was in here with her.

Again, she felt something; it touched her arm this time. She tried desperately to kick and splash, but she was exhausted. She gave up.

Two solid and firm limbs wrapped around her shoulders and, although she tried her best to resist them, pulled her through the darkness. She had no idea which way she was going. Was she going up? Down? Left? Right? She was at the mercy of this powerful force pulling her against the water. It simply wouldn't let her go.

To her surprise, Ellora emerged from the water.

She gasped desperately for breath, greedily gulping it down as fast as she could, soothing her sore lungs and chest.

There was still a pair of strong arms wrapped around her.

Hunter.

He was in the water beside her, holding onto her to stop her from being flung away. He had jumped in after her.

The moment she saw it was him, she wrapped her arms around his shoulders, clinging onto him tightly.

The water, although calmer than before, was still rough, and neither of them could stay above the darkness for more than a few seconds at a time. But slowly, they made their way back over to the boat, and Hunter boosted her up as she hoisted herself back onto the vessel, landing inside and panting but refusing to let herself stop until Hunter was back in the boat with her.

Hunter's head ducked below the water again, and Ellora reached over, holding out a hand for him to grab. But he didn't come back up.

His dark hair blended in with the water so seamlessly that Ellora had no chance of spotting him in the inky pool. She screamed, "Hunter!" Her throat and chest burned, but she screamed again, "Hunter!"

Finally, his head reemerged, and he grabbed desperately onto her hand.

"Help!" she called for the others. The rain was still falling heavily onto them and wet strands of her her hair stuck to her face and her lips as she pulled him up.

Clara appeared behind her and reached down, grabbing Hunter's other arm and together, they dragged him up and back onto the boat.

He collapsed onto the bottom of the boat, panting for breath, as Ellora did the same.

His jet-black hair was somehow even darker now that it was soaked. Individual strands clung to his forehead, dripping water droplets down his flushed face.

"You came after me," she whispered, still breathing heavily, as she wiped the hair from his eyes. "You came after me."

Hunter remained silent and unmoving. Had he passed out?

Before she could move to check, she heard his voice, so soft she couldn't be sure she really heard him. "Of course I did."

Every breath simultaneously felt like fire coursing through her and like ice soothing her very being.

She lost consciousness lying next to Hunter, but another harsh wave jostled her and caressed her with determination. She needed to get up, and they needed to get through this.

For Oriel.

She heaved herself onto her feet and grabbed onto the side of the boat with one hand, wrapping her other around Hunter's wrist. She would sooner die than let anything happen to him.

Although she was so drenched already that her hair stuck to her skin, dripping water down her face, and her clothes clung tightly to her frame, she could feel the difference when the hot tears began to flow from her eyes as she looked at him.

A series of smaller waves crashed into the side of the boat, and Ellora lost her balance, almost falling on top of Hunter. But she grabbed on. It was when the third wave hit that Ellora had to let go and heave Hunter up into a sitting position. The bottom of the boat, once again, was quickly filling with water, and if she had left him down there, it would have been to drown.

Ellora felt a warmth on her face and wiped at it, sure she was crying again. But her face was dry. She looked up to see the grey clouds finally open up, allowing a stream of sunlight into the boat.

They looked at each other in relief.

They had made it through the storm.

Slowly, Hunter's eyes opened, and he coughed a few times, spluttering out water. Ellora rubbed his back gently, and he lay his head, silent and weak, on Ellora's shoulder.

"Is it over?" pleaded Dan, finally breaking the silence that felt so loud after being surrounded by the sounds of a storm.

But he spoke too soon. Before anybody could reply, a jolt of lightning shot down from the sky, directly striking the middle of the boat and shattering it into countless wooden pieces.

Luckily, they had cleared the storm now, and so the water was calm and clear. Behind them, the storm still raged, but ahead were only blue skies. One by one, they emerged from the water again, using the broken pieces of wood to stay afloat.

Ellora kept her arm under Hunter, who was drifting in and out of consciousness, refusing to let him go.

The storm was no longer an issue, but there was no land in sight; they still had a long journey to go and no boat to take them.

"Is everyone okay?" called Belle, who was hanging onto a larger piece of wood with Clara.

"What are we going to do?" exclaimed Clara, panicked.

"Belle, can you try your Aura again?" suggested Melody.

Belle lifted her hand and made a few swirling motions but to no avail. "It's hopeless."

There was a quiet but hopeful sound coming from behind Ellora. A giggle.

She turned to see Melody looking down at the water, chuckling softly. But the chuckle turned into full-blown laughter, and the others frowned. Was she having a breakdown? Melody didn't like to swim anyway, and after the incident with the Hydra last year, she was even more terrified of water than usual. Not that anybody could blame her. In fact, Ellora was surprised she had even agreed to get into this boat in the first place. What could she have to laugh about?

After only a moment of Melody giggling uncontrollably, Dan joined in. Ellora was about to ask them what had happened when she felt something brush against her ankle, tickling her.

From the water rose majestic creatures that looked somewhat like horses, only made from water. They galloped majestically around them in circles. One came to a stop in front of Ellora and bowed down its head. She reached out to touch it and felt that, although it looked like it was made from water, it was very much solid.

Not only were they solid, but they looked very strong. She backed away slowly, still holding on tight to Hunter. There was a splashing sound, and Ellora turned to see Melody gracefully hoist herself onto one of the creatures.

"It is okay. Zhey are 'ere to 'elp us," she said happily. "Climb on!"

Dan was the first to listen and climbed on easily, followed quickly by Clara and then Belle. Ellora, however, took a little more time. With the help of the creature in front of her, she put Hunter on its back first, before climbing on herself, positioning herself behind him in case he fell.

"Ready?" asked Melody.

Ellora adjusted Hunter and herself, making sure they were secure and nodded.

"All good," Melody said, leaning down to talk to her creature and rubbing its head fondly.

They shot off at once, galloping smoothly across the water and leaving the furious clouds and water behind them. The journey was surprisingly swift and easy, not bumpy at all like it would be if they had been on land horses. Ellora smiled and gulped in the fresh air as they moved, exhilarated.

A journey that would have easily taken hours without the boat, or perhaps even *with* the boat, took only minutes, and soon the animals came to a stop on a black sand beach to drop them off. One by one, they each bowed deeply to Melody before turning and galloping back into the sea.

"That was impressive, Melody!" Belle cried in awe.

"How in the Realms did you do that?" asked Clara.

Melody simply shrugged, looking just as confused and impressed as the rest of them. "I suppose zhey sensed zhat we needed zhem and zhey came to 'elp us."

Ellora looked worriedly at Hunter, who woke up again on the ride in a state of confusion.

"How are you feeling?" Ellora asked in a hushed voice, placing a hand on his arm to try and help him into a sitting position.

"Fine," he said gruffly, shaking her off. He was definitely not fine, although Ellora kept quiet. "Dan," Hunter called him and gestured feebly towards his backpack. Dan nodded and dug through his bag, fishing out and tossing Hunter another bottle of red liquid and a chocolate bar, both of which Hunter struggled to catch.

"Where are we?" asked Clara, looking around with trepidation.

They landed on a dark and sandy beach which looked like a battlefield. The sand was a strange mixture of coal black and dark crimson. There were a few metres of sand before it turned to jagged black rocks. Ellora could see nothing else, no sign of life. No trees or flowers and certainly no animals. Although they had expected to find a wasteland, this felt rather eerie to her. There was a horrible feeling of nothingness, of not knowing what was out there, that made her skin crawl.

"Zhis used to be zhe Obscuri Kingdom?" asked Melody.

"Onwards and upwards," said Dan, his words hopeful but his voice reflecting the same feeling of uneasiness coursing through them all.

"Before we do anything else," Belle began before sweeping her arm in a wide gesture over them.

"Thank the Spirits," Hunter murmured. With an effortless wave, Belle dried them all. Even their clothes and hair felt normal again.

"Well then," said Ellora, fidgeting with her hands. "I guess we're off to find the herb."

CHAPTER TWENTY ONE

The Herb of Asphodel

In this dark wasteland which, unbelievably, used to be the Obscuri Kingdom, everything looked almost exactly the same.

"It would have been useful if the signs were still up, really," sighed Belle. They had been walking for thirty minutes and somehow ended up back on the beach three times already.

"Maybe we should think about splitting up?" suggested Clara.

"I don't think that's a good idea," Replied Dan. "We have no idea where we are, so we would have no idea how to find each other again."

They trudged forward in silence for a few more minutes.

"Are we sure the herb grows here? I haven't seen a single sign of life," stated Hunter with a frown.

"Clara, you used to come with your dad, right?" asked Ellora.

"Yeah, as a kid, but I don't remember how we navigated this place. I do remember the herb being really rare, though. If dad spotted a patch, he'd harvest the whole thing because we didn't know if we'd find anymore."

"Perfect," Hunter muttered under his breath.

"It's fine. Let's just keep our eyes out, shall we?" Ellora said.

"Clara, could you per'aps use your Aura to locate zhe 'erb?" asked Melody.

"That's a great idea!" exclaimed Belle.

"I've never tried to do that before, but maybe?" Clara seemed unsure, but she closed her eyes tightly. She bent down and touched the tips of her fingers to the ground, breathing deeply and keeping her eyes shut.

"This is hopeless," Hunter grumbled under his breath so quietly that Ellora was the only one to hear him.

"Why are you being so grumpy?" she asked just as quietly.

"I'm not grumpy."

"You sure as Spirits are."

"Well, maybe I am, but I think anybody would be after almost drowning."

Ellora bit her lip. She stayed silent for a few moments before finally whispering, "sorry."

"Got it!" Clara declared excitedly. "I think I've found some. It doesn't seem to be too far away."

"Well, what are we waiting for?" asked Belle. "Let's go!"

Clara led the way forwards, directing them towards where she could sense the herb. Belle, Dan and Melody followed closely behind, and Ellora moved to catch up, but Hunter grabbed her wrist.

She looked questioningly at him. "We'll lose them."

"Why did you apologise?"

She shrugged. "I'm the reason you almost drowned?"

"I didn't want an apology."

"You seemed to be upset with me. I can't blame you. If I almost drowned for somebody, I would probably be annoyed, too."

"No, you wouldn't."

"Hunter, can we go?" he looked down at his hand, which was still gripping tightly onto her wrist. He released her.

Ellora frowned at him but didn't want to waste any time. She turned and hurried to catch up with the others.

"What are those?" asked Belle, pointing to some creatures moving through the sky. They all stopped immediately. Having seen no sign of life at all so far, it was unclear if this was a good sign or a bad one.

"I zhink zhey are Loriana," Melody said, watching them with gleaming eyes. "Zhey are birds native to zhe Lynchi Kindom zhat were said to 'ave died and became extinct in zhe war. Zhey 'ave not been spotted in years!"

"They're beautiful," Clara commented as the six of them watched in awe and the beautiful white birds glided through the air, elegant and majestic.

A pristine feather drifted down from one of the birds and landed on Hunter's head, the whiteness of the feather a stark contrast with his inky black hair. Ellora plucked the feather from his tresses and held it up to the light; it sparkled in the sun.

"But why are they here?" asked Hunter.

"What do you mean?" Belle countered.

"They're native to the Lynchi Kingdom, and yet they're flying around the Obscuri lands," said Hunter with a frown. "Something's off."

"I think I can answer that one," replied Clara with a grim face. "In the past, sending over an animal like the Loraiana to another Kingdom would be considered a sign of war."

"War?" Ellora swallowed.

Clara nodded. "The Lynchi Obscuri War, remember? The Lynchi Kingdom must have sent the birds to declare war, and they stayed and bred, and now they live here."

"But I zhought it was zhe Obscuri Kingdom zhat started zhe war," Melody added. "At least zhat was what I 'ad read."

"I don't think anyone really knows what happened," replied Hunter. "No history book has the same recount of events as another, and none of the teachers seem to want to go into too much detail about it."

"Maybe we should leave the birds in peace and continue looking for the herb?" offered Dan.

"You're right," said Clara. "It's close by, anyway."

Ellora tucked the beautiful feather into her jacket pocket as they followed Clara; it was too beautiful just to discard.

"On the bright side, to survive, the birds need some sort of food and water," Belle spoke as they walked. "Maybe we're near an oasis or something like that?"

"Zhere!" called Melody suddenly, pointing to a small patch of bright green that stood out against the black rock beneath it.

"The Herb of Asphodel," whispered Belle excitedly.

For something so rare, so important, and so delicate, it looked rather like an average garden weed to Ellora.

"How much do you think we'll need?" pondered Clara.

"I have no idea," replied Ellora. "Let's just take as much of it as we can get?"

"Okay, I'll harness all three cloves," Clara replied, taking the scythe from Belle and carefully clipping each individual herb from the root.

"I suppose we need a way back now," said Dan, looking around anxiously.

"Well, the boat is definitely no option," said Belle.

"And zhe animals will not take us zhrough zhe storm," added Melody.

"So maybe we should keep walking?" suggested Ellora. "There may be another way without going through a storm. And like Belle said, the birds must be getting their nutrients from somewhere; maybe we can find something to eat too or cap out for the night."

"I think it's best to turn back where we came from," Dan disagreed quickly.

"Back where?" Ellora asked with an empty laugh. She had no idea why he was so stressed, but if he wouldn't share it with them, then there was nothing they could do. "There's nothing for us back there."

"We'll figure something out," said Dan. Ellora frowned at him, and Hunter raised an eyebrow. "I just think it's better than going into unknown territory."

"We've come this far into the island already," argued Hunter, "and all we've encountered was a peaceful pack of birds in the sky and a group of weeds."

"And I don't see how we have any other options," Ellora added in agreement.

"Fine," said Dan in resignation. "But we need to be careful." He looked around nervously as if something would appear out of nowhere and devour them whole.

"What is zhat?" asked Melody before they could begin moving, pointing over at a large vehicle that was unlike anything Ellora had ever seen before. It was sitting dormant a few hundred metres from them and seemed to be made of metal with large wheels. It was nothing like a car and didn't seem to have any sort of engine or anything else to pull it along.

"Strange," Clara said as they walked over to examine it. "Someone must have been here at some point, right? This can't have just appeared out of nowhere."

Melody crouched down to examine it. "It does not look rusted or anyzhing at all. It cannot 'ave been 'ere for too long."

"Maybe step away from it," suggested Belle. "We don't know what it is and—"

There was a loud sound, and the six of them were suddenly surrounded by a strange ring of purple flames.

"What in the Realms?!" Hunter shouted.

"What's going on?" whispered Melody, inching closer to the group.

"Stick together, guys," Belle said in a firm voice.

The ring tightened around the six of them, and they huddled closer and closer together.

A small, thin gap opened up in the purple flame, and Belle moved to the front of the group.

They watched as a small, dark, cloaked figure walked through the gap, followed by another. Their faces were hidden by the shadows of the tall flames.

But when they stepped into the light, Ellora felt her heart leap into her throat.

The second figure was a tall woman with long hair, the vibrant colour of fire. It flowed elegantly, and yet somehow dangerously, behind her. It was familiar.

But it was the first figure who really caused goosebumps to prickle on Ellora's skin. She had grown, that was for sure, but those deep brown eyes and silky dark hair Ellora could never forget.

"Dan," the first girl said with a sigh. "It's you."

Could it be?

"Who are all these people you've brought with you, Dan?" the girl asked.

Belle, Melody, Hunter and Clara all turned to look at Dan in shock, but Ellora couldn't take her eyes off the little girl she once knew.

She walked forward slowly, her legs shaking and her lip wavering.

"Ophelia. "

Afterword

Thank you for visiting The Aura Realm again! I really hope you enjoyed Drako's Fire. It truly means the world that you would take a chance on a small indie author like me.

Reviews mean the world to us as authors (especially independently published authors), so if you did enjoy Drako's, I would be incredibly grateful if you could leave a quick rating and review.

Castina's Wish (the third and final instalment of this series) is coming out in May, and I'm so excited to share it with you. You can pre-order Castina's Wish now!

You can also sign up for my newsletter to get exclusive updates about my upcoming books (there are a lot coming this year) and be the first to learn about new releases!

THANK YOU

I would like to start by saying a huge thank you to you—my readers. All of your kind messages, your comments and your reviews really do push me to keep writing and publishing the best books I possibly can for you. I really hope you enjoyed it and that you will be joining us in The Aura Realm again in May! Thank you so much for taking a chance on a new and young author like myself.

To my friends and family—you know who you are, and you know I could not do this without you. I know I say thank you a lot, but let me say it again. Thank you.

Isha, you read the first chapters I ever wrote. I will always remember that and be grateful. Without your honest feedback and words of encouragement, I wouldn't be where I am today.

Thank you to you all. I love each and every one of you.

ABOUT AUTHOR

Maya Unadkat is a multi-genre UK-based author of young adult fantasy and romance novels. She is a student at Royal Holloway, University of London working to acquire her

Bachelor of Arts degree in French and Spanish. When she was just sixteen, she discovered her love and passion for writing and when, at age nineteen, she was hospitalised due to appendicitis, she decided to begin working on her first novel. She hasn't stopped writing since. Her passions include stories, chocolate and Jane Austen.

Printed in Great Britain
by Amazon

17397444R10182